U0140547

广东外语外贸大学 2010 年科研学术著作出版资助

The Construction of Prosecution-Defense-Judge Relationship:

A Frame Analysis of Judges' Courtroom Discourse Processing

控辩审关系的建构

——法官庭审语篇处理的框架分析

陈金诗　著

科学出版社

北　京

图书在版编目(CIP)数据

控辩审关系的建构：法官庭审语篇处理的框架分析 = The Construction of Prosecution-Defense-Judge Relationship: A Frame Analysis of Judges' Courtroom Discourse Processing: 英文 / 陈金诗著. —北京：科学出版社，2011.5

　ISBN 978-7-03-030929-7

Ⅰ. ①控…　Ⅱ. ①陈…　Ⅲ. ①审判 – 语言分析 – 研究 – 英文　Ⅳ. ①D915.04

中国版本图书馆 CIP 数据核字(2011)第 077387 号

责任编辑：刘彦慧 / 责任校对：胡小洁
责任印制：赵德静 / 封面设计：无极书装

联系电话：010-6401 9074　电子邮箱：liuyanhui@mail.sciencep.com

科 学 出 版 社 出版
北京东黄城根北街 16 号
邮政编码：100717
http://www.sciencep.com
中国科学院印刷厂 印刷
科学出版社编务公司排版制作
科学出版社发行　各地新华书店经销

*

2011 年 6 月第 一 版　　开本：A5 (890×1240)
2011 年 6 月第一次印刷　　印张：9
印数：1—2 500　　字数：375 000

定价：48.00 元
（如有印装质量问题，我社负责调换〈科印〉）

序

运用语言学理论和方法分析、解决法律问题是法律语言学的宗旨所在,陈金诗博士的著作《控辩审关系的建构——法官庭审语篇处理的框架分析》充分体现了这一宗旨。该著作即将出版,受其委托代为写序。作为导师,我对作者在写作过程中付出的种种艰辛非常了解,对其孜孜以求、勇于探索的开拓精神印象深刻。

法官的庭审语篇是法律语言学研究的重要课题,并受到越来越多国内外法律语言研究者的关注。刑事庭审中的控辩审关系是法学界研究的热点,从法官的语篇分析切入进行探讨,具有鲜明的现实意义。作者选择此课题体现了法律语言学为我国法治建设服务的研究指向。作者基于机构性语篇的框架分析理论,运用语篇树状信息结构的分析手段,构建了"控辩审关系建构的多维度框架分析模型",并对法官庭审语篇建构控辩审关系的表现、原因和语篇处理策略进行了深入细致的分析和研究。语言的使用必须植根于一定的社会环境,受到社会因素的影响,尽管我国法治化进程不断推进,法官的庭审语篇仍存在建构倒三角控辩审关系的现象,作者因此提出在中国法制背景下法官如何通过语篇处理策略构建合理的控辩审关系。如通过信息层次降级、信息层级移位或共享分类修改等手段改变法官角色,通过信息单位增补、信息单位合并、冗余信息删除、信息单位融合、信息点更换、信息单位重复或信息单位共享等手段进行再框定等。这些基于语料分析和验证而提出的语篇处理手段试图从语言学角度解决控辩审关系建构这一法律问题,具有较强的理论意义和实践价值。

作者在本书中构建的分析模型基于框架理论,但是为了避免框架分析的抽象性,作者经常与我讨论、与学界同行切磋,最终形成了此分析模型——把互动性框架、框定和语篇立足点迁移融为一体,并采用了语篇信息分析的手段，解决了框架认定难题，形成了一套微观、中观和宏观兼具的多维分析框架。该模型的构建，是法律语言学理论建设中的一种成功尝试。作者严肃认真的态度贯穿整个写作过程，作为导师我深感欣慰。此书的出版，是他本人的收获，也是法律语言学界的幸事，值得祝贺。相信陈金诗博士在今后的学术研究中能持之以恒，多出成果，出好成果，为中国法律语言学的发展做出更大的贡献。

是为序。

杜金榜

2011 年 1 月于广州白云山下

Acknowledgements

I could not accomplish this book without the help of many people, and I am glad to be able to acknowledge their help and express my appreciation here.

First and foremost, I will be eternally indebted to my respected supervisor, Professor Du Jinbang (杜金榜) for his guidance and continuous support throughout the course of this study. He was always there to listen and to give advice. He was a very careful reader, which is almost beyond description. He helped me complete the writing of this book as well as the challenging research that lies behind it. Especially, he taught me how to write academic papers and express my ideas. Without his priceless support, constant encouragement, and valuable advice throughout my academic journey, this book would never have been accomplished. He has been and continues to be the example for me as a devoted researcher and a wonderful human being.

My sincere appreciation goes to Dr. Zhang Xinhong (张新红), Dr. Xu Zhanghong (徐章宏) and Dr. Yuan Chuanyou (袁传有) for their insightful comments and valuable suggestions on how to improve the research. I would also like to extend my heartfelt gratitude to Professor Zhao Junfeng (赵军峰), Professor Liu Jianfu (刘件福), Dr. Huang Yongping (黄永平), Dr. Zhong Caishun (钟彩顺), Dr. Xu Youping (徐优平) and Dr. Li Yuekai (李跃凯). Their generous help and cordial encouragement have made me realize that true friendship is not conditioned.

I feel greatly obliged to Ms. Zhang Xinrong (张新荣) who has

always shown deep concern for my work and offered great help for my life in the past few years.

I am deeply grateful to the other scholars like Professor Liu Jianda (刘建达), Professor Huo Yongshou (霍永寿), Professor Ouyang Huhua (欧阳护华), and Professor Shen Sanshan (沈三山) whose inspiring lectures are of great help for my understanding of linguistics and academic writing.

I owe a particular debt of gratitude to Professor Liu Weiming (刘蔚铭) in Northwest University of Politics and Law for his warm recommendation for publishing the book, and to Ms. Liu Yanhui (刘彦慧) in Science Press for her enthusiastic help and meticulous editing.

My sincere thanks is also expressed to my best friend, also my former classmate Zhang Gang (张刚), whose moral and economic support will forever be cherished.

I cannot thank enough my parents Chen Xuezhi (陈学志) and Zou Qun (邹群), my brother Chen Yinshi (陈银诗) and my lovely daughter Chen Haoran (陈浩然), who all have provided me with their love and support.

My special thanks go to my beloved wife Wan Hong (万红) for her understanding and patience. It is her love and encouragement that have always been inspiring me to persevere in the face of formidable challenges and spurring me forward along the academic road.

This entire page is devoted to thank them. Finally, I would like to say that all the accomplishment that I would make in the future is greatly indebted to these people.

内 容 简 介

控辩审关系是司法实践的重要内容之一，也是刑事诉讼研究的一个重要课题。此前，从法官的庭审语篇操控入手研究控辩审关系的建构尚属空白。而法官的裁判权通过庭审互动来实现，法官的语篇处理会影响到庭审中各方关系的建构，因此法官如何通过语篇处理建构合理的控辩审关系成为本研究的关注焦点。

本研究构建了一个描写、分析和解释法官庭审语篇的分析框架。该分析框架基于框架理论，并结合相关分析工具，从微观、中观和宏观三个维度进行分析，涉及框架分析的三个核心内容：互动性框架、框定和语篇立足点迁移。整个研究主要是对从法律语料库中抽取的语料进行语篇信息的定性分析。

语料分析表明，法官有时在庭审互动过程中建构出控辩审间的倒三角关系。在操控庭审的过程中，法官的独白偶尔会具有"控审合作"倾向，违背庭审程序。法庭对话中，法官也会使用有违庭审程序的"有罪推定"语篇信息。而法庭问答内容最为丰富，法官的语篇信息处理不当可能也会导致"有罪推定"、"控审合作"或"控辩不平等对抗"等违背司法公正的后果。这些都不利于维护被告人的诉讼权利。

分析还揭示了在法官的语篇信息处理中影响控辩审关系建构的各种因素，详述了法官庭审语篇如何遵循或违背了司法公正。分析发现，法官的定位、中立性和对当事人的信任性与程序公正密切相关。法官的目的和动机、个人因素或非个人因素影响着庭审中的分配公正；而惩罚公正的违背主要源于应得惩处、惩处对象、惩处手段以及惩处力度。根据司法公正原则可知，分配公正和惩罚公正的违背最终导致程序公正的破坏。

同时通过比较研究，归纳出法官通过语篇手段重构控辩审关系的框定策略。在语篇立足点迁移的策略分析中，归纳了法官的三种语篇立足点，即"语篇实践者"、"语篇实践者+语篇作者"、"语篇实践者+语篇作者+语篇委托者"。在互动中，信息层次降级、信息层级移位或共享分类修改等语篇手段会引起语篇立足点迁移。在分析再框定的策略时，归纳出了框架紧缩、框架延展和框架合意三种次级策略。框架紧缩主要通过信息单位增补或信息单位合并等手段以实现框架的具体化；框架延展是通过冗余信息删除或信息单位融合等手段来完成；框架合意则通过信息点更换、信息单位重复或信息单位共享等手段来实现。在中国法制背景下，这些策略和具体的语篇手段有助于避免控辩审正三角关系重构中的司法不公。

　　本研究的主要创新点在于基于语篇信息的框架分析解决了控辩审关系的建构问题。语料分析证实了该分析框架的适用性和有效性。本研究提出系统的语篇处理策略和具体的语言实现手段，为司法公正相关课题提供了语言研究视角和研究方法。另外，本研究的分析框架具有综合性和多维性特征。它把互动性框架、框定和语篇立足点迁移融为一体，构成了框架分析的三个核心成分。并应用了"法律语篇树状信息结构"这一操作性强的分析工具，有效地支持了框架的认定和定性、语篇立足点的分类和迁移、框定过程和策略分析。此外，本研究为与刑事诉讼相关的教学提供了更为丰富的内容，对有志于从事司法工作尤其是从事法官工作的学习者也具有启发意义。该研究强调保障被告人合法权益、维护程序公正、分配公正和惩罚公正，因此对中国司法改革具有参照作用。

　　本书用英文出版，便于向国外推广，加深国外法律语言学界对中国法律语言的认识。本著作可能尚存不当之处，敬请读者批评指正。

Abstract

Prosecution-Defense-Judge (PDJ) relationship is a major concern both in judicial practice and in the study of criminal litigation. Up to now, the research on this topic from judges' discursive perspective in particular remains fairly insufficient at home and abroad. However, now that judges' jurisdiction is exercised in the courtroom interaction, judges' discourse processing will influence the construction of the relations among all the parties in trials. Thus, how judges construct rational PDJ relationship via discourse processing becomes the focus of the present research.

To accomplish the research objective in the present study, an analytical framework is constructed for the description, analysis and interpretation of the language used by judges in court. On the basis of frame theory integrated with some other tools, the analytical framework is concerned with judges' discourse processing at the micro-level, meso-level and macro-level, which involves such constituents of frame analysis as interactive frames, framing and footing shifts. All these constituents are mainly investigated through the qualitative analysis of discourse information from a legal corpus.

Data analysis shows that judges may sometimes construct PDJ relationship as an inverted triangle in the courtroom interactive process. In the manipulation of trials, judges' monologue occasionally violates trial procedures, inclining to "Prosecution-Judge (PJ) cooperation". In courtroom dialogue, judges may use the discourse information with guilt presumption, which always violates trial procedures. As for courtroom questioning, judges' discourse information processing may result in "presumption of guilt", "PJ cooperation" or "Prosecution-Defense (PD) adversarial inequality". All these phenomena are detrimental to the maintenance of defendants' litigant rights.

Data analysis also reveals that various variables affecting judges' discourse information processing lead to the observation or the violation of judicial justice on the three dimensions relevant to the PDJ relationship. Judges' standing, neutrality and trust are closely related to procedural justice; judges' goal and motivation, individual or non-individual factors influence distributive justice; and deserving punishment, criminal punished, punishment means or punishment severity are pertinent to retributive justice. Based on the principles of judicial justice, the violation of distributive justice or retributive justice eventually leads to the destruction of procedural justice.

Through comparative analysis, judges' framing strategies are generalized for the reconstruction of PDJ relationship, which have been realized in the discursive way. In the courtroom interaction, judges' footing is categorized as "animator", "animator + author" or "animator + author + principal". Judges' footing shifts, as a strategy in reconstructing PDJ relationship, can be utilized by means of such discursive devices as degradation of information levels, displacement of information levels or modification of knowledge categories. As another strategy, reframing involves frame contraction, frame expansion and frame negotiation. Frame contraction can be employed to specify frames via addition of information units or combination of information units. Frame can be expanded by deletion of redundant information or assimilation of information units. Frame negotiation can be achieved by alteration of knowledge categories, repetition of information units or sharing of information units. These findings bring the research to the conclusion that judges' appropriate footing shifts or reframing in an appropriate way constitutes effective means to avoid the violation of judicial justice in the reconstruction of a "regular-triangled" PDJ relationship in China's legal context.

The major contribution of the present research lies in addressing judges' construction of PDJ relationship via the information-based frame analysis. Data analysis has proven the applicability and validity of the analytical framework used in attaining the research objective of this study. Our discursive approach focuses on the authentic data of courtroom discourse, brings forth some relevant discursive strategies and specific devices of discourse processing and provides a linguistic perspective for relevant legal issues to judicial justice.

Moreover, the analytical framework is characterized by the comprehensive and tridimensional interactive frame analysis. Interactive frames, framing and footing shifts have been integrated, which form the three constituents of frame analysis. The framework has employed "Tree Information Structure of Legal Discourse (TISLD)" as an operable and feasible tool. The identification and characterization of frames, the categorization and shifts of footings, and the process and strategies of framing are all mainly attributed to the analysis of discourse information processing.

In addition, the present research has provided the new content for the teaching of criminal litigation and offered some implications to the future legal workers, especially the learners who are determined to be judges.

It is also hoped that the research can be of value to China's judicial reform, as it lays much emphasis on protecting and safeguarding the defendants' legitimate rights and interests, upholding and maintaining procedural justice, distributive justice and retributive justice.

Key words: PDJ relationship; construction; courtroom discourse; discourse processing; frame analysis

Transcription Conventions

?	Inquiring intonation
,	Continuation
.	Falling, stopping intornation
......	Omission
=	Contiguous utterances
::	Prolonged syllable; the more colons, the more elongation
↑	Raising intonation
↓	Falling intonation
(0.5)(2.6)	Examples of timed pause
(.)	Micro pause (shorter than 0.5 seconds)
<u>word</u>	Stressed word
°word°	Quieter and softer speech
><	Speeding up utterance
<>	Slowing down utterance
(word)	Comments made by the researcher
[ ]	The start and end of overlapping speech
Bold	Speech that is obviously louder than surrounding speech
▬	Cut-off of the preceding sound
--	A short, untimed interval without talk
⊥	repair

Abbreviations

PDJ	Prosecution-Defense-Judge
PD	Prosecution-Defense
PJ	Prosecution-Judge
JD	Judge -Defense
FA	frame analysis
TISLD	Tree Information Structure of Legal Discourse
CA	conversation analysis
IS	interactional sociolinguistics
CLIPS	the Corpus for the Legal Information Processing System
CPL	The Criminal Procedure Law of the People's Republic of China (1996)
KN	Kernel Proposition
WT	What Thing
WB	What Basis
WF	What Fact
WI	What Inference
WP	What Disposal
WO	Who
WN	When
WR	Where
HW	How
WY	Why
WE	What Effect
WC	What Condition
WA	What Attitude
WG	What Change
WJ	What Judgment

Contents

Introduction

The pursuit of judicial justice and legal equality is the main goal for which people in different societies have been struggling. With the advancement of the legal system in China nowadays, criminal trials tend to be transparent, just and equal. However, there is quite a long way to go to realize the rational construction of Prosecution-Defense-Judge (PDJ) relationship, which attracts special attention in China's criminal courtroom. Supported by the current legal system, such a legal issue is also influenced by the actions of the participants in trial, specifically referring to their courtroom discourse practice.

Judges' courtroom discourse will be the special focus in the present research, as judges constitute the best role in the construction of PDJ relationship (Li, 2006). The study of legal issues by means of linguistic theories and methods, which is the nature of forensic linguistics, provides us with an incentive to adopt a discourse analytical approach to the hot legal issue. Based on frame analysis, this study will integrate some other analytical tools to describe, analyze, and interpret the language used by judges in court with the expectation of promoting the criminal trial reform, strengthening the criminal defense system and enhancing judicial justice in China.

This introductory chapter will define the key working terms, observe the research background, justify the rationale of the present study, state the general research objective, raise some research questions, and outline the organization of the present research.

1.1   Key Concepts

The three key concepts *discourse, frame* and *PDJ relationship* need to be defined since they are utilized as the working terms in the present study.

1.1.1   Discourse

As the subject of heated debate, the notion of *discourse* has been defined both from common sense and from theoretical sense by many scholars in various disciplines. Not only linguists and discourse analysts, but also sociologists, use the word quite often in their research.

Linguists define discourse as the use of language(Brown & Yule, 1983), the designation of any spoken or written variety of language use (Verschueren, 1999), or a social one produced within a communicative event (Bloor & Bloor, 1995) or used in social context (Martin & Rose, 2003).

Discourse analysts all agree that discourse is a form of language use, but they want to include some other essential components in the concept, namely *who* uses language, *how*, *why* and *when* (van Dijk, 1997a).

In social sciences, Foucault defines discourse as systems of thoughts composed of ideas, attitudes, courses of action, beliefs and practices that systematically construct the subjects and the worlds of which they speak (Lessa, 2006). Modernist theorists view discourse as "a being relative to talking or way of talking and understood discourse to be functional" and postmodern theorists "embark on analyzing discourses such as texts, language, policies and practices" (Strega, 2005).

All in all, no matter what kind of definition is given, the term holds two senses, one linguistic and one social. Conley and O'Barr argue that (1998) the former, which overlaps with language and will be called microdiscourse, is illustrated by phrases such as everyday discourse and courtroom discourse; the latter by phrases such as the discourse of social factors and the discourse of cognitive factors, sensed as macro-discourse. In the present study, the working term discourse can be defined as an institutionalized way of thinking in an interactional or cognitive process, which can be manifested through language within its social and ideological context.

1.1.2   Frame

The academic term "frame" can be traced back to the work of Bateson (1955). It was in his first major work, *The Presentation of Self in Everyday Life* that Erving Goffman (1959) introduced "frame" to sociology and then made it an important notion in qualitative study. Bateson and Goffman understood frames as being our conceptual or cognitive views of particular situations (Chenail, 1995). Goffman's (1974) basic opinion on frame is that people interpret events or strips of activity in situations with schemata that cognitively encircle or frame what is occurring.

To Gamson, a frame is a "central organizing idea or story line that provides meaning" (Gamson & Modigliani, 1987: 143) to events related to an issue. It is the core of a larger unit of public discourse, called a "package" that also contains various policy positions that may be derived from the frame as well as a set of "symbolic devices" (Gamson & Modigliani, 1987: 143) that signify the presence of frames and policy positions. Frames are underlying structures or organizing principles that hold together and give coherence to a diverse array of symbols and idea elements (Creed, Langstraat & Scully, 2002) and can be signified through some symbolic devices (Gamson & Lasch, 1983;

Gamson & Modigliani, 1989).

Tannen (1993) argues that frames—interactive and cognitive mechanisms—act as structures of expectation that enable social actors to define or redefine the situation, to relate their structures of experience to what is actually taking place in the interaction, or to participate coherently in the communicative exchange.

> Interactive frames are the mechanisms whereby those taking part in an interaction evoke and interpret the activity they are co-constructing. They correspond essentially to the concept of frame put forward by Goffman (1974), who sees them as principles for social interaction and organization. According to Goffman (1974), social activities are perceived by speakers in terms of their participation frameworks, which not only serve to provide their actions with meaning, but also involve and commit them to the communicative exchange...
>
> (Tannen & Wallat, 1993)

In contrast, knowledge schemas represent the cognitive dimension of the frames (ibid).

> They refer to participants' expectations about people, objects, events and settings in the world, in contrast to the alignments being negotiated in a particular interaction. At all events, ... knowledge schemas and interactive frames must not be seen as separate mechanisms. To a certain extent, they represent two sides of the same coin, as they act together during interaction. Indeed, a mismatch between knowledge schemas would lead to changes in interactive frames.
>
> (Tannen & Wallat, 1993)

Given the judges' discourse orientation of this study, we will integrate the definitions by Goffman (1974), Gamson (1987) and Tannen (1993) as our working one, in that it lends itself to the analysis of textual messages. Frames, which can be signified through linguistic devices, are the combination of interactive and cognitive mechanisms and act as structures of expectation that enable social actors to define or redefine the situation, to relate their structures of experience to what is actually taking place in the interaction, or to participate coherently in the communicative exchange. Frame is used to analyze how people understand situations and activities while framing is the process by which a communication source defines and constructs a social issue or public controversy.

1.1.3   PDJ Relationship

The ideal PDJ relationship in trial is the one like an equilateral triangle, or like a balance in which the prosecution and the defense are two trays supported justly by judges (Bian, 2007). Therefore, judges' action will either bring Prosecution-Defense (PD) balance or lead to the PD unbalance. At present, the law theories in both the common law system and the continental law system universally accept the PDJ relationship—"equality between the prosecution and the defense with the neutral judge" as an inherent element in the trial justice (Chen, 1997: 261).

The Criminal Procedure Law of the People's Republic of China (CPL) (1996) stipulates that the courtroom PDJ relationship in China is PD balance with the neutral judge, which constitutes the definition in the present study. According to the law, the prosecution in courtroom includes prosecutors and victims; the defense includes defendants and their defenders; and the judge includes presiding judges, judges and people's assessors.

1.2 Research Background

1.2.1 Judges in the Courtroom Interaction

1.2.1.1 Judges' Role in the Courtroom Interaction

Olsen (1991) has examined the basic nature of social interaction, the enactment of social roles within social life and illustrated (Figure 1-1) the idea that social relationships develop as social actors (participants) interact through social actions.

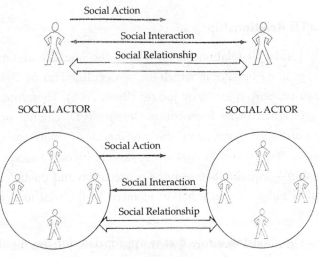

Figure 1-1   Social actors, social actions, social interactions, and social relationships (Olsen, 1991)

In his opinion, "roles are dynamic sets of expectations and actions that individuals enact in relevant situations. Frequently, however, we want to locate a particular role or set of roles within an established relationship or organization." (ibid: 21) Successful role enactment, which needs three steps diagrammed in Figure 1-2, has two major benefits of individuals: first, roles provide guidelines for our social actions; second, roles give regularity and predictability to our social interactions.

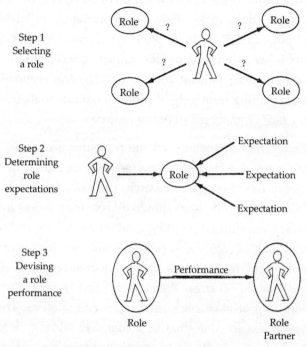

Step 1
Selecting
a role

Step 2
Determining
role
expectations

Step 3
Devising
a role
performance

Figure 1-2   Steps in role enactment (Olsen, 1991)

According to Olsen (1991), the first step in role enactment is role selection, or choosing a role that is appropriate for the situation, the other people involved, and oneself; the second is determining the expectations of the role one has chosen to enact in a given situation; and the third is devising a role performance based on the expectations for the chosen role, situational conditions, and one's role partners. Olsen's opinion will help us conceptualize our theoretical framework because discursive strategies constitute the key part of performance (Duranti, 1997).

Qu (2006) argues that judges' multi-role conflicts exist between powerful role and legal role, between cultural role and legal role, and between social role and legal role for the reason that any trial at present will be the result from the competition among various judges' roles. Firstly, judges make decisions dependently in trials because irrational power relations lie in the current power system. Secondly, judges' trials are influenced by the conflict between traditional legal culture and modern judicial conception. Thirdly, economic factors result in the shifting from judges' professional role to their social role when they face promotional or economic lure.

Although he has anatomized the headstream of those conflicts, Qu (2006) does not propose some specific measures to avoid or resolve them. Based on Qu's research, Li (2007) argues that judges' legal role originates from law[1] (powerful role from power institutions, cultural role from cultural traditions, values and ethics, and social role from social life). Li (2007) also puts forward two suggestions on the solution of judges' role conflicts. One is about judges themselves, that is, judges should change their ideas and accept just judicial conceptions to protect citizen's legal rights and interests. The other is about system construction, that is, a complete set of systems clearly oriented to judges' role should be established to ensure judicial justice. In addition, Wang (2006) believes that the realization of judicial justice in court requires the intensive training of judges' ethical role.

Scholars abroad have been studying judges' role from the perspective of linguistics. Cotterill (2003) argues that the judge plays a dual role to keep order in court: first, as representative of the Law; second, and more significantly from the point of view of interactional dynamics, as controller and moderator of the talk produced by all the other participants.

---

1. "Judges are judicial persons who exercise the judicial authority of the State according to law" in Article 2 of Judges Law of the People's Republic of China. (translated by the present author)

The judge has the greatest degree of linguistic freedom, commensurate with his status, in terms of his own turns as well as his control over those of the other interactants in court. The judge is responsible for managing the day-to-day running of the trial and has the freedom to address all members of the courtroom cast; from lawyers and witnesses to the jury, press corps and public gallery, the judge has the right not only to address any of those present in court, but also to restrict the turns of these participants.

(Cotterill, 2003: 93)

Cotterill's categorization of judges' role, oriented to the American trial process, is not of universal applicability, but the linguistic technique of exploring the role gives us some implications for the exploration of judges' discursive behavior in the criminal courtroom.

In the courtroom interaction, judges need to position themselves in the construction of PDJ relationship. The research on judges' role helps us to explicate reasons why judges employ some linguistic devices to frame certain PDJ relationship and suggest how they should shift their footings to manipulate discourse information to construct rational PDJ relationship.

1.2.1.2   Judges' Courtroom Discourse

In the court setting, it is the role of the jury or judge to communicate different messages to decide which witnesses to believe and whose testimony to hold above others in reconciling difference (O'Barr, 1982). Obviously, judges' discourse is one of the main topics in the courtroom discourse study (Du, 2003).

Some scholars at home and abroad have explored the specific language use in courtroom.

According to Shuy's (2007) review of the studies on judges' language, Conley and O'Barr (1990) describe research on the efforts of litigants to make their case in small claims courts. Those who follow the rules that reflect the language of the courts are successful. Those who describe their problems using the language of broad social terms tend not to succeed. Philips also explores how the syntactic form of judges' questions (e.g., *yes/no* questions vs. *wh*-questions) greatly affects the nature of the answers that those questions will elicit (Berk-Seligson, 1990). In his work *The Language of Judges*, Solan (1993) utilizes Chomsky's TG grammar to analyze judges' trial language meticulously and shows how various linguistic features and terms are handled by judges, including "plain language', the "and/or" rule, and how antecedents and pronouns are used and interpreted by the courts.

Wu (2002) believes that both the importance of judges' language and the inevitability of judges' decision-making in court account for the study of judges' discourse. Through the analysis of some authentic courtroom records, Xu and Li (2006) adopt adaptation theory to examine *overinformative response* in courtroom interaction, investigate language users' psychological and social factors, and suggest that judges should discern respondents' language strategies to improve the quality of their questions.

Their studies remind us that both litigants' and judges' linguistic strategies or devices play an important role in the final judgment of relevant cases. The research also demonstrates that the study on courtroom discursive strategies constitutes an indispensable part in the field of forensic linguistics, for example, judges can employ plain language to explain difficult legal terms to illiterate litigants in trials.

Some other experts pay special attention to the study on the relations between judges' discourse and power.

Conley and O'Barr (1998) also examine judges' courtroom discourse from such three aspects as language, discourse and power in their book *Just Words: Law, language, and power*. Moreover, Philips' book, *Ideology in the Language of Judges* (1998), is an ethnographic study of the power of judges who apparently believe that they simply follow and apply the law in a neutral and apolitical way but who still fall deeply into individual interpretation of it.

Starting from discourse resource used and discourse freedom owned by judges and parties in court, Lü (2006) analyzes the discourse model of courtroom interaction and reveals the phenomenon of judges' power manipulation and power relations between different participants in courtroom communication.

The study on discourse and power proves that judges' courtroom discourse influence judicial justice in trials greatly through their exercise of authority. It also offers the implication that the research on judges' discursive actions should be made from different perspectives, for example, judges' discursive construction of PDJ relationship in court cannot be separated from their discourse affected by their authority.

All the researches above provide us with implications on courtroom discourse analysis, in which not only linguistic features and discursive patterns are involved, but psychological and social factors might be discussed as discourse is produced in interaction. Du (2004) also holds the opinion that forensic linguistic research should be placed in the sociological framework and emphasizes that the study of judges' discourse should be based on the sociological background. It is Du's opinion that helps shape the standpoint of the present research.

1.2.2   PDJ Relationship in Courtroom

1.2.2.1   Judicial Justice in Court

Judges' discursive practice in court is inevitably involved with judicial justice, which has always been studied from the jurisprudential perspective and the legal sociological perspective.

Some scholars have explored the relationship between judicial justice and the reform of legal system in China. Kuang (2000) maintains that the process of the reform, in which the legal supervision system should be improved, depends on the constitution and starts from the leading system of the judicial organs, financial management, and the internal working system of the court. Actually judicial justice is reflected partly by the independence and neutrality of the court, which play the roles of the prerequisites and conditions in the legal practice. Therefore, it can be introduced to advance the judicial reform that the common international criteria proposed in United Nations focus on the independence of the court in the maintenance of judicial justice (Bai, 2003).

The equality between the prosecution and the defense constitutes the core of the criminal judicial justice. Ji (2007) holds that equality of arms, equal protection, adversarial equality and equal cooperation have composed the modern connotation of the PD balance. This requires procedural justice and substantive justice, taking just trial as the core. The justice includes some rights and principles. The former includes the rights to keep silence, defend, learn the truth and lodge an appeal, which are given to the accused as the means in litigation. The latter includes that no person can be forced to give evidence that may incriminate himself, no person can be presumed guilty before the pronouncement of judgment, the procedures should be regulated by law and illegal evidence should be excluded as the guarantee.

PDJ relationship is related directly to courtroom judicial justice, which is discussed by Sanders and Hamilton (2000) from three dimensions. They maintain that justice is particularly important in legal contexts: Nowhere are justice concerns closer to the surface than in law and we look to law to assess the direction of our moral compass. Consequently, justice in legal institutions has also been explored from the three core dimensions: retributive justice, procedural justice, and distributive justice. Retributive justice and distributive justice constitute the whole of substantive justice.

According to Sanders and Hamilton (2000), retributive justice, concerned with punishment, explores the desire for retribution and revenge, which focuses somewhat more on the subjective psychological reaction of the victim. To the degree, this is the case; retributive justice is more concerned with what happens to a wrongdoer. Most research on retribution has taken place within the context of formal legal processes, especially those involving criminal justice issues.

Distributive justice centers on fairness in the distribution of rights or resources, i.e. it examines the conditions under which allocations will be defined as just or equitable. When individuals are instructed to pursue fairness, they apply different allocation rules depending on the situation (ibid).

Additionally, procedural justice concerns the fairness and the transparency of the processes by which decisions are made, and may be contrasted with distributive justice and retributive justice. Hearing all parties before a decision is made is one step which would be considered appropriate to be taken in order that a process may then be characterized as procedurally fair (ibid).

The previous study provides with the implication that PDJ relationship has always been related to the three dimensions of judicial justice. Procedural justice actually means the impartiality in the process of judgment while substantive justice is a relative domain that must be achieved through procedural justice. PD balance in PDJ relationship is the requirement of procedural justice and influenced seriously by substantive justice.

In courtroom, judges' neutral performance determines PD balance to some extent (Song, 2003; Li, 2006). According to Brennan (1996), a judge serves the community in the pivotal role of administering justice according to law, especially presides at a trial. The judge's function is to keep the ring, not to enter the fight. The present criminal procedure law in China offers judges favorable conditions juridical neutrality to investigate criminal cases. Judges keep their neutral position and give equal opportunities to the prosecution and the defense to clarify cases. This is necessary to the realization of both procedural and substantive justice (Li, 2006).

Juridical neutrality is the core sense of judges' courtroom role (Li, 2007) which is evoked by means of discourse. It is difficult to tell if judges' role embodies judicial justice in the construction of PDJ relationship. "Justice must not only be done, but must be seen to be done[2]." Since judges' judicial behavior actually takes on discourse practice (Zhong, 2009), the exploration of PDJ relationship can be made based on judges' performance and the three dimensions of judicial justice (Sanders & Hamilton, 2000) through the adoption of a discourse approach.

Specifically speaking, procedural justice will be embodied through the way in which whether judges' discourse processing in the manipulation of trial procedures observes relevant laws and regulations (Sanders & Hamilton, 2000). Distributive justice reflects the rationality and fairness of judges' allocating discursive power to the other parties in court since it relates to the allocation of interest (ibid). Besides, whether retributive justice is complied with depends on punishment means and severity (ibid) based on relevant laws and regulations, which are expressed through judges' discourse.

---

2. A legal proverb

1.2.2.2   Opinions on PDJ Relationship

Not only has the study of courtroom discourse drawn a great deal of attention in China, but also PD relationship in court has always been appealing to many scholars, especially those in the field of law. Although they take different perspectives or adopt different approaches for different purposes, these scholars have made insightful studies on this issue. In this section, previous researches are reviewed in order to present a relatively complete picture of the status quo of the research.

Criminal prosecution has developed from the inquisitorial system in feudal society to the adversary system in the Anglo-Saxon Law System and the inquisitorial and adversary system in the Continental Law System, which boasts one important feature—to safeguard the rights of the defendant (Feng, 1998). Furthermore, as related to each other closely, the equality between the prosecution and the defense can demonstrate the rights of the defendant adequately (ibid). China's new criminal procedure law has obviously revised the part of safeguarding of the rights and interests of the defendant that provides the procedure support for the equality between the prosecution and the defense (Shen, 2001). At present, the study on the equality between the prosecution and the defense is mostly made from the procedural perspective.

From the legal thought and the theories of law, it is clear to see that the issue about the equality between the prosecution and the defense has always been discussed in both China and foreign countries. Locke's emphasis on everybody's equality before law in the era of Bourgeois Revolution, Jefferson's view on human rights given by the God and Dworkin's theory of citizen's rights—all these have provided the basis for the equality between the prosecution and the defense from the angle of legal thought (Gu, 2000). Since the core of procedural justice is to protect the rights of defendants' individuals and restrict the state power, Dershowitz[3] in the US and Radbruch (1963) in Germany have stressed that both the prosecution and the defense should enjoy procedural equity and justice.

Similar to the Principle of Equivalent Means proposed in the foreign theories of criminal procedures, the minimum justice standard has been put forward by Chinese scholars (Shen, 2001): 1) People influenced directly by criminal judgment should have sufficient rights to participate in the trial process. 2) Judges should be neutral to the prosecution and the defense. 3) The prosecution and the defense should be treated equally. 4) The trial procedures should be rational. 5) The judgment should be made in the trial process. 6) The judgment should be made in time so that the defendant's criminal responsibility will be ascertained. Ma (1998), Yang (1999) and Feng (1998) have also explored the equality between the prosecution and the defense in China based on the trial procedures, and they agree that the basic meaning of judicial justice is the maintenance and embodiment of equity and justice in the judicial process and result.

Although they have done little research on PDJ relationship, forensic linguists have contributed to the study of judicial justice from the linguistic perspective. Gibbons (1994a) argues that "sometimes injustice is deliberately enacted by politicians, with the support of some or most of the population. In other cases it is the result of the way the legal system itself operates. In either case these injustices can involve language as it is used in the law." And he has also implemented frame analysis in the study of unequal treatment in the justice system (Gibbons, 2003: 224). In consequence, whether judicial justice exists can be demonstrated by the legal process including

---

3.《"最好的辩护"来到中国——本刊总编与美国著名律师艾伦·德肖微茨对话》，载自《中国律师》2001 年第 7 期。

language use as the detail of law application. Liao (2006) explores "formulation" in Chinese courtroom discourse that influences judicial justice, and reveals the nature and the characteristics of the phenomenon. He argues that formulation is one of the reasons that cause misjudged cases. Zhang and Liu (2006) argue that the trial language of the judge falls in the domain of the metalanguage that affects the representation of the case, i.e. the trial content. Evidence from their data analysis shows the dilemma for judge's impartiality in court that there is certainly a kind of intervention, which might undermine people's perception of judicial justice. Du (2008) maintains that judges' manipulation of information flow facilitates the steady and orderly progress of the trials, and directly affects trial justice and efficiency because judges determine trial procedures and allot discourse power.

The previous research shows that firstly, hardly has the issue of PDJ relationship been explored by means of integrated analytical tools. The production of discourse is affected by various factors and the role played by discourse is reflected on multi-levels, so it may be propitious to fully anatomize the present issue by multi-approach from multi-perspective. Secondly, scholars from the field of law and the field of linguistics drive the vehicles for exploring the issue on the two paralleled roads. Although both concern judicial justice, the former pays special attention to jurisprudential research while the latter takes great interest in courtroom discourse. Since the above literature demonstrates that PDJ relationship is directly relevant to judicial justice and is affected enormously by their courtroom discourse, it may be feasible and valuable to bridge judges' discourse processing and the construction of PDJ relationship on the three dimensions, i.e. procedural justice, distributive justice and retributive justice.

1.3 Rationale

Although the reform of China's trial has developed steadily, especially with the trial procedures having become ever-increasingly normalized, PDJ relationship still remains a hot legal issue mainly argued about and delved into, sporadically explored in the discourse study.

The rationale for adopting the topic is that legal discourse analysis, as one of the most important branches of forensic linguistics, has attracted more and more attention in this field. Nevertheless, it is an area of virgin soil to study PDJ relationship in China's criminal courtroom from the judges' discursive angle. Thus, we have chosen it so as to provide a new perspective for the study of PDJ relationship and make a certain contribution to forensic linguistics.

1.3.1 The Status Quo of Research on the Topic

Since forensic linguistics is interdisciplinary in nature, this topic is prompted and initiated by the following concerns involving the studies from sociological, jurisprudential and linguistic perspectives.

Firstly, as the first virtue of social institutions (Rawls, 1999: 3), justice should be studied in social science, with its essential requirements being focused on. Feagin (2006) claims that researchers should think deeply of social justice and engage sociologically in its study to aid in building more just and egalitarian human societies. A just balance preserves justice.[4] Starting with a sociologically informed theory of justice provided by Fraser, the collection *(Mis)recognition, Social Inequality and Social Justice* edited by Lovell (2007) considers some of the conceptual and philosophical contentions that Fraser's

---

4. A Latin proverb

(2007) model has provoked and presents some compelling issues of social justice in which the relationship between participants and justice is included.

Secondly, the construction of PDJ relationship is one of indispensable elements in law, especially the requirement of judicial justice in court (Xia, 2000; Cui, 2006; Wang, 2006; Li, 2007). According to Samaha (1997), judges affect decision making in criminal justice because judges, prosecutors, and defense attorneys should not oppose each other in competition for the truth as they are a team, negotiating the best settlement possible with minimal dispute and maximum harmony within the courtroom work group. Neubaucer (1988) considers the prime concern about judges' role is how the judge shapes the courtroom and in turn is shaped by the courtroom work group. Sanders & Hamilton (2000) consider retributive justice, procedural justice, and distributive justice as "three basic building blocks" of legal justice, "when any of these are violated we are often left with a sense of injustice". As for the topic of the construction of PDJ relationship, most scholars have explored from the perspective of legal systems, hardly concerning the dimensions of judicial justice.

Thirdly, linguists also exhibit their interests in language and justice. Participants have many different roles which affect the production and comprehension of discourse, so van Dijk (2001) assumes that judges are aware they are in the area of Law labeled as the global social domain while speaking and their discourse (local action) will engage in justice (global action). In fact, forensic linguists have made great contributions to the study of judges' courtroom discourse (O'Barr, 1982; Solan, 1993; Conley & O'Barr, 1998; Gibbons, 1994c, 2003; Cotterill, 2002, 2003; Solan & Tiersma, 2005). Although the study of courtroom language focuses on the research on the legal language applied practically in the specific situation with the help of forensic linguistic theories and approaches, there is lack of judges' discourse study on the present topic both at home and abroad.

Nowadays China's legal system stipulates the equality between the prosecution and the defense to protect the defense's rights and interests on the one hand; it endows the prosecution with the rights to supervise judges' trial on the other hand. Judges will be positioning themselves as a neutral role before the prosecution and the defense, and be facing the supervision from the prosecution as well. As a matter of fact, the discourse implying the presumption of guilt and the unjust discourse distribution both lead to PD unbalance. Therefore, it is necessary to study whether judges' action in court can keep PD balance and what role judges should play in the pursuit of judicial justice.

1.3.2 Frame Analysis as a Practicable Approach

Frame analysis is a multi-disciplinary method in social science research, which of course can be applied to the present study. It is a broad theoretical approach that has been put in use in communication studies, news, politics, and social movements among other applications. Social relations can be constructed through framing specific situations and events (Fisher, 1997), for example, Goffman uses the term "footing" to study roles in the frame theory, Fauconnier and Turner (2002) exemplify the buyer-seller relationship frame and the nature of the relevant activity, events and participants are specified in organizing frames.

What's more, discourse and frame are often utilized together in the organizational and institutional research because frames are indispensable for communications (Goffman, 1974; Gitlin, 1980; Gamson, 1987) and are essential to any speech activity and to any interaction (Hoyle, 1993). Operating at all levels of discourse, frames are sets of concepts that help an individual organize and interpret language and experience, and they are essential for understanding and producing situated and motivated discourse (Downs, 2002). The study of frame starts with analyzing language in that frames develop in discourse (van Dijk, 1980; Donati, 1992; Triandafyllidou, 1995) or in parallel with discourse (Fisher, 1997). Furthermore frame analysis is accordingly used to explore discursive strategies through which some social issues will be embodied or solved (Goffman, 1981; Tannen, 1989; Macgilchrist, 2007).

According to Goffman (1983), face-to-face communication titled as the interaction order, a domain that is warranted for employing the social situation as the basic working unit in its study. A trial progresses in a certain interaction order within some specific frames. Once some inappropriate information appears in an inappropriate procedure, the interaction order will be broken and PDJ relationship might be influenced. So the courtroom PDJ relationship can be bridged via appropriateness of discourse, which concerns the adjustment of one's language usage to suit the situation in which a communicative event takes place. Specifically speaking, PDJ relationship will be influenced by the participants' recognition of speech events, identification of particular contexts, application of language, and use of rule of speaking, which are corresponding to their social roles (Ferenčík, 2004).

1.4   Research Objective and Questions

The research objective is to study how judges construct rational PDJ relationship in the discursive way while performing their duty in China's courtroom and hence contribute to the reform of legal system and enrich legal discourse analysis. To achieve such a research objective, this study aims to answer the following research questions in view of what is stated in the rationale and in conformity to the theories relevant to discourse.

(1) What manifestations of PDJ relationship are framed by judges' discourse in the criminal courtroom interaction?

The goal of frame analysis is to understand how certain idea elements are linked together into packages of meaning, potentially encoded into sound-bite-like signifiers that stand for those packages of meaning, and deployed in situated discursive activity (Creed, Langstraat & Scully, 2002). Therefore, starting with monologue, dialogue and questioning, we will analyze how judges engage in courtroom discursive practice to frame PDJ relationship and how the specific frames are recognized. Since shifts between frames are a normal feature of conversation (Goffman, 1974), we will also explore the dynamic and interactive features of the frames identified.

(2) What factors influence the construction of PDJ relationship in judges' courtroom discourse practice?

With the trial proceeding and due to information exchange at different levels, it is of great importance to explore what factors impact on PDJ relationship in court by examining how judges' information processing observe or violate procedural justice, distributive justice or retributive justice. This demands a deep and sufficient analysis of judges' discourse information processing, and requires the look inside and outside the law to perceptions of justice in the society at large (Sanders & Hamilton, 2000).

(3) How are framing strategies employed by judges to construct PDJ relationship?

The framing strategies are embodied through discourse information manipulation in the courtroom interaction. To explore PDJ relationship, we need to verify whether judges' discourse made conforming to justice norms within the legal context. With footing shifts and reframing, judges manipulate discourse information overtly or covertly to help construct courtroom PDJ relationship. Here we will investigate comparatively and contrastively whether judges' discourse information processing accords with the three dimensions of judicial justice and how judges can enact framing strategies to overcome injustice and keep PD balance.

These three questions are formulated on the basis of frame theory and the research on justice for solving legal problems via discourse analysis. Therefore, discourse forms a string that links such three key points in the present research as judges, PDJ relationship and judicial justice.

1.5   Organization of the Book

This book will be organized as follows:

Chapter 1 introduces the scope of the present study, the rationale for the choice of the research topic, the objectives of the study, and the research questions we will answer.

Chapter 2 presents the theoretical backgrounds of frame analysis approach so as to formulate a conceptual framework for the current study of judges' discourse, including the application of frame theory to discourse analysis, some analytical approaches to legal discourse, and their relevance to the current research. It also explicates the core dimensions of constructing PDJ relationship and provides the methodology, which will include data collection, data analysis and specific research procedures.

The following three chapters concentrate on the discussion of the results of analyzing the relevant data from the corpus to answer the preceding three research questions. Chapter 3 will deal with judges' discourse and discourse information for the purpose of recognizing the types of PDJ relationship and identifying these frames in court, Chapter 4 will focus on the specific factors that affect PDJ relationship in judges' discourse practice with the shifts of frames, and Chapter 5 will explore judges' discursive strategies to construct PDJ relationship.

Chapter 6 is the closing part of this book. It will give a summary of the findings and discuss the theoretical and practical implications for judicial reform and legal discourse analysis. The limitations of the study and suggestions for future research are also included.

Chapter 2

Theoretical Framework

2.1 Introduction

On the strength of the rationale and the research objective, this chapter is devoted to the construction of the theoretical framework for the current topic. To guarantee the validity of ensuing discussions, we intend to recapitulate our conception of the relationship between judges' discourse and PDJ relationship. To offer the theoretical basis and methodological implications for the contextualization of this research, we will provide a brief overview of frame analysis, which is often employed in institutional discourse study. Integrating frame analysis with the overview of analytical dimensions, we will also develop a feasible and operable theoretical construct for our empirical research.

2.2 Theoretical Basis

Even after more than fifty years since its inception, frame theory remains less than unified and clear-cut as it has been subjected to numerous interpretations by theorists working within the fields of sociology (Goffman, 1974; Snow, 1986; Benford, 1994), cognitive psychology (Minsky, 1975; Fillmore, 1982; Frake, 1977; Tannen & Wallat, 1993) and linguistics (Gamson, 1987; van Dijk, 1977a, 1980, 1985).

2.2.1   Frame Theory

2.2.1.1   Sociological Perspective

Frame analysis originates from sociology (Goffman, 1959), with its service followed for sociological studies. Therefore, the overview of frame theory starts with the research from the sociological perspective.

(1) Goffman's Frame Analysis

Sociologists, and in particular, Erving Goffman (1974), have investigated framing as a process through which societies reproduce meaning and frame analysis promises a socio-semiological methodology, a technique for analyzing data.

Goffman argues that frame analysis addresses an experiential issue: how do individuals make sense of any given strip of activity? A strip is defined as "any arbitrary slice or cut from the stream of ongoing activity" (ibid: 10) that serves as the place where analysis starts (Smith, 2006). Any strip of activity, Goffman (1974: 8) noted, can pose a sense-making problem for individuals: "what is it that is going on here". Applying the relevant frame to the strip provides the solution.

The core of frame analysis rests on distinctions between three types of frame: the primary framework and two transformations or reworkings of the primary framework: the key and the fabrication (or design). A strip is rendered intelligible by a primary framework. It is primary in that it is the elemental interpretive scheme enabling the individual to make sense of activity that is otherwise meaningless. The use of primary frameworks is such a massive and omnipresent feature of social life that:

> We can hardly glance at anything without applying a primary framework, thereby forming conjectures as to what occurred before and expectations of what is likely to happen now … mere

perceiving, then, is a much more active penetration of the world than at first might be thought.

(ibid: 38)

Goffman suggested that each culture produces two types of primary frameworks: natural frameworks and social frameworks. Natural frameworks develop from purely physical experiences which people understand "to be due totally, from start to finish, to natural determinants", as distinct from experiences with which people associate a willful agent who both has the power and desire to influence at least some aspect of the experience (ibid: 22). As a result, "success or failure in regard to these events is not imaginable; no negative or positive sanctions are involved" (ibid: 22). In contrast, social frameworks arise from the willful exertions of "an intelligence, a live agency, the chief one being the human being" (ibid: 22). Frames organize information drawn from real experiences and about people and objects actually in the world. Keys, or stagings, mimic primary frameworks, but do not fully duplicate them (ibid).

> Primary frameworks can be transformed into either keys or fabrications (which might be thought of as secondary frameworks, although Goffman does not use this term). In the case of keyed frames, all the participants are aware that the activity is transformed. In the case of fabrications (or designs) there is an asymmetry: the mark has a false belief about the activity, unaware of the true nature of the transformation that has occurred.

(Smith, 2006: 57)

Goffman states that his frame perspective is situational, which amounts to "a concern for what one individual can be alive to at a particular moment, this often involving a few other particular individuals, and not necessarily restricted to the mutually monitored arena of a face-to-face gathering" (1974: 8). Frame analysis shifts the scope of his work towards the individual's experience and away from the interaction order that up until now had provided the analytic anchor for his studies.

His remark that "the first issue is not interaction but frame" (ibid: 127) suggests that frame analysis was intended to undergird his sociology of the interaction order up to this point (Smith, 2006). However, in the last decade of his life Goffman used frame concepts to deepen his interactional analysis. Frame analysis is especially effective in dealing with an issue his earlier interactional analyses tended to overlook: "context" (Scheff, 2005). Frame supplies the sense in which a strip of interaction is to be taken (Smith, 2006). Moreover, Goffman's opinion that shifts between frames are a normal feature of conversation has also been accepted by other scholars like Labov and Fanshel who identify in their data a configuration of different style associated with different frames (Fairclough, 1992).

In addition, Goffman (1981) uses the term FOOTING to refer to the alignments that people take up in relation to the social context. He suggests that both speakers and hearers are of different types. For hearers, he makes a distinction (made by others in different terms) between "addressed" and "unaddressed" recipients. For speakers, Goffman (1981) distinguished the roles of ANIMATOR, AUTHOR, and PRINCIPAL. The animator actually speaks the words, or "animator, referred to as the "sounding box", is the one who produces or gives a voice to the message that is being conveyed" (Duranti, 1997: 297). The author originally wrote or spoke those words, or it refers to "the one who is responsible for the selection of words and sentiments that are being expressed" (ibid: 297). And the principal (a term Goffman borrows from legal discourse) believes in those word, or it refers to "the person or institution whose position or beliefs are being represented by those words" and "also the one who is held responsible for whatever position is being presented" (ibid: 297).

> Goffman argues that situations vary as to the speaker and hearer roles that are available, and as to how they can be combined. The particular combinations for a given situation constitute its participation framework. The FOOTING or alignment of a participant toward an utterance will vary, depending on the combination of speaker roles held by the animator, which provide the "production" format of the utterance. Thus when I am reciting someone else's poem, my footing is different than when I am reciting my own poem; and the difference in footing produces a difference in framing.
>
> (Philips, 1983)

Taking the following conversations as examples to illustrate footings as "a frame is constructed through participants" signaling their footings and recognizing and ratifying another's footing—which often changes from moment to moment" (Ribeiro, 2006).

Example 1

1　John: The doctor believes that by any number of neurologists' standards that mom has mild cognitive decline.

2　Louis: Yeah.

3　John: He said that—based on what he has seen, that there is likely to be improvement in her condition.

Now that footing is "the linguistic expression of one's stance" (Kinney, 1998: 34), in Turns 1 and 3 John takes a footing as ANIMATOR of the doctor's beliefs. He uses indirect speech to paraphrase, animating the doctor's words, so he plays the role of "sounding box". Meanwhile, Turn 3 in this example provides the information that the doctor takes the footing as both AUTHOR and PRINCIPAL, because he has said those words and believed in the hopeful evaluation that "there is likely to be improvement in her condition."

Although Goffman has defined FOOTING clearly, the version of his frame analysis contains some methodological imperfections. Goffman gives little consideration to the development of frames in the first place, including the processes by which originators generate frames and the questions of who can produce frames, what conditions permit frame production, and what constraints influence that production (Fisher, 1997).

Succeeding to Goffman, sociological scholars like Snow and Benford have applied frame analysis to explore the processes by which social movements come to understand problems and to sell their perspectives to a wider audience. They suggest that frames overlap and organize the values and beliefs of movement activists, and that individual people control frame production.

(2) Snow and Benford's Application of Frame Analysis

Snow and Benford build on Goffman's work in their bid to account for the factors which contribute to the success or failure of social movements. Snow and Benford criticize social movement theories for taking a static view of participation (Snow et al., 1986). They contend that social movements not only frame the world in which they are acting, but also frame social problems (ibid, 1986).

A functional definition of frame analysis that advances this ontological claim has been developed by Snow and Benford (1988): frames are collections of idea elements tied together by a unifying concept that serve to punctuate, elaborate, and motivate action on a given topic, and framing as the process by which ordinary people make sense of public issues (Benford, 1994). People work with two types of frames: domain-specific interpretative frames, which organize sets of behaviors and individual lifestyles; and global interpretative frames or master frames which signify meaning on a broader scope and which organize sets of domain-specific frames (Snow et al., 1986).

Although they emphasize the dynamic feature of frame, Snow and Benford do not locate frames within the discourse patterns. In addition, they ignore the question of how social scientists might test the reliability and validity of frames. They do not address the question of how they identified the frames they discuss. Like Goffman, Snow and Benford raise the prospect that some frames are "truthful", while others are "misframings", but also like Goffman, they neglect the question of how researchers delineate between the two (ibid).

Goffman's opinion and Snow and Benford's application provide with necessity and feasibility to conduct frame analysis from the social perspective. However, frame is related to cognition, which requires cognitive analysis cannot be separated from frame analysis.

2.2.1.2 Cognitive Perspective

Frames have been described as "problem solving schemata, stored in memory, for the interpretive task of making sense of presenting situations (Johnston, 1995: 217)." because one of the central tenets of frame analysis is the idea that frames are cognitive constructs that are used to organize interpretations of, and responses to, particular situations (Kretsedemas, 2000). Therefore, some scholars have built an understanding of frames that is closely linked with cognition.

(1) Minsky's Static Concept

In contrast with the anthropological/sociological characterization of frames as an interactional unit with social meaning, Minsky (1974) holds a static concept of frame, rooted in the computer model of artificial intelligence. Minsky propounds the notion of frame as an all-inclusive term that is "a data-structure for representing a stereotyped situation, like being in a certain kind of living room, or going to a child's birthday party. Attached to each frame are several kinds of information. Some of this information is about how to use the frame. Some is about what one can expect to happen next. Some is about what to do if these expectations are not confirmed." (1974: 212).

For Minsky, this term denotes such event sequences as a birthday party, but also indicates expectations about objects and setting (e.g. a certain kind of living room). Minsky distinguishes at least four levels of frames: surface syntactic frames, surface semantic frames, thematic frames, and narrative frames (Tannen, 1993).

Although it represents a particularly coherent, complete, and readable formulation of the theory, Minsky's explication of frame theory just provides a static concept which has had resounding impact on the field of artificial intelligence and cannot be appropriately applied to the analysis of natural conversation or institutional discourse.

(2) Fillmore's Cognitive Opinion

Fillmore (1982) proposes frame theory in his works *Frame Semantics*, in which frame is considered as a coherent cognitive structure, related knowledge and concepts of recurring experiences, the stereotype of an object or an event, and the interface between pure language knowledge and conceptual knowledge.

Fillmore (ibid) also believes that the elaboration of any concept must touch upon other relevant concepts in the same frame; and there are at least two main relations between different frames, that is hierarchy and sub-frame relation. Framing is a process in which someone or something will be considered as a part of a frame so that the relations between different parts can be established (Figure 2-1).

From the translation of the figure in Zhu (2005), the figure concludes the role relations. When one participant in the communication frames a role, the other framed may enter the frame or may not. When

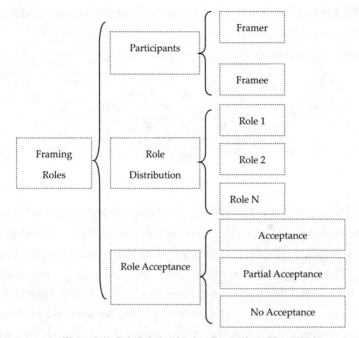

Figure 2-1   Role Relationship in a Frame (from Zhu, 2005)

someone frames the social roles of himself and others, role relations involved may be the simple "one-to-one", but "one-to-many", "many-to-one" or "many-to-many" may also exist. Moreover, role distribution concerns both the role chosen for oneself and the attitude including acceptance, partial acceptance or no acceptance adopted by the other participant in the communication (ibid).

In spite of special emphasis placed on cognition, Fillmore's frame theory is useful in three areas: "analysis of discourse, acquisition of word meaning, and the boundary problem for linguistic categories" (Tannen, 1993).

(3) Frake's Cognitive Notion

From the cognitive anthropological perspective, Frake (1977) holds a dynamic notion of frames in favor of an interactive model and has broadened the concept from its linguistic application to isolated sentences to a sequence of conversational exchange (Figure 2-2).

Figure 2-2   Contextual Model of Frame

He notes that in the cognitive anthropological notion of frame, the element A is specified by its contextual constraints X, Y, and by its relation to other elements B, that can occur in the same context. Frake (1977: 33-34) suggests that "the unique, and still poorly appreciated, contribution that the cognitive anthropologist made to this contextual model was that the context was not limited to portions of single, isolated sentences. A frame was construed as an inquiry matched with a set of responses. The unit of analysis was a question-answer sequence, a conversational exchange." Thus, the anthropological/ sociological view stresses frame as a relational concept. In his paper, Frake (1977) ends with the extended metaphor of people as mapmakers whose "culture does not provide a cognitive map, but rather a set of principles for mapmaking and navigation," resulting in "a whole chart case of rough, improvised, continually revised sketch maps". This metaphorical chart case seems awfully like a set of overlapping, intertwining, and developing scripts (Tannen, 1993).

Despite the importance attached to the context, the contextual model has not offered the concrete variables of frames or put forward practicable measures to conduct frame analysis. Therefore, other models need introducing for the deep analysis.

(4) Tannen and Wallat's Dynamic View

The dynamic view of frame has been utilized by Tannen and Wallet (1993) to make an analysis of some specific discourse—a pediatric examination. In their paper *Interactive Frames and Knowledge Schemas in Interaction*, Tannen and Wallat (1993) demonstrate a relationship between interactive frames and knowledge schemas by which a mismatch in schemas triggers a shifting of frames. They argue that interactive frames and knowledge schemas are two sides of the same coin and they cannot separate from each other.

As for frame theory, Goffman has developed a complex system of terms and concepts to illustrate how people use multiple frameworks to make sense of events even as they construct those events. Exploring in more detail the linguistic basis of such frameworks, Goffman (1981) introduced the term "footing" to describe how participants frame events; they negotiate the interpersonal relationships, or "alignments", that constitute those events. Succeeding to Goffman's frame theory, Tannen and Wallat (1993) refer the interactive frame to a definition of what is going on in interaction, without which no utterance (or movement or gesture) could be interpreted; also refers to a sense of what activity is being engaged in, how speakers mean what they say. They (1993) refer the term knowledge schema to participants' expectation that is corresponding to linguistic semanticists' interest and observation that even the literal meaning of an utterance can be understood only by reference to a pattern of prior knowledge.

Tannen and Wallat (1993) holds the opinion that not only interactive frames but knowledge schema are dynamic because all types of structures of expectations are dynamic as Frake (1977) has emphasized. This can be exemplified by the shifting frames triggered in a specific pediatric examination, in which the three most important frames are the social encounter, examination of the child and a related outer frame of its videotaping, and consultation with the mother. Tannen and Wallat's (1993) analysis demonstrates when participants have different schemas, the result can be confusion and talking at cross-purposes, and, frequently, the triggering of switches in interactive frames.

Just as Tannen and Wallat (1993) say, their viewpoint of frame analysis goes beyond the disciplinary limits of medical settings. There is every reason to believe that frames and schemas operate in similar ways in all face-to-face interaction, although the particular frames and schemas will necessarily differ in different settings.

2.2.1.3 Linguistic Perspective

The sociological and cognitive studies demonstrate frame analysis cannot conduct without discourse analysis since language serves as one of the main media in the construction of specific frames at the social level or cognitive level. The following will present Gamson's linguistic opinion on frame analysis and van Dijk's multi-dimensional practice in performing frame analysis.

(1) Gamson's Signature Matrix

Gamson has developed the sociological concept frame proposed by Goffman even further. To Gamson, a frame is a "central organizing idea or story line that provides meaning" (Gamson & Modigliani, 1987) to events related to an issue. It is the core of a larger unit of public discourse, called a "package", that also contains various policy positions that may be derived from the frame as well as a set of "symbolic devices" (Gamson & Modigliani, 1987) that signify the presence of frames and policy positions.   Five devices signify the uses of frames: metaphors, exemplars, catchphrases, depictions, and visual images (Gamson & Lasch, 1983; Gamson & Modigliani, 1989).

For Gamson, the underlying assumption of frame analysis is that a frame is a necessary property of a text—where text is broadly conceived to include discourses, patterned behavior, and systems of meaning, policy logics, constitutional principles, and deep cultural narratives (Creed, Langstraat & Scully, 2002).

Gamson and Lasch (1983) use frame analysis to sort out underlying logics. They provide one of the most basic and highly accessible ways of approaching frame analysis by laying out a "signature matrix" for sorting the specific idea elements of a set of texts into categories such as metaphors, exemplars, catchphrases, depictions, visual images, roots, consequences, and appeals to principle.

One goal of a frame analysis, and of a signature matrix as a particular technique, is to direct careful attention to how these diverse idea elements are deployed in integrated ways. This approach enables the analyst to discern the connections among these elements and to identify and distinguish the different unifying structures or frames that hold them together. A frame analysis not only clusters the texts, it also explains why any single text is meaningful (Creed, Langstraat & Scully, 2002). The text below has been analyzed as an example to exemplify signature matrix in frame analysis (ibid).

The principal idea of social investing is to support economic organizations that have a positive impact on society. This means a positive impact on all members of society, including gay, lesbian, bisexual and transgender people. We support the right of all people to obtain and keep employment based on merit, to live in decent housing, to raise children and live free of violence. We support the right of all people to a healthy life and to obtain health care insurance. In this regard, we think the views expressed by Genesis on gay and lesbian issues are not consistent with the values of social investing. (Letter to the organizer of the Making a Profit While Making a Difference conference, cited in Torbert, 1991b)

"The text represents a conflict over the meaning of socially responsible investing (SRI), unfolding in a contest of how to frame the core principles of the SRI movement. It also reveals how social forces impinge on organizations as their members try to figure out what stance to take on lesbian/gay/bisexual/transgendered (LGBT) issues. We use this case throughout to illustrate how and why to use frame analysis. (Creed, Langstraat & Scully, 2002)"

Table 2-1   Signature Matrix for Primary Frames in SRI Text

	Social Justice Frame
Metaphors	Meritocracy; democracy
Exemplars	Positive: People who value employment, housing, families, freedom from violence
Catchphrases	The "right[s] of all people"
Depictions	The rights of LGBT people
Visual images	None noted in this text
Roots	Economic organizations can have negative effects on society; corporate social responsibility
Consequences	People suffer when investors do not act responsibly; LGBT people will suffer if SRI screens them out
Appeals to principle	The goal is a positive impact for all; LGBT people should have the same basic human rights

The authors identify idea elements and sort them into a signature matrix (Table 2-1), asking what holds the diverse elements together. Then they give provisional labels to the primary frames of the text above. They find what they identify is the primary frame called "Social Justice Frame" in the text. The signature matrix demonstrates that frame contains such elements as linguistic means (metaphors, catchphrases or depictions) and nonlinguistic factors (visual images, exemplars, roots, consequences or appeals to principle). These idea elements require to be situated in specific context for deeper analysis, i.e. "the contextualization of framing activity comes into play" (Creed, Langstraat & Scully, 2002).

They also hold that the text also contains elements of other frames. For example, implicit in the text are what they might label the "correcting the negative impact of business", the "universal human rights", and the "inclusivity" frames. Such labels provide initial shorthand for the essence of each idea package; they should be grounded in the text and may even be directly quoted phrases (ibid).

After analyzing the identification of frames, the authors situate these frames in a context for further discussion. For instance, in the discourse about SRI, the meaning of the phrases "socially responsible" and "investing around our values" take on different meanings depending on who is using the terms and in what contexts.

Overall, these devices in the signature matrix above show not only the means by which an author or a speaker frames a situation, but also the way in which a reader or a listener identify a frame. The approach is a useful way to analyze frames based on precise measures of idea elements, laying the groundwork for the micro-analysis strategy. Meanwhile, idea elements have been considered as the constituents of a frame, which supports our opinion on frame analysis by means of different linguistic devices. In addition, Gamson's discovery of primary frames and sub-frames in a discourse has also proved that the hierarchical structure in discourse. Lastly, the matrix provides a more intuitionistic and visual model to make frame analysis, especially to identify a specific frame.

However, the approach needs to be improved for analyzing other kinds of institutional discourse in that the variables in the signature matrix should tally with what is being analyzed. The analysis at the linguistic level (metaphors, catchphrases and depiction) cannot be made sufficiently as it is known that metaphor cannot exist in every discourse and depiction is too general for the analysis. Moreover, the variable exemplars actually belong to cognitive factors, which can be specified in concrete analysis. The last three variables in the signature matrix are relevant to social factors, which can also be illustrated more clearly while frame analysis is being conducted.

Due to its application at linguistic, social and cognitive level, Gamson's approach proves its values in the frame analysis of institutional discourse. van Dijk's context analysis in frame analysis and discursive structures as frame analysis may provide more detailed and tangible variables in the actual exploration.

(2) van Dijk's Context Analysis in Frames

Context analysis (van Dijk, 1977a) highlights the relations between frames in social and cognitive contexts in the interaction.

van Dijk (1977a) notes that social context in a frame is "an abstract construct with respect to actual social situations". Social context analysis begins at the level of general social context, which may be characterized by the following categories: 1) private; 2) public; 3) institutional/formal; and 4) informal. Meanwhile, the different social contexts globally characterized are in turn defined by the following properties: 1) positions (e.g. roles, status etc.); 2) properties (e.g. sex, age, etc.); 3) relations (e.g. dominance, authority); and 4) functions (e.g. "father", "waitress", "judge", etc.)

van Dijk (ibid) also maintains context is a cognitive abstraction. The analysis of a particular context in terms of the concepts mentioned above is possible only with respect to general knowledge of social structure. The internal structure of the speaker, in terms of: 1) knowledge, beliefs; 2) want, desires, preferences; 3) attitudes; and 4) feelings, emotions. van Dijk says one of the most obvious examples of cognitive processing devices is based on the typical structure of the sentence: "if an interrogative structure is given, we may provisionally conclude that a question or request is made."

Finally, context analysis also involves self-analysis of the hearer. In order to understand that the particular speech act is appropriate to him, he must be aware of his own (previous) activities and the underlying knowledge, wishes, attitudes and emotions.

van Dijk (ibid) illustrates context analysis through the analysis of the example below, which will be construed from an institutional context.

"May I see your ticket, please?"

Although there is set of possible contexts with respect to which this utterance, taken as a request, may be appropriate, only one example will be given, viz. that of ticket inspection on trains, or means of public transport in general. The analysis based on social context has been carried out below, to which cognitive interpretation may complement.

> Social context type: Institutional. Public.
> Institution: Public Transport
> *Frame*: Ticket Inspection
> A. *Frame structure*
>   a. *Setting:*   train (during operation)
>   b. *Functions:* F(x): official ticket-inspector
>   G(y): passenger
>   c. *Properties:* x has visible signs of being inspector of the (railroad) company; and/or x can identify himself as being an

inspector of the (railroad) company;

x actually performs his task of ticket inspection;

y is the obvious ticket-holder (e.g. not a child travelling with his parent)

d. *Relations:* $F(x)$ has authority over $G(y)$;

e. *Positions:* (see functions): y is checked by x

x is checking y

B. *Frame conventions* (rules, norms, etc.)

1. Each passenger must have a valid ticket when on means of public transport;

2. Each passenger must show his ticket upon request to officials of the railroad company;

3. A passenger which is not in the possession of a valid ticket will be fined $25.00.

n. It belongs to the duties of ticket-inspectors to inspect tickets (...)

Contextual course of action:

Macro-action: x takes train to Z.

Previous acts: -x went to station

-x bought a ticket (=> has ticket)

-x entered carriage (=> is on train)

-x sees/looks at/hears inspector

-(x begins search for ticket)

"It is roughly in this kind of context that an utterance as this example may successfully be performed as an acceptable request. That is, the hearer will not only conclude from the form of the utterance itself that it is a request, but also that the request satisfies the specific request conditions as well as the grounds for these conditions, as defined by the social structure. Only those hearers who have the information available about the context as specified will be able to judge whether these grounds are sufficient for the acceptability of the act of requesting, and hence whether the request should be complied with or not" (van Dijk, 1977a).

"Thus, if one of the contextual features does not obtain the request may become spurious and hence socially unacceptable (at least to some degree). If I am not on the train, no request for my train ticket may be made; similarly if the inspector has neither a uniform nor identification: I need not show my ticket to any passenger requesting so; etc. Note that the frame conventions are the basis from which specific knowledge, beliefs, duties/ obligations, etc. may be derived. Hence, passenger x (= hearer) knows that by regulation (law) B.1. he should also have a ticket, a knowledge which is a condition for actually buying the ticket, and for feeling the obligation to show it to an inspector, when requested (as by B. 2)" (ibid).

van Dijk's model in frames is of benefit to the more concrete analysis, which has been embodied through the micro-categorization of social and cognitive variables. "Discourse is not simply a representation of related facts; it also must respect various information processing constraints, from both a cognitive and an interactional or social point of view (van Dijk, 1985)". These categories have actually specified the social and cognitive variables in Gamson's signature matrix model. Therefore, the integration of the two models may be valuable to explore in conduction frame analysis. Besides, van Dijk's model also highlights the analysis in the interaction in that the involvement of hearers should be considered. Now that van Dijk (1977a) holds that contexts are "not static, but dynamic", this model conforms to one of the important features of frames, i.e. interactive frames (Tannen & Wallet, 1993).

Meanwhile, van Dijk's frame analysis has also attached great importance to micro-linguistic investigation, which can be demonstrated through his utterance analysis of discursive structures.

(3) van Dijk's Discursive Structures as Frame Analysis

van Dijk's frame analysis provides us with a relatively general view on discourse. Discourses are in principle characterized by an overall meaning or macrostructure that formalizes the theme or topic of the discourse as a whole, and the local coherence of discourse is to be formulated in terms of propositional relationships denoting relations between facts in some possible world (van Dijk, 1985).

van Dijk identifies procedures in his study of macrostructures or discursive structures as frame analysis. van Dijk (1977b) argues that language, discourse, and social behavior arise from the cognitive processes by which people perceive, interpret, organize, and represent their knowledge of the world and language represents meaning on both a micro or local level and a macro or global level. That is, the rationality of discourse information distribution is embodied by discourse coherence both at the level of proposition sequences and at the level of a whole discourse (van Dijk, 1985).

The local coherence depends on rules and strategies for ordering sentences and expressing spatial, temporal, and conditional relations between propositions and facts. It has been emphasized that coherence always should be defined in terms of full propositions and the facts they denote and that coherence is relative to the world knowledge of speaker and hearer (ibid).

Example 1
a. *We went to an expensive restaurant.*
b1. *John ordered a big Chevrolet.*
b2. *John ordered a big turkey.*

Although (b1) is a meaningful sentence in isolation, it does not meaningfully relate to the previous sentence if it is interpreted as an action performed at the restaurant. Conversely, (b2) is appropriate to follow (a) in a coherent discourse. Our world knowledge about eating in restaurants organized in so-called scripts tells us that ordering a car "Chevrolet" is not a normal thing to do in restaurants, but "a big turkey" is. Hence, the meaningfulness of discourse also depends on what we assume to be the normalcy of the facts, episode, or situation described.

Another aspect of a meaningful discourse resides at a global (or macrostructural) level. A macrostructure is a theoretical reconstruction of intuitive notions such as topic or theme of a discourse. It explains what is most relevant, important, or prominent in the semantic information of the discourse as a whole. At the same time, the macrostructure of a discourse defines its global coherence (ibid).

Without such a global coherence, there would be no overall control upon the local connections and continuations. Sentences might be connected appropriately according to the given local coherence criteria, but the sequence would simply go astray without some constraint on what it should be about globally:

Example 2
This morning I had a toothache. I went to the dentist.
The dentist has a big car.
The car was bought in New York.
New York has had serious financial troubles.

Example 3
This morning I had a toothache. I went to the dentist.
The dentist asked me to open my mouth for examination.
After it, he drew out the bad tooth and filled the hole with some medicine.
Then the dentist asked me to have a good rest at home.

The facts in Example 2 may be related locally, but they are not related to one central issue or topic. However, Example 3 is both locally and globally coherent as the macrostructure—the process of seeing the dentist is the semantic information that provides this overall unity to a discourse. Often such underlying macrostructures are expressed by the text itself, for example, in announcements, titles, summaries, thematic sentences, or the expression of plans for action (ibid).

van Dijk's postulation of global and local discursive structures gives prominence to discourse elements mapping (van Dijk, 1980). Discursive structural analysis facilitates the analysis of how people construct individual discourse to achieve a particular communication goal. One could use this methodology to compare framing strategies of people who attempt the same communication goal in producing the same type of discourse, or to compare uses of a particular discursive frame by different people.

Although van Dijk concerns the narrow sense of frame, but the meaning-extensive concept plays an important role in the semantic micro-analysis of discourse (Han & Chen, 2003).

The above overview gives emphasis to three dimensions of frame analysis, that is, social frame, cognitive frame and linguistic frame covering their nature, property, as well as the condition of application to discourse analysis. It also displays that frame analysis cannot be conducted only from one of the three perspectives in that it always bond well to discourse analysis.

The overview demonstrates that discourse analysis is the key anchor for frame theory. This analysis has the potential of shedding light on such issues as the exercise of control in organizations, and employee resistance and submission to management control—issues of interest to scholars of discursive dynamics (Chreim, 2006).

Institutional discourse study can benefit from frame analysis (Creed, Langstraat & Scully, 2002), but such discourse exists in the context at different levels. Alvesson and Karreman provide the basis on which we now build our own conception of frame analysis. As different levels of context can be conceptualized and included in studies of discourse and frames, Alvesson and Karreman indicate that studies of discourse vary in terms of the assumptions they make regarding the scope and scale of discourse. The micro-discourse approach focuses on language use in a particular micro context, the meso-discourse approach attends to language use in context but goes beyond the material in the text, and the macro-discourse (grand-discourse) approach emphasizes the dominating power of ideologies and their impact on organizational frames (Alvesson & Karreman, 2000). The three approaches are naturally corresponding to the linguistic level, social level and cognitive level, which constitute a comprehensive analytical model for the research of institutional discourse.

2.2.2   Discourse Analysis and Frame Analysis

Rooted in a range of theoretical traditions, discourse analysis can be defined as the study of how segments or texts are structured and how they are used in communication (Conley & O'Barr, 1998: 7). Although different analytical approaches emphasize different aspects of language use, they all view language as social interaction and are concerned with the social contexts, in which discourse is embedded. And they help us analyze the exchanges between characters in order to facilitate the understanding of the text and how conversation works, and assist us to see things in the text that other forms of analysis might have allowed us to miss and so on (Thornborrow & Wareing, 1998). Therefore, to explore judges' discourse in court, it is indispensable to study the relations between discourse and context, discourse and interaction, and discourse and cognition.

2.2.2.1   Tree Information Structure of Legal Discourse

Due to the above overview of frame theory, we can connect Tree

Information Structure of Legal Discourse (TISLD) (Du, 2007) with frame analysis. Gamson's opinion on idea elements in frames corresponds to information chunks, which may be refined through discourse information analysis. This can also compensate for the weakness of linguistic analysis in signature matrix. Although the significance of Goffman's frame analysis is of far-reaching, the exploration of footing has always lacked the sufficiency of linguistic analysis, which is expected to be addressed through discourse information analysis. Moreover, van Dijk's view on macrostructural and microstructural coherence reflects the tree structure of discourse system, which tallies with the model of TISLD. Thus, it is a good way to combine macro-oriented and micro-oriented frame analysis. Meanwhile, van Dijk's macro-structure and micro-structure are based on the proposition, which is also consistent with the TISLD. Different from van Dijk's argument, TISLD can be utilized to make a much deeper analysis at the micro-discursive level. In the process of identifying frames and analyzing discourse, the application of TISLD may contribute more to the observation of information distribution in frames.

Accordingly, Tree Information Structure of Legal Discourse will be introduced as follows for the sake of concrete frame analysis.

Tree Information Structure of Legal Discourse (TISLD) is appropriate for analyzing both written and oral discourses. The terms information and information structure are endowed with meanings different from those in information theory and "language information' in common sense (Du, 2007).

The term information here is defined as a proposition with a relatively independent structure, which is a minimal meaningful unit for communication. Meanwhile discourse information structure refers to the structure of the content conveyed in a discursive way by discourse users. The information in a discourse is woven into a network in which the information in different parts relates to each other and bears such relations as primary and secondary, upper and lower, former and latter, etc. Here discourse information structure is different from discourse structure which refers to the surface structure of a discourse and emphasizes language, and also different from discourse proposition structure which refers to the network formed by propositions.

(1) Tree Information Structure

　　Discourse network is a hierarchical system in which a discourse has a kernel proposition surrounded by all information at different levels. Thus, discourse network can be described as a tree structure (Figure 2-3).

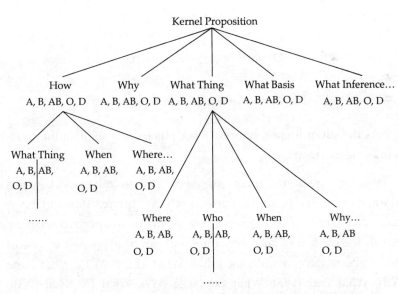

Figure 2-3　Tree Information Structure of Legal Discourse (from Du, 2007)

(2) Information Units and Information Knots

　　Discourse information structure is composed of information units each of which acts as the smallest meaningful unit based on a proposition. Information units relate to each other and each develops its superordinate information unit from some aspect. For example,

a. "I didn't participate in the discussion." (information unit)
b. "Firstly, I wasn't mentally equipped," (information unit)
c. "Secondly, I was unfamiliar with the topic." (information unit)

The relationship between a, b and c is as follows (Figure 2-4):

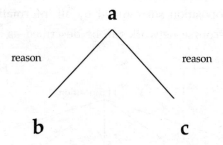

Figure 2-4   Relationship between a, b and c (from Du, 2009a)

As the subordinates, Information Units b and c explain the cause of Information Unit a.

Besides "reason", there are some other relations between information units in a discourse, such as "place, time, manner, thing…" which can be expressed by means of interrogative words. That is, the content of an information unit can be expressed by one of the 15 interrogative words, including What Thing (WT), What Basis (WB), What Fact (WF), What Inference (WI), What Disposal (WP), Who (WO), When (WN), Where (WR), How (HW), Why (WY), What Effect (WE), What Condition (WC), What Attitude (WA), What Change (WG) and What Judgment (WJ). The interrogative words actually denote from what aspect subordinate information units specify their superordinate ones. Moreover, the interrogative words, endowed with new meaning—the hierarchical relation between information units, are called information knots.

An information knot is different from an information unit. The former expresses relations and has more than ten types of alternatives (Table 2-2) and the latter is the minimal meaningful unit bearing the content.

Table 2-2 Types of Information Knots

Interrogative Words	Labels	Interrogative Words	Labels
What Thing	WT	How	HW
What Basis	WB	Why	WY
What Fact	WF	What Effect	WE
What Inference	WI	What Condition	WC
What Disposal	WP	What Attitude	WA
Who	WO	What Change	WG
When	WN	What Judgment	WJ
Where	WR		

Knowledge Categories

In addition, knowledge categories have been put forward in Tree Information Structure of Legal Discourse (Table 2-3).

Table 2-3 Knowledge Categories

Context	Knowledge Categories	Notes
monolog	A, B, C, E, O, D	C=AB, E=BA(known to neither)
question	a, b, c, e, o, d	Corresponding to the ones in monolog
dialogue	R, S, T, Y, Z, U	Corresponding to the ones in monolog

According to Table 2-3, A in monolog represents A-events which is known to A, but not to B, B is known to B, but not to A, C is known to both A and B; E is known to neither, O is known to everyone present, and D is known to be disputable. "a, b, c, e, o, d' in question and "R, S, T, Y, Z, U" in dialogue have the corresponding meanings to "A, B, C, E, O, D" in monolog. Knowledge categories can also be supported by Zhang and He's (2001) argument. They holds that in order to transmit information successfully, speakers or authors must presuppose listeners or readers' ability to comprehend discourse and even all the indispensable background information and contextual features in a discourse, and presuppose their ability to deduce the implicate meanings of discourse; the less background information speakers or authors presuppose, the more details they provide in discourse.

Tree Information Structure of Legal Discourse can be integrated with frame analysis to identify specific frames, framing process and footing shifts based on information levels, information units, information knots and their relations.

Firstly, frames activated by judges' discourse can be revealed through the exploration of the interaction order in court combined with the analysis of information levels and their relations. Labov (1977) argues that the use of basic language rules depends on the particular shared knowledge of participants, which forms the basic mechanism of requests, rejections and other rules. Therefore, the use of knowledge categories, together with concrete legal context, is helpful to study judges' discourse from the cognitive and social aspects.

Secondly, with the aid of analyzing discourse information, the frame identification process might be made more visible and systematic in the interaction between judges and other parties in court. So far, many studies have left the reader in the dark about the actual process of empirical frame detection. Thus, the first step towards the present study is the construction of frame taxonomy, distinguishing discourse information structural schemes from frames that focus more on content (Benford, 1997) or that are "principles of selection, emphasis and presentation composed of little tacit theories about what exists, what happens, and what matters" (Gitlin, 1980: 6).

Thirdly, framing process and footing shifts can be investigated by means of TISLD which sorts the specific idea elements of a set of texts into categories. One goal of a frame analysis is to direct careful attention to how these diverse idea elements are deployed in integrated ways (Creed, Langstraat & Scully, 2002). A frame analysis not only clusters the texts, it also explains why any single text is meaningful (Creed, Langstraat & Scully, 2002), the choice of information knots and knowledge categories, and the arrangement of information levels make it clearer that how judges' build certain frames and shift their footings in the construction of PDJ relationship.

All in all, frame analysis by means of TISLD not only manifests the way in which judges deal with courtroom discourse information at such micro-levels as information knots and levels, but also provides the cognitive observation of the effect of knowledge categories exerted on the PDJ relationship.

Meanwhile, frame analysis, mainly adopted in sociological research, requires the aid of conversation analysis and interactional sociolinguistics from the social perspective. Discourse analysts holds interests in the relations between text (discourse) and context, the relations between discourse and interaction, the relations between discourse and cognition and memory and so on. Accordingly, discourse analysis is also conducted by means of such analytical approaches as conversation analysis and interactional sociolinguistics, which originate form frame analysis and with which frame is often integrated while the analysis is conducted (Tannen, 1993; Sarangi and Roberts, 1999; Prego-Vazquez's, 2007).

2.2.2.2 Conversation Analysis

A Dictionary of Sociology (Marshall, 1998) defines conversation analysis as a research method that takes conversations in real-life settings as the object of study, and as a window on to the roles, social relationships, and power relations of participants.

Since its derivation from ethnomethodology and sociolinguistics, conversation analysis has emerged as a major and distinctively sociological contribution to the analysis of discourse. Its research findings have proved useful in elucidating many hidden aspects of human interaction which have wider interest in understanding real-life as well as research interviews (Marshall, 1998). More specifically speaking, conversation analysis are concerned with conduct or action in every social setting and in institutional contexts (Pomerantz & Fehr, 1997), and it has been focusing on conversations including both ordinary conversation and institutional talk since the late 1970s.

From the methodological perspective, the study of legal language as a process has always adopted conversation analysis because of its suitability rather than its popularity (Liao, 2004). Although conversation analysis focuses extensively on issues of meaning and context in interaction, the relationship between conversation analysis and institutional talk, and turn-taking system will be introduced for the purpose of the present research.

(1) Conversation Analysis and Institutional Talk

Drew and Heritage's *Talk at Work* (1992) establishes institutional talk as an analytical phenomenon. Conversation analysis studies of interactions in institutional settings demonstrate how social order is built and recognized in the talk between "clients" and "representatives" of an institution (Nielsen & Wagner, 2007). In recent years, the number of studies of institutional interaction has increased significantly, as can be seen from studies of medical interactions (Heritage & Maynard, 2006), news interviews (Clayman & Heritage, 2002), negotiation (Firth, 1995), and courtroom discourse (Conley & O'Barr, 1998) to mention just a few.

Heritage (1998) explores the relationship between conversation analysis and institutional interaction, and he argues that conversation analysis of talk in institutions starts with the view that context is both a project and a product of the participants' actions.

> The assumption is that it is fundamentally through interaction that context is built, invoked and managed, and that it is through interaction that institutional imperatives originating from outside the interaction are evidenced and made real and enforceable for the participants. We want to find out how that works. Empirically, this means showing that the participants build the context of their talk in and through their talk.

> (Heritage, 1998)

It is often very demanding that in addition to the normal conversation analysis tasks of analyzing the conduct of the participants and the underlying organization of their activities, that conduct and its organization must additionally be demonstrated to embody orientations which are specifically institutional (Heritage, 1998). Just as Schegloff (1991) has argued, if it is to be claimed that some interaction has a specifically institutional character, then the relevance and procedural consequentiality of the institutional context and its associated roles, tasks and identities must be shown in the details of the participants' conduct.

Although Schegloff (1991) observes that it is difficult to specify activities organized differently in institutional settings precisely and to demonstrate their underlying institutional moorings, Conley and O'Barr (1998) explores principles of conversation analysis in courtroom discourse analysis. They suggest participants in such institutional setting such as a courtroom employ the basic rules of conversation analysis but modify them in important ways because the courtroom environment has distinctive feature not present in everyday conversations.

> From an everyday perspective, it would be very peculiar to limit some speakers so that their only type of turn is asking questions, while restricting others to giving answers to whatever questions they are asked. Such institutional constraints introduce into courtroom interactions a degree of rigidity not found in everyday contexts and thereby help the court do its assigned task of trying cases. … From the outset, the structural arrangements for talking in court do not privilege all speakers in the same way. … This imbalance of power is present in all courtroom dialogue.
>
> (Conley and O'Barr, 1998: 20)

Through the modification of the basic rules, Conley and O'Barr (1998) employ conversation analysis to scrutinize the discourse between lawyers and witnesses.

Owing to the particularity of courtroom discourse, the relevant domains will be investigated without delay. In their earlier papers, Drew and Heritage identified six distinct domains of interactional phenomena which might be investigated for their relevance to the nature of institutional interaction (Drew & Heritage, 1992; Heritage, 1998). These domains are: 1) Turn-taking organization; 2) Overall structural organization of the interaction; 3) Sequence organization; 4) Turn design; 5) Lexical choice; 6) Epistemological and other forms of asymmetry.

A judge acts as referee to oversee the system of turn-taking, monitor the substance of what is discussed and resolve complex interactional problems when they arise (Conley & O'Barr, 1998). Thus, turn-taking system should especially be focused on in the research.

(2) Turn-taking and Interruption

Turn-taking is one of the fundamental organizations and the nature of conversation. The turn-taking model for conversation was arrived at inductively through empirical investigation of field recordings of conversation and fitted to such observationally arrived at fact as overwhelmingly, participants in conversation talk one at a time. The fundamental objective of conversation analysis research is to explicate the ways in which co-participants make sense of one another's talk, and how they design their own turns at talk so as to be appropriate next moves. Thus the sequential patterns which analysis uncovers are the emergent products of participants' understandings of what each other said in a prior turn, and their response to that in their "next turn" (Drew, 1998: 166-167).

Turn-taking is defined by Sacks, Schegloff and Jefferson (1974) as a process by which interactants allocate the right or obligation to participate in an interactional activity. Besides, they formulate a set of rules for turn-taking which are context free. Schegloff (1992) updates "intersubjective understandings" in talk-in-interaction.

Schegloff's update manifests that a turn's construction involves speaker selecting a relevant or appropriate next action in response to the perceived action in a co-participant's prior turn: in other words, a turn is constructed with respect to its placement in a sequence of actions (Drew, 1998). "However, a further aspect of turn construction or design should be emphasized, that of "recipient design". The descriptive terms which speakers select are contextually sensitive: they take into account not only the topic of conversation, but also contextual circumstances relevant to the talk (ibid, 1998: 167-168)."

Accordingly, such an explanation also updates the understanding of sequence organization which concerns how actions are ordered in conversation.

With the primary aim to examine the sequential organization of courtroom participants' turns at talk, Atkinson and Drew (1979) has employed a conversational analytic methodology to illustrate the essential asymmetry of spoken legal discourse in UK courtroom, by reference to the turn-taking mechanisms of interaction in coroners' courts and tribunal hearings.

Interruption is a common phenomenon in turn-taking system. Speakers use interruptions to disrupt another's utterance and gain the floor for a competing turn. The use of interruptions violates turn-taking rules. It is therefore a special kind of language and social act. Sacks et al. (1974) demonstrate that when speakers design their turns at talk they occur in constructional units of talk and the endpoint of these units are transition relevance places (TRPs) and it is at these TRPs that a change of speaker can occur. If a speaker does not produce his words at TRPs, the phenomenon interruption might occur.

Although the study on interruption has obtained a strong accomplishment in mundane conversation, the phenomenon affects the "moment-by-moment" allocation of turns in institutional discourse. For instance, based on the transcription of authentic mediation discourse, Lü (2005) analyzes the conflicting interruption with regard to the interrupter's power, and points out that interruption is an important conversational strategy, which will help the mediation participants to achieve their expected goal if used properly. Zhang (2006) studies the interruptions made by the judges in civil courts and draws a conclusion that there is a contradiction between judges' frequent interruption and their identities in court.

As a methodological tool consistent with investigating a phenomenon of talk-in-interaction, conversation analysis has been often utilized to explore courtroom discourse (Drew, 1985, 1992; Matoesian, 1993, 1997, 2001, 2005; Stygall, 1994; Cotterill, 2003). For example, Cotterill (2003) makes a comprehensive conversation analysis of the opening and closing statements and witness examinations of the O. J. Simpson trial to demonstrate the asymmetrical power relationships between the participants to the case. She discusses macro-, micro- and multiple narratives in court in criminal cases and applies turn-taking system to elaborate on witness examination in the form of question and answer. Additionally, based on Goffman's identification of two basic categories of hearer (the ratified and the unratified), Cotterill (2003) construes the role the jury play in the court.

Under the guidance of frame theory and with the aid of Goffman's (1983) interaction order, Sarangi and Roberts' (1999) institutional order, discourse analysts can also probe into judges' performance in trial by means of such conversation analytical techniques as turns distribution, interruptions and so on.

2.2.2.3   Interactional Sociolinguistics

Interactional sociolinguistics is concerned with how speakers signal and interpret meaning in social interaction. The term and the perspective are grounded in the work of Gumperz (1982a, 1982b) who blended insights and tools from anthropology, linguistics, pragmatics, and conversation analysis into an interpretive framework for analyzing such meanings. Interactional sociolinguistics acts as a bridge builder, combining wider contextual knowledge with linguistic and conversational analysis to illuminate the interpretive processes of interaction (Sarangi & Roberts, 1999) and attempts to bridge the gulf between empirical communicative forms (e.g. words, prosody, register shifts) and what speakers and listeners take themselves to be doing with these forms. Methodologically, it relies on close discourse analysis of audio- or video-recorded interaction. Such methodology is central to uncovering meaning-making processes because many conventions for signaling and interpreting meaning in talk are fleeting, unconscious, and culturally variable.

(1) Contextualization Cues

Verbal and non-verbal behaviors that give clues about meaning and underlying assumptions within an interaction allow participants to predict what will come next. It refers to the process whereby people understand what kind of activity is taking place during an interaction, and therefore how an utterance is to be interpreted. Take the following as examples (Gumperz, 1982a),

> T: Can you guess what does this word mean?
> S: I don't know (contextualization cue with rising intonation which indicates for further support or encouragement)
> T: Then, who can guess the meaning of this word? (misinterpretation of the contextualization cue as unwillingness to answer the question)

(2) Theoretical Significance

Firstly, interactional sociolinguistics places emphasis on the dynamic context. Gumperz argued that we communicate rapidly shifting interpretive frames through conventionalized surface forms, which he calls contextualization cues. These contextualization cues, like "constellations of surface features of message form", are "the means by which speakers signal and listeners interpret what the activity is, how semantic content is to be understood and how each sentence relates to what precedes or follows" (Gumperz, 1982a: 131).

Secondly, it constitutes the key theoretical contribution to illustrate a way in which social background knowledge is implicated in the signaling and interpreting of meaning. Such interpretive approach is taken to explore the nature of interaction in the social context.

Thirdly, it integrates macro-analysis and micro-analysis through two ways, of which one is the study of contextualization and contextualization cues to investigate the relations between interactional processes, the other is the simultaneous examination of several interactional processes of discourse to reveal the relations between them on the temporal, spatial and social dimensions (Sun, 2007).

(3) Application in Frame Analysis

Developed in an anthropological context, interactional sociolinguistics has the most salient explanatory value. The perspective has been applied to the performance of social identity through talk and it can be applied to any interaction. Much of the empirical work that falls under discourse analysis in communication owes a debt to this perspective, which is exemplified by Prego-Vazquez's (2007) works.

From its beginning in the 1980s, interactional sociolinguistics has been concerned with the analysis of the link between communicative misunderstandings and social inequality. Based on frame analysis, Prego-Vazquez (2007) employs multi-method approach including conversation analysis and interactional sociolinguistics to explore the frame conflict and social inequality in the workplace. In the paper, three types of conflicting frames have been revealed:

1) The customer introduces interactional patterns that fail to correspond to the sequential rules of organization that are in keeping with the institutional context.

2) The customer uses code-switching and code-mixing, resources that are traditionally associated with spontaneous conversation (Gumperz, 1982a), as a contextualization cue for the negotiation of professional and personal frames.

3) The customer introduces personal and conversational topics that contrast sharply with the professional topics traditionally associated with the institutional context. The resulting conflict is the result of the differences in the knowledge schemas used by the participants and restricted access to bureaucratic and professional discursive skills.

Through the analysis, Prego-Vazquez (2007) draws the conclusion as follows:

The sequential and critical microanalysis of the data has managed to explain the role and sociodiscursive impact of linguistic resources on the negotiation of interactive frames and interactional asymmetries. In addition, it has enabled us to link frame conflicts and interactional asymmetries with the reproduction of inequality and the power differences that separate institutions and citizens. A qualitative and detailed analysis of the data shows how frame conflicts are connected, on the one hand, with citizens' limited access to the professional discursive domains of the water company, and, on the other hand, with institutional interactive routines.

Koester (2006) has commented the relations between contextualization cues and frame analysis—at the global level, contextualization cues are indicative activity and converge with the notion "frame". So interactional sociolinguistics provides us with a useful tool to analyze courtroom discourse at a higher level and endows us with a broad social research background.

Focusing on the theoretical basis and methodological investigation, the foregoing section has introduced frame theory and its applications in the social science research and some other topics related to the present study. Based on frame theory, judges' discourse and judicial justice can be bridged. However, frame analysis requires combined analytical tools in its practical use for solving specific social problems.

Consequently, related discourse analytical tools have also examined, such as tree information structure of legal discourse, conversation analysis, and interactional sociolinguistics, which can integrated with each other for the fulfillment of the research objective. Conversation analysis and interactional sociolinguistics come down in one continuous line with frame theory and they can be taken up to impel our research towards a socio-interactional discourse analysis. Although conversation analysis and interactional sociolinguistics are always involved in frame analysis, the two analytical tools have not solved the problem of identifying frames except that some specific linguistic analysis can be employed in making frame analysis.

However, tree information structure of legal discourse proposed within a social framework can be exploited to help penetrate into judges' courtroom discourse. This model concerns both social and cognitive factors, accentuates both deep micro-linguistic analysis and macro-discursive construction, and avails to analyze both oral and written discourse. Meanwhile, since it has reified idea elements in Gamson's signature matrix by means of information levels, information units, information knots and knowledge categories, the model may be integrated to identify concrete frames via signature matrix. Moreover, in agreement with van Dijk's frame analysis based on global coherence and local coherence, the model benefits discourse analysis on multi-levels.

Thus, frame theory and relevant tools are deliberate arrangements to form an interconnected theoretical and analytical system that is to highlight the present study.

2.3 Conceptual Framework of Frame Analysis

2.3.1 Interactive Frames Activated by Discourse at Multiple Levels

Discourses contain frames, which are manifested by the presence or absence of certain keywords, stock phrases, stereotyped images, sources of information, and sentences that provide thematically reinforcing clusters of facts or judgments (Kweon, 2000). Hence, frame analysis is often conducted through the analysis of different institutional discourse in which frame is articulated by discourse (Coburn, 2006; Pick, 2006), activated by discourse (Prego-Vázquez, 2007) or socially enacted by discourse (Creed, Langstraat & Scully, 2002).

Communicators consciously or unconsciously produce frames and receivers are guided in their interpretation of communicators' frames by their own frames, in which the audience does selective mental information processing (Kweon, 2000). Speakers might change their footings or embed one footing within another to produce discourse, which results in frame shifting as a normal feature of discourse (Goffman, 1974). Not only does transferring discourse information signal shifting frames in the interactive activities (Tannen & Wallat, 1993), but also frames account for interaction in discourse (ibid) and guide interactants to appropriate interpretations of what is going on in situations at each moment (Watanabe, 1993). What's more, frame conflict might be engendered with interactive frames. Linked to the situations of interactional asymmetry, frame conflict can be a struggle between professional and local frames presented in discourse analyzed or occur as a result of the differences between the systems of values and knowledge of the institutional and lay worlds (Prego-Vázquez, 2007).

In interactions, some specific frames can be triggered through such discursive activities as micro-level ones—strategic lexicalization (Cotterill, 2003), meso-level ones—context (Chreim, 2006) and macro-level ones—expectation (Tannen, 1993). Therefore, framing has also been recognized "as a key strategy in persuasively communicating" in legal settings (Hallahan, 1999) and a strategy towards a satisfactory end in conversation (Appelrouth, 1999; Prego-Vázquez, 2007).

Therefore, the present study starts with recognition and identification of frames in trial via judges' discourse analysis in which different discourse information hold together at different level from lower to higher. It also concerns frame existence and shifts in the process of language use and information progress. Overall, the whole study will focus on the linguistic use, social contexts and cognitive factors to explore judges' discourse practice on the grounds that workplace communication needs to be analyzed at various levels (Sarangi & Roberts, 1999).

2.3.2 Application of Framing

Although it has always been ignored in the interpretation of discourse and reference in discourse analysis theories (Fauconnier, 1994), framing is the process of frame-constructing that helps us organize information in patterns that serve as cognitive maps. Framing makes for organizing knowledge and predicting the meaning of new information, events, and experiences. Parties in a dispute develop considerably different frames about what the dispute is about, who should do what about it, and how and when they should do it. They often resolve frame conflicts in the interactive process during which there is deliberate reconsideration of existing frames.

Framing discussed by Kweon (2000) provides an answer for the question of how news texts are framed by media style, and among business focus, general news focus, and media focus. Furthermore, the discussion proves that an analysis of news frames is a useful theoretical model that provides news texts on various dimensions. Through content analysis, one could get the answer to the news framing style, format, timing, and nature for both media and non-media.

Pan and Kosicki (1993) maintains that framing analysis is presented as a constructivist approach to examine news discourse with the primary focus on conceptualizing news texts into empirically operationalizable dimensions—syntactical, script, thematic, and rhetorical structures—so that evidence of the news media's framing of issues in news texts may be gathered. The two authors have also illustrated the applications of this conceptual framework of news texts as these framing devices are practical and functional.

In addition to its feasible use of analyzing news texts, framing has also been applied in forensic linguistic study.

Baunach (1977) outlines arguments supporting the approach framing to the evaluation of criminal justice programs and cites two examples in which the "under what conditions...?" question guides the focus and structure of the research effort.

Aldridge & Luchjenbroers (2007) holds framing questions can be used as linguistic manipulations in legal discourse. In their research, they pay special attention to a consideration of how the lexical choices in the questions posed to a witness encourage a particular perception of her testimony. The concepts being discussed include conceptual frames and smuggling information, and they offer a qualitative consideration of how the semantic features of a lawyer's lexical choices can support a representation of either the witness or her experiences that is not in her interests. The appropriateness of a lawyer's chosen frame is of key importance to "smuggling information', a term used when a lawyer's question inserts (negative) information into a witness's testimony through suggestion. They look at how such linguistic manipulations can weaken a witness's account by suggesting that she is to blame, and/or is lying or perhaps has simply misunderstood the situation. Their analysis offers an explanation as to why vulnerable witnesses may not be believed in court.

The above-mentioned research reflects that framing, as a discursive strategy, can be effectively taken to explore certain social issues from linguistic, social and cognitive perspectives.

2.3.3　Footing Shifts in Frame Analysis

Footing is identified as a re-working of "the frame analysis of talk" (Philips, 1983) because a frame is constructed through participants' signaling their footings and recognizing and ratifying another's footing—which often changes from time to time (Ribeiro, 2006).

Footing shifts appear not only in everyday communication, but in institutional discourse. Different speakers may talk about the same thing with different footings in the interactive process. Other times speakers switch to an institutional voice whereby they mark what they say not so much as their own personal opinion but as what they happen to think or want as representative of a certain group (an office, a firm, a school, a team, a family, a political group)—these are also contexts in which speakers often switch to the first person plural "we" (Duranti, 1997: 298).

For example, one member in a patient's family sometimes takes a footing as animator of the doctor's beliefs while reporting the doctor's clinical evaluation (ibid); "the Press Secretary typically acts as the animator of words that may have been authored by someone else (one or more of the White House writers) and that are said on behalf of the President (the principal) (Duranti, 1997: 297)"; or the use of the alternative footings of speakers will be made to avoid waging frame conflict, to attenuate it or dissolve it (Bonito & Sanders, 2002).

Although speakers often assume all the three footings at the same time, the roles need to be distinguished in more cases than we might think (Duranti, 1997: 297). The exploration of footings helps to examine judges' self-identifications in trials. The footing befitting a judge conforms to the construction of rational PDJ relationship; otherwise, it will violate judicial justice.

Accordingly, a three-dimensional conceptual framework can be formulated in Figure 2-5, which serves the aim of the present research.

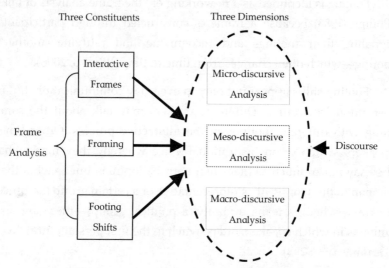

Figure 2-5　A Conceptual Framework of Frame Analysis

According to the theoretical framework, frame analysis can be conducted on the three dimensions which is favored by scholars like Fairclough (1992), van Dijk (1997a; 2001), Cotterill (2003) and so on to explore discursive practice.

Fairclough (1992: 85) maintains that micro-analysis and macro-analysis should be combined for the analysis of discursive practice. Complemented with macro-analysis, the former is the sort of analysis at which conversation analysts excel, and micro-analysis is the best place to uncover that information which provides evidence for macro-analysis, so micro- and macro-analysis are consequently mutual requisites (ibid). This opinion follows his three-dimensional framework (textual analysis, discursive analysis and social analysis), which can mediate the relationship between the dimensions of social practice and text: it is the nature of the social practice that determines the macro-processes of discursive practice, and it is the micro-processes that shape the text (see Fairclough, 1992).

van Dijk (2001) believes each role of a participant differentially affects discourse production which is involved in the contexts of social relations and cognition. Social relations may be expressed or enacted virtually everywhere in linguistic forms and pragmatic use, and cognition including ideologies is the very basis of a host of semantic and pragmatic properties of discourse.

As a matter of fact, Alvesson and Karreman (2000) happen to have an identical view as van Dijk's. They hold that studies of discourse regarding the scope and scale of discourse include the following approaches. Micro-discourse approach focuses on language use in a particular micro context. Meso-discourse approach attends to language use in context but goes beyond the material in the text. Grand discourse approach emphasizes the dominating power of ideologies and their impact on organizational frames. Besides, mega-discourse approach addresses more or less standardized ways of referring to or constructing a certain type of phenomenon, e.g. courtroom practice. The first one is concerned with linguistic level, which is micro-discursive analysis; meso-discourse approach in fact refers to the analysis of discourse in van Dijk's social context. The last two can be integrated into macro-discursive analysis corresponding to van Dijk's cognitive dimension (van Dijk, 1997a, 2001).

2.4   Analytical Framework

Considering the analytical concerns in the research, and according to the particularity of judges' discourse in China's courtroom settings and the need for solving the practical problems in the research, we attempt to develop the following analytical framework of the study, which entails the conceptual framework of frame analysis configured above.

The whole process of frame analysis will resort mainly to discourse information processing. Tree information structure of legal discourse suggests that a proposition may not necessarily appear as a complete grammatical structure. But where the context is sufficient, a fragment of a grammatical structure can be taken as a proposition. A single proposition can be taken as a piece of information. Due to the distinctions of courtroom discourse, conversation analysis and interactional sociolinguistics will also be applied when they are needed.

In courtroom context, PDJ relationship construction cannot be separated from judges' discursive practice, since some conflict may occur in the process of participants' interaction. In addition to the factors from legal systems, whether judges' action in court influences judicial justice and how it does if so might result from judges' discourse information processing on the multi-dimensions mentioned above.

In the process of criminal trials, judges' framing strategies are inevitable in the construction of PDJ relationship, which requires being explored. Pan and Kosicki (1993) argue that framing devices can be explored on such four dimensions as syntactical structure, script structure, thematic structure, and rhetorical structure. Their opinion, combined with Yuan's findings that specific discursive strategies or devices can be provided to solve relevant legal issues (Yuan, 2007), affords us the access to the investigation of judges' framing strategies based on their discourse information processing.

Accordingly, solid theoretical foundations have been laid for a comprehensive analytical framework formulated as in Figure 2-6, which contributes to the concrete analysis of the data in this research.

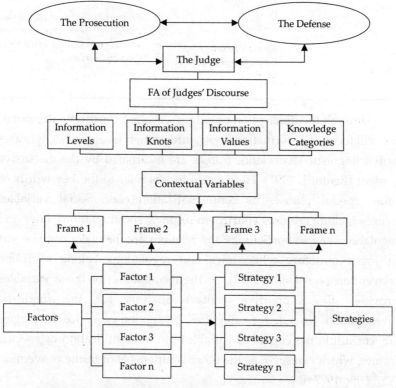

Figure 2-6   An Analytical Framework for Exploring PDJ relationship

Discourse analysis can start with the identification of specific primary frames and sub-frames (see Table 2-4) in the interaction, which involves the variables on the three dimensions we have conceptualized above.

Table 2-4   Signature Matrix for Frame Identification and Framing

Dimensions	Variables	Frames
linguistic	Information levels Information knots Catchphrases ...	A frame will be identified based on the analysis of the variables in the process of discourse articulation.
social	Settings Rules Relations ...	Framing will be explored via analyzing how speakers or writers employ these variables to construct a frame.
cognitive	Knowledge categories Perception of justice Ideologies ...	

Through the description of judges' criminal courtroom discourse, we will focus on information knots, information levels or catchphrases at the linguistic-levels since frames are incarnated by the discursive content (Benford, 1997). Here catchphrases refer to the key words or other special phrases as contextualization cues. Social variables mainly include criminal courtroom settings, social relations, laws and regulations and so on. Settings and relations are the major components in frame structure while laws and regulations belong to frame convention (van Dijk, 1977a), so the examination of those variables provides the supportive context analysis for the linguistic investigation. Knowledge categories, perception of justice, ideologies etc. constitute the cognitive variables in the identification of specific frames, which can serve as the other components of frame convention (van Dijk, 1977a).

Overall, the reification of frames will be accomplished by the exploration of discourse information chunks in both social and cognitive contexts.

The second concern in Figure 2-6 is the factors that influence the PDJ relationship constructed in the courtroom. We will make the description of the extent to which the PDJ relationship is corresponding to the three core dimensions of judicial justice. Based on interactive frames, footing and framing, we will then explain various factors concerning legal system, cultures, knowledge schema, ideology, power, etc. We conduct the investigation of interactive frames and framing according to the signature matrix in Table 2-4 and explore specific footings in virtue of participation framework (Goffman, 1981).

Unquestionably, judges' framing strategies in the construction of PDJ relationship are the ultimate purpose of the research. The strategies should be put forward aiming at the foregoing description and explanation of the phenomena and reasons. All the factors influencing PDJ relationship have always been embodied by discursive practice in trials, so have framing strategies. With the shifts of frames, judges adjust their discourse information to the process of a trial, which reflects whether PD balance can be kept, whether judges preside over the trial neutrally, and whether justice on the three dimensions is maintained. We categorize these strategies and interpret which should be reserved, which should be discarded and which should be amended so as to help construct rational PDJ relationship.

In the next section, we will present research methodology for the present study and explain how the data are collected and analyzed.

2.5   Research Methodology

In virtue of the theoretical framework constructed based on frame theory, this research is to implement an exploratory and explanatory analysis of judges' courtroom discourse. This conforms to the principles of frame theory at both technical level and operational level (Zhang, 2001).

In the first place, the present research is a data-based empirical research of PDJ relationship constructed. Given the inclination of frame analysis, the qualitative approach is adopted to represent the characteristics of judges' judicial discourse information processing.

Methodologically, this research takes an integration of Deductive (Top-down) approach and Inductive (Bottom-up) approach. It is deductive in that we investigate PDJ relationship from the top, the theories as mentioned above, which are conducive to the construction of the present theoretical framework. Meanwhile, it is inductive in that we start from the bottom by focusing on the data: identifying specific frames, classifying factors and proposing framing strategies.

Contrastive and comparative analysis is also employed in this research to describe judges' discourse information processing in similar cases. This analysis is intended to observe what types of discursive devices used by judges are propitious to the construction of rational PDJ relationship.

2.5.1 Data Collection

In order to ensure the reliability and validity of the present research, the data on criminal trials analyzed will be extracted from the CLIPS (Corpus for the Legal Information Processing System[5]) in which all the data have been tagged by following the tagging convention of Tree Information Structure of Legal Discourse. Texts of 36 trials have been involved in which 34 of them have been extracted randomly, the other 2 concerning the same case have been chosen for

---

5. This corpus was developed in Guangdong University of Foreign Studies, consisting of various genres of legal discourse.

the purpose of contrastive analysis.

2.5.2   Data Analysis

The data analysis will be implemented in the light of the analytical framework we have constructed above. Since all the data have been sampled from the CLIPS, Tree Information Structure of Legal Discourse will be exploited and integrated with other analytical tools based on frame analysis. We will categorize judges' discourse according to information types, considering the context of each information unit as well.

For each legal discourse, we can identify the kernel proposition (KN) and its subordinate information units. Therefore, the information structure of a legal discourse can be displayed as a tree diagram like the one in Figure 2-7. Every information unit corresponds to an information knot in the tree diagram. Besides interrogative words, the tagging of information units also includes level codes, information source and knowledge categories.

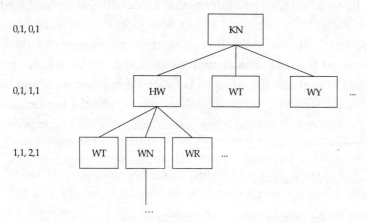

Figure 2-7   Tree Information Structure of Legal Discourse (Du, 2009)

Level codes are composed of level number and position number of the information knot and its superordinate information knot. In Figure 2-7, KN (kernel proposition) is the information focus of the whole discourse. It is at the top of the tree structure, so we give it the level code "0, 1, 0, 1". It is developed into subordinate information knots, in this figure HW, WT and WY, at the first lower level. Their level codes are "0, 1, 1, 1", "0, 1, 1, 2" and "0, 1, 1, 3" respectively. Knot HW has its own subordinate knots WT, WN and WR, the level codes of which are "1, 1, 2, 1", "1, 1, 2, 2" and "1, 1, 2, 3". "1, 1, 2, 3" means knot WR takes up the third position (tagged as 3) at level 2. It is subordinate to knot HW which is at the first position (tagged as 1) of level 1.

It will be an attempt made for the present research that the two micro-analytical tools are combined with tree information structure of legal discourse. The integration of information levels and information units with turn-taking and interruptions is useful to explore how frames are articulated in the courtroom and how they interact with each other along the progress of discourse.

Information level and information knots will also be employed to parse judges' discourse and detect how judges evaluate or identify legal facts. At the same time discourse processing can be best interpreted through context analysis (van Dijk, 1992), which can be utilized to explicate the relations between information units and legal contextual variables. Such an analysis serves both the exploration of interactive frames and the inquiry about judges' discourse processing and discursive strategies.

The second concern in discourse analysis is social context in which discourse is produced as frames are socially enacted by discourse (Creed, Langstraat & Scully, 2002). As a conceptual tool, frame analysis is particularly suited for understanding how people construct meaning from moment to moment (Ribeiro, 2006). As discourse is being produced, understood and analyzed relative to such context features as participants, their roles and purposes, as well as properties of a setting (van Dijk, 1997b), judges' discourse does not appear in vacuo and the study cannot be independent of such social factors as social power, social relations, social status and social role. The meso-discursive analysis will elucidate how judges perform their duties through the information exchange and clarify whether symmetry/asymmetry exists in the process of courtroom information flow.

Since the study of legal language is based on the social context (Du, 2004), interactional sociolinguistics, a useful analytical tool, can be applied at the meso-level to explore shifting frames (Gumperz, 1999). It has contributed a series of tools that can be used in the interpretative and inferential analysis of the data (Prego-Vázquez, 2007). For example, the study of contextualization cues is crucial in order to explain how frames shift in the interactions studied. Thus it has enabled us to observe the way in which social order is built up from interactional order, revealing the role played by frames, linguistic resources and interactional asymmetry in reproducing the power differences that separate institutions and citizens (Prego-Vázquez, 2007).

Thirdly, we also need to extend our analysis into macro-context in which cognitive factors will be involved. The discursive level of discourse represents more than the sum of the individual parts of sentences and fragments in text, but at some point, the researcher must draw inferential conjectures about "black box" operations of the human mind to identify the markers of the frame in the text (Fisher, 1997). The outstanding achievements made in the cognitive research dwell in analyzing cognitive process of discourse, thus a series of models and important concepts have been put forward like schema (Rumelhart & Ortony, 1977), frame (Minsky, 1975), script (Schank & Abelson, 1977). Besides cognitive analysis from the psychological perspective, macrostructure (van Dijk, 1977b; van Dijk & Kintsch, 1983) has been brought into the cognitive analysis from discursive perspective and a comprehensive research has also been made in discourse comprehension strategies (van Dijk & Kintsch, 1983). So we need to make cognitive analysis which concentrates on the psychological representation and emphasizes the analysis of macro-discursive structure and discursive structural elements (e.g. propositions and propositional network) (Du, 2008a).

Since the frames that give form to our experience are cognitive and are grounded in strips (Smith, 2006), judges choose the corresponding types of discourse information to construct frames. As a result, knowledge categories can be adopted to study how judges make their articulated and shifting frames accepted by other participants in court. For example, judges will construct a frame to organize a trial, in which certain expressions can be perceived and accepted by other participants as the activity of controlling the trial, because this activity may be existing as ideology in the social cognition shared by social groups (van Dijk, 2001).

In conclusion, we will begin our analysis with the linguistic features of discourse, which pin down the context in which discourse is produced. Thus, both social and cognitive factors will be involved in scrutinizing judges' discourse.

Chapter 3

PDJ Relationship Constructed by Judges in Court

3.1 Introduction

Data analysis will be implemented in the light of the analytical framework we construct above. Since all the data have been sampled from CLIPS, Tree Information Structure of Legal Discourse will be exploited and integrated with other analytical tools based on frame analysis. Meanwhile, we will classify judges' discourse into such three categories as monologue, dialogue and questioning (Du, 2007) for the convenience of exploring the relationship construction.

Data analysis starts with the categorization of judges' discourse information according to information types, considering the context of each information unit as well. According to Searle's revision of speech act theory, sentences have been taxonomized as such five types as assertives, directives, commissives, expressive and declaratives, which have close relations with propositions (Searl, 1969, 1975). Based on Searle's categorization and the judge's duties regulated by law, judges' discourse information units can be categorized as declarative information, directive information, confirmative information and expressive information, which help to explore how different manifestations of PDJ relationship are framed in court.

In accordance with the description of judges' discourse and the analysis of courtroom context, we will recognize primary trial frames and sub-frames which focus on content (information knots, information levels, knowledge categories and key words, etc.) (Gamson & Lasch, 1983; Gamson & Modigliani, 1989; Benford, 1997). The primary frames identified are so pervasive that they can be used in almost any criminal trial in China. Thus, they actually manifest general PDJ relationship in the criminal courtroom interaction, while in each primary frame or with the frame shifts sub-frames activated or articulated will manifest PDJ relationship specifically. Then we will explore specific manifestations of PDJ relationship constructed by courtroom discourse in different frames, through frame shifts or due to frame conflicts. The relationship constructed depends on linguistic features, courtroom background and knowledge schemas.

We will make a comprehensive and detailed analysis of discourse information structure in the data extracted randomly from CLIPS. Moreover, the data constitute the discourse transcribed and tagged from 33 cases in the criminal courtroom. Take the information unit "<0, 1, 1, 1, WT, P, A, 现在开庭>审判长：**区人民法院刑事审判庭现在开庭。 (The Criminal Court of ... is now in session.)" as an example to explain what aspects of discourse information we will analyze according to specific extracts and concrete necessities. "0,1,1,1" here represents the information levels in this unit, "WT" the information knots, "P" the information value, "A" knowledge category, and "现在开庭" the key word of the information unit.

Discourse structure concerns "what elements or episodes are combined in what ways and what order to constitute (Fairclough, 1992: 77)", e.g. a job interview or a criminal trial. The conventions in the examples can give a lot of insight into the systems of knowledge and belief and the assumptions about social relationships and social identities that are built into the conventions of discourse types (ibid).

As Fairclough (1992) suggests, we are concerned with monologue, dialogue and questioning in criminal trials.

3.2 PDJ Relationship Manifested in Monologue

The right to produce monologue is an illustration of the hierarchical structure of courtroom talk. As the institutionally more powerful participants in court, judges are sanctioned to produce monologue, which is of even greater importance in the trial process (Cotterill, 2003). Therefore, this section will deal with PDJ relationship manifested in judges' monologue in details.

3.2.1 Monologue in Judges' Discourse

In the criminal court, judges' manipulation of the trial procedures can be embodied by their processing of discourse information. It is essential that judges' monologue be scrutinized based on frame analysis. Moreover, the framing process can also be revealed by analyzing the features of courtroom interaction.

Extract 3-1

1 <0, 1, 1, 1, WT, P, A, 现在开庭>审判长:＊＊区人民法院刑事审判庭现在开庭。

Presiding Judge: The Criminal Court of … is now in session.

2 <0, 1, 1, 2, WT, P, A, 法庭调查>审判长:现在开始法庭调查。

Presiding Judge: Now proceed to the court investigation.

3 <1, 2, 2, 7, WT, P, A, 举证质证>审判长:现在由控辩双方举证、质证。

Presiding Judge: Now the prosecution and the defense start presenting and challenging the evidence.

4 <0, 1, 1, 3, WT, P, A, 法庭辩论>审判长:现在开始法庭辩论……

Presiding Judge: Now proceed to the court debate. …

5 <1，3，2，49，WT，P，A，结束辩论>审判长：法庭辩论结束……

Presiding Judge: The court debate is over. ...

6 <0，1，1，4，WT，P，A，法庭宣判>审判长：现在进行法庭宣判……

Presiding Judge: Now proceed to the court pronouncement. ...

7 <1，4，2，61，WT，P，A，闭庭>审判长：现在闭庭。

Presiding Judge: It's time for closing of the court.

The information units in Extract 3-1 represent the declaration of the key stages in almost all the criminal trials. We can describe the characteristics of these information units as follows.

The information levels are Level 1 or Level 2, among which Level 2 information unit "<举证质证> (presenting and challenging the evidence)" is one of the subordinates of Level 1 information "<法庭调查> (court investigation)". All the information knots are WT. Knowledge categories are A, which means only judges know when to shift a trial stage to another. Meanwhile all the information values are all P, which means the information produced is positive to the father information through which a trial proceeds smoothly.

To explain specific frames articulated and illustrate the PDJ relationship constructed by the presiding judges' declarative information, we will map a characterization of a signature matrix, in which linguistic, social and cognitive analysis will be conducted with the consideration of legal reasons. This can be supported by the "architecture" of discourse, and specifically higher-level design features (Fairclough, 1992). The signature matrix (Table 3-1) has been thus formulated for the discourse information at Level 1 in Turns 1, 2, 4 and 6.

All the information knots are WT which plays an important role in reminding all the parties in court including the audience of the

Table 3-1   **Signature Matrix of Primary Trial Frames**

Dimensions	Variables	Frame 1	Frame 2	Frame 3	Frame 4
	Information levels	0,1,1,1	0,1,1,2	0,1,1,3	0,1,1,4
	Information knots	WT	WT	WT	WT
linguistic	Information values	P	P	P	P
	Catchphrases	now	It's time…	It's time…	It's time…
	…				
	Settings	criminal trial	criminal trial	criminal trial	criminal trial
social	Rules	CPL	CPL	CPL	CPL
	Relations	domination	domination	domination	domination
	…				
	Knowledge categories	A	A	A	A
cognitive	Perception of justice	conform to law	conform to law	conform to law	conform to law
	Ideologies	power	power	power	power
	…				

Note: CPL=The criminal Procedure Law of the People's Republic of China (1996)

transition from one stage to another in trials. Meanwhile, these WT information knots enjoy higher position (at Level 1), which means all the other information knots will develop the discourse centering on the WT information. The four WT information knots, together with their subordinates, will have formed four information chunks. Each chunk represents a stage in a trial and each WT information knot symbolizes a transition of a stage.

In the information articulating process, the Chinese phrase "现在 (now)" in judges' monologue is a contextualization cue which triggers the other parties' cognitive mechanism to know the shift of trial stages or the start of a new stage. Thus the catchphrase "现在 (now)" embodies the implicit interaction between judges and the other parties. The information value P indicates that all the four units support their father information (the kernel proposition) in a discourse.

From the social and cognitive perspectives, the judges' discourse information processing conforms to the relevant law while exercising their power in the criminal trials. Boasting one of the organizational discourse features, these information units are completely new turns, aiming to advance a trial smoothly and to avoid the disorder in the trial process because the knowledge categories are all A that means only judges know when to shift a trial stage to another.

The analysis above demonstrates the major components of frames necessary in the comprehension and acceptance of the judges' monologue as declaration. Therefore, we can generalize that the primary frames (see Figure 3-1) in criminal court can be identified through the combination of information structures and contextual factors. In addition, Turns 3, 5 and 7, generating some sub-frames[6], can also be analyzed in another signature matrix. These information units are at Level 2, which is a higher level too. The other variables are similar to and even the same as those in Turns 1, 2, 4 and 6.

In conclusion, the analysis shows that judges' monologue functions as information declaration. They use all the declarative information units above before directing the other parties in court to perform their duties in the advancement of a trial. These high-level information units, like the main branches, dominate a courtroom discourse tree (see Figure 3-1). From the social interactional perspective, all the information units perform their functions to inform all the other parties of the trial stage and to switch from one stage to another. That is, judges utilize these information units to advance trials smoothly and realize their trial tasks. Without considering turn-taking and other contextual factors, the analysis of these declarative information units

---

6. The recognition of the other frames or sub-frames will be the same as that of the primary frames in Table 3-1.

demonstrates that judges in criminal courts have constructed the rational PDJ relationship conforming to the relevant law.

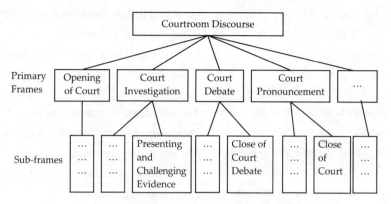

Figure 3-1   Primary Frames Activated in a Courtroom Discourse Tree

However, the analysis based on the interactional nature in the legal context predicts that some manifestations of PDJ relationship may be framed in the actual criminal courtroom by declarative WT information. Whether the prediction will come true or not lies in the result from deeper analysis of judges' language in the interactional process. The subsequent further analysis of deeper discourse features and discourse connotations also involves the cognitive factors, social background and linguistic use. Specifically speaking, we focus on the interaction between all judges and the other parties in court rather than analyze judges' discourse in isolation. Starting with the investigation of some extracts from a certain specific trial, the analysis will explore whether judges make turn-takings at the appropriate situation or transmit discourse information to shift primary frames or sub-frames at appropriate time.

3.2.2   PDJ Relationship in the Monologic Interactions

In terms of the following data analysis, we will justify whether specific PDJ relationship can be constructed by means of primary frame shifting or in the process of sub-frame activating.

Extract 3-2 (Case 05)

<3，37，4，43，WF，P，b，有无新证据>审判长：公诉人有无新的证据？

Presiding Judge: Does the prosecutor have any new evidence?

<3，37，4，43，WF，P，b，举证>公诉人：福建商会的证明和田**家属提供的收条（提供证据）。

Prosecutor: The proof from Fujian Chamber of Commerce and the receipt offered by a member of Tian**'s family. (*offering evidence*)

<2，14，3，38，WT，P，A，举证质证结束>审判长：……现在不再进行举证、质证。<0，1，1，3，WT，P，A，法庭调查结束>法庭调查结束……

Presiding Judge: …Now, there is no need to continue presenting and challenging the evidence. The court investigation is over.

In Extract 3-2, the judge shifts the frame "法庭调查 (*court investigation*)" to the next one by declaring the end of "举证质证 (*presenting and challenging evidence*)" at an irrational situation in the courtroom interaction. In this extract, the prosecutor produces a WF information knot and provides the court with evidence to reply to the judge's request. Generally, a directive information unit for challenging evidence in a trial should follow such an evidence-presenting behavior, but the judge uses a declarative information unit to terminate the stage of presenting and challenging evidence rather than produces two WA information knots to ask both the defendant and the lawyer for challenging evidence. Turn-taking, concerned with how people get to talk and for how long and with what consequences (Schegloff, 2007), has been particularly impressive and influential (Fairclough, 1992). Here the turn taking through discourse information omission has obviously violated the procedural criminal law and the judge's information shift is positive to the prosecution but negative to the defense, which breaks the PD balance.

Extract 3-3 (Case 05)

1 <1，3，2，21，WT，有无新意见>审判长：辩护人和被告人有无新的辩护意见？

Presiding Judge: Defender and defendant, do you have any new points of defense?

2 <1，3，2，21，WT，建议>辩护人：建议给予被告人从轻、减轻处罚。

Defender: I suggest that the defendant should receive lenient punishment or mitigated punishment.

3 <1，3，2，22，WT，有话说>被告人：审判长，我有要说的。

<2，22，3，45，WO，提出三个证人>关于证人有三个人，一个是佟**；第二个是张**，他是我与被害人的朋友；第三个是在十二建要账。

<2，22，3，46，WT，希望证实>我希望法庭可以找这几个证人证实。

Defendant: Presiding judge, I have something to say. With regard to the witnesses, there are three—one is Tong**, another is Zhang**, who is a friend of the victim's and mine, the third one is the person in charge of collecting debts in No.12 Building Firm of ... I hope that the court will ask the above- mentioned witnesses to appear in court.

4 <1，3，2，23，WT，P，A，公诉人答辩>公诉人：审判长，我进行答辩。<2，23，3，47，WO，无人证实利润>第一，谁能够证实田**与被告人有30%的利润？<2，23，3，48，WO，债权债务不明>第二，谁能证实有多少钱是被告人要的或者是被告人帮田**要的？<2，23，3，48，WO，债权债务不明>谁能证实田**与被告人有多少债权债务。<2，23，3，49，WO，证据明确>关于要账的问题，我们控方的证据已经很明确了。

Prosecutor: Presiding judge, I will give a reply to the claim. Firstly, who can prove that Tian** and the defendant have 30% of the profit? Secondly, who can prove the exact amount of money requested by the defendant or by the defendant instead of Tian**? Who can prove the exact amount of credit and debt between the defendant and Tian**? As for collecting the debt, the evidence from the prosecutor is very clear.

5 <1，3，2，25，WT，辩论结束>

审判长：……法庭辩论到此结   Presiding Judge: ...The court
束。   debate is over.

In the extract above, the judge's declaration of the end of "*法庭辩论 (court debate)*" at inappropriate situation leads to unfairness to the defense.

The judge has not interdicted the prosecutor from his chiming in as the conversation between the judge and the defense or interrupted the prosecutor when he is producing some irrational debating discourse information. The extract begins with Turns 1-3 in the conversation between the judge and the defense with the topic whether the defense has new defending opinions or not. However, in Turn 4 the prosecutor has interrupted them without the permission from the judge and has been pouring forth his so-called defending in a torrent. In the presentation, the prosecutor produces WO information by means of three rhetorical questions. Here the prosecutor has forgotten his duty that "the one who prosecutes has to presents evidence[7]" and he has even used the duty to produce his defending reasons. However, not only does the judge not stop or interrupt him, but his higher-level declarative information unit "<1, 3, 2, 25, *辩论结束*> *(The court debate is over.)*" in Turn 5 will shift one primary frame to another, which makes the prosecutor's defending rational and the defense's reply much weaker.

It is doubtful that the collegial panel will take account of the defense's opinion. Maybe the collegial panel will discuss the issue of new witnesses raised by the defense and the prosecutor in the process of the "*法庭辩论 (court debate)*". However, the question lies in whether the collegial panel will require the prosecution for new witnesses, whether the collegial panel will accept the opinion of the

---

7. The Criminal Procedure Law of the People's Republic of China (CPL) (1996)

prosecutor, and whether the defense has rights and competence to bring new witnesses.

Through the information analysis of the whole discourse, the answer to these questions can be found that the collegial panel entirely supports the prosecution, for the judge has not required the prosecution to bring in the witnesses and has not given the defense an opportunity to find new witnesses.

Extract 3-4 (Case 06)

<1, 1, 2, 19, WT, 普通程序简化审>审判长：公诉机关建议本案适用普通程序简便审理，<2, 19, 3, 21, WA, 询问被告人意见>对此，被告人马**是否有意见？

<2, 19, 3, 21, WA, 没意见>马**：没有。

<0, 1, 1, 2, WT, 宣布法庭调查>审判长：现在开始法庭调查。

Presiding Judge: The public prosecution organ proposes that the case should be heard in summary procedure. Do you agree with it, Defendant Ma**?

Defendant: Yes.

Judge: Now proceed to the court investigation.

Extract 3-5 (Case 08)

<1, 1, 2, 14, WT, 普通程序简化审>审判长：公诉机关建议本案适用普通程序简便审理，<2, 14, 3, 1, WA, 询问被告人意见>对此，被告人于**是否有意见？

<1, 1, 2, 14, WA, 没意见>被告人：没有。

<0, 1, 1, 2, WT, 宣布法庭调查>审判长：现在开始法庭调查。

Presiding Judge: The public prosecution organ proposes that the case should be heard in summary procedure. Do you agree with it, Defendant Yu**?

Defendant: Yes.

Presiding Judge: Now proceed to the court investigation.

The two extracts above show the irrationality in the rational summary procedure applied to a trial due to the insufficient discourse information provided by the judges. In such cases as those from which the data extracted, the judges have not produced sufficient information to interpret the conditions and requirements to the defense and have not asked the defenders for agreement. Instead, they immediately declared the beginning of the "法庭调查 *(court investigation)*" after imposing the prosecution's suggestion upon the defense with only two information units (WT and WA). The judges' information shift from insufficient knots at the lower levels (*<1, 1, 2, 19>*, *<2, 19, 3, 21>*, *<1, 1, 2, 14>*, *<2, 14, 3, 1>*) to the declarative knots at higher level (*<0, 1, 1, 2>*) will result in an unclear frame of the summary procedure in the defendant's mind. It seems that the defense has no rights to learn the conditions or the nature of summary procedure applied to the trials. Therefore, the declarative information by the judges has symbolized that the judges seemingly side with the prosecution, which tips the balance of justice.

Extract 3-6 (Case 04)

<1, 4, 2, 61, WT, P, A, 闭庭>审判长：现在闭庭。	Presiding Judge: It's time for closing of the court.
<0, 1, 1, 5, WT, P, A, 判后释法>审判长：根据**区人民法院刑事审判第一庭深化刑事审判方式改革若干规定的要求，下面进行判后释法。	Presiding Judge: Based on the requirements of the relevant regulations on deepening the reform of the mode of criminal trials in the 1st Criminal Court of ... Now proceed to the interpretation of law after judgment.

The stage of interpreting the law relevant to the judgment in Extract 3-6 constructs another primary frame and reflects the procedural justice of the criminal trial. Actually, it seems that the trial work should end with the presiding judge's declaration of closing court after the verdict. But the presiding judge firstly puts forward the legal basis of interpreting the relevant law with the phrase "根据······要求 *(based on the requirements of ...)*", then activates the new primary frame by means of the key word "判后释法 *(interpretation of law after judgment)"*. Thus, the production of the two WT information knots has realized the shifting of two primary frames—the trial judgment to the interpretation of relevant law. The frame shifting then has added one more stage to the normal criminal trial and has made both the parties (namely the prosecution and the defense), and the audience more aware of the legal basis of the final judgment. In fact, the shifting frames the specific relation between the judge, the prosecution and the defense in court. That is to say, the judge maintains the rights and interests of both the prosecution and the defense, renders the judgment based on the relevant law, and hence forms the contradiction solver. As a result, the primary frame of interpreting the relevant law avails to facilitate the reform of criminal trial and to realize the judicial justice.

Extract 3-7 (Case 04)

<1, 1, 2, 16, WB, 依法审案>审判长: 根据《中华人民共和国刑事诉讼法》第 152 条的规定, 本庭依法公开开庭审理**区人民检察院提起公诉的被告人姜**诈骗一案。<1, 1, 2, 17, WO, 合议庭成员>本合议庭由本院审判员陈**担任审判长、审判员曹**和人民陪审员印**组成。<1, 1, 2, 18, WO, 书记员>书记员刘**担任法庭记录。<1, 1, 2, 19, WO, 公诉人>**区人民检察院指派检察员毛**、代理检察员顾**出庭支持公诉。<1, 1, 2, 20, WO, 辩护人>**律师事务所律师翟**担任被告人姜**的

Presiding Judge: In terms of the relevant regulation in Article 152 of "CPL", the court conducts a public trial of the fraud case filed by the People's Procuratorate of ** against the defendant Jiang**. The collegial panel is composed of the presiding judge undertaken by the judge Chen** from the present court, the judge Cao** and the people's assessor Yin**. The recorder Liu** undertakes the job as a court recorder. The People's Procuratorate of ** assigns the prosecutor Mao** and the acting prosecutor Gu** to appear in court to support the public prosecution. The lawyer Zhai** from the Law Office

辩护人。   of ** undertakes the defender of the
                                     defendant Jiang**.

Here, the presiding judge constructs two sub-frames of the primary frame "开庭情况 (situation of opening the trial)", namely "依法审案 (trial by law)" and "法庭人员组成 (court staff)". The declarative information, which the presiding judge provides before the opening of each trial, embodies the judge's performance of the duty of judging based on the relevant law and the acceleration of implementing trial procedures. Meanwhile the declarative information has constructed the relationships among all the parties in court within the specific legislative scope.

In the first sub-frame at Level 2 "<1, 1, 2, 16>", the judge makes use of WB information to transmit the legal basis of the trial to activate the legal frame "依法审案 (trial by law)" in all the other parties' cognition, and make the sub-frame shifting undergo smoothly into the transmission of another sequence of declarative information.

In the second sub-frame at Level 2 "<1, 1, 2, 17>, <1, 1, 2, 18>, <1, 1, 2, 19> and <1, 1, 2, 20>", all the other parties can both acquire the relevant information about the members of collegial panel and the prosecutors, and witness that the lawyer defends the defendant. Surely all the parties can be aware of the rationality of the members of the collegial panel and the prosecution. In this way, the legal triangle PDJ relationship can be basically constructed in the trial—the judge conducts the trial based on the relevant law, the prosecutor appears in court to support the public prosecution and the defender defends for the accused.

However, Liu Jinghua, a vice presiding judge of the 1st Court of the Beijing High People's Court, said that within such a legal system there exists a tendency with more emphasis on cooperation and less on constrain between each other in the public security organs, the people's procuratorates and the people's courts[8]. A vivid saying can illustrate this tendency well, i.e. the public security organs are the cook, the people's procuratorates the persons delivering the meal and the people's courts the persons who enjoy it[9]. Professor Chen Weidong said that judges always believe prosecutors' and scouts' statements by instinct, but ignore defendants' or lawyers' defending[10].

The analysis of judges' monologue above demonstrates that in trial judges may shift turns when the prosecution is at an advantage but end a conversation sequence or shift to another primary frame when the prosecution is at a disadvantage. Meanwhile, judges will also omit intentionally some questions to the defense or interpretation to the defense, which should exist in the trial. All the information processing by judges has seriously violated the procedural justice in trial and has revealed certain relations between the judge and the prosecution. Actually, judges have constructed the relationship as "PJ cooperation (Bian & Li, 2004; Li, 2006)" by means of the framing device as "information omission or information shifting".

3.3   PDJ Relationship Manifested in Dialogue

Dialogic discourse can be found in various cultures and certain specific contexts such as institutional settings (Prego-Vázquez, 2007). The structure of dialogue involves turn-taking systems and conventions for organizing the exchange of speaker turns, as well as conventions for the stages in conversations (Fairclough, 1992). Therefore, it is necessary to investigate the dialogue between judges and the other parties in criminal courts.

---

8. http://news.sohu.com/20050414/n225174602.shtml
9. http://news.sohu.com/20050414/n225174602.shtml
10. http://news.sohu.com/20050414/n225174602.shtml

3.3.1   Dialogue as Judges' Directive Information

The illocutionary point of a DIRECTIVE is to get the hearer to do something (Hu, 454). Judges' directive information functions as the requirement for the prosecution or the defense to perform some act in the trial interaction. Meanwhile, the information also plays an important role in the achievement of judicial justice.

Extract 3-8 (Case 02)

<1，2，2，5，WT，P，R>
审判长：……首先由公诉人宣读起诉书。

Presiding Judge: ... Firstly, let the prosecutor read out the indictment.

<1，2，2，7，WT，P，R>
审判长：下面由被告人对起诉书指控的犯罪事实向法庭进行供述。

Presiding Judge: Next, let the defendant make a statement of the criminal facts charged in the indictment to the court.

<2，8，3，42，WT，P，R>
审判长：……首先由公诉人向法庭出示相关证据。

Presiding Judge: ... Firstly, the prosecutor can show the related evidence to the court.

<1，3，2，11，WT，P，R>
审判长：下面由被告人杨**的辩护人发表辩护意见。

Presiding Judge: Next, the defender of the defendant Yang ** can state the defensive opinion.

<1，3，2，24，WT，P，R>
审判长：……被告人作最后陈述。

Presiding Judge: ... Now the defendant can make a final statement.

In Extract 3-8, it can be seen that this type of judges' discourse information is transmitted in the period when the transition between trial stages succeeds, directing the prosecution or the defense to fulfill their rights or duties of interrogation, presenting or challenging evidence, defending, presenting opinions.

All these information knots are WTs, which constitute typical dialogue in the courtroom interaction. These knots have definitely assigned the communicative tasks, on which all the subordinates center for the advancement of the trials.

The interaction between the judge and the prosecution or between the judge and the defense is triggered by such contextualization cues as "首先由…… (Firstly)", "下面由…… (Next, let ***... or *** can...)", "进行…… (make)" or "作…… (make)", which are followed by the other parties to perform some acts in trials.

All the information values are P, which supports the father information while knowledge category R indicates that the presiding judges know what to do at the present time. The value P and knowledge category R thus conform to the duties fulfilled by judges to switch trial stages.

The analysis shows that all the information units will influence the development of the subsequent or subordinating information since they are positioned at higher levels (Levels 2 or 3).

3.3.2   PDJ Relationship in the Dialogic Interactions

With the turn-taking made in the interactive process, diverse frames will shift from one to another for the realization of certain communicative purposes (Goffman, 1974). In this section, frame shifts will be explored to reveal PDJ relationship manifested in the interactive process.

3.3.2.1   Primary Frame Shifting

A trial develops with the transition of different stages, which means the switches between primary trial frames constructed by judges' discourse information. The judges' discourse information triggering the shifts will subsequently be scrutinized.

Extract 3-9 (Case 02)

<2，2，3，9，WT，O，提被告入庭>审判　Presiding Judge: Fetch the
长：提被告人杨**到庭。　　　　　　defendant Yang** to be

<0，1，1，1，WT，A，现在开庭>**区人 民法院刑事审判庭现在开庭。 interrogated! The Criminal Court of ** is now in session.

Before the opening of a trial, the judge frames the defendant guilt with the use of WT information with the word "*提 (fetch the defendant to be interrogated)*".

In a criminal trial, it is possible for a judge to use such kinds of phrases as "*传被告人到庭 (call upon the defendant to the court)*", "*带被 告人到庭 (bring the defendant to the court)*", "*提被告人到庭 (fetch the defendant to the court)*", among which "*传 (call upon)*" and "*带 (bring)*" are neutral words that do not frame the presumption of defendants' guilt but embody defendants as a subject in a suit as well. On the contrary, "*提 (fetch)*", as a derogative word based on *Dictionary of Modern Chinese* (5th edn.) (Lü & Ding, 2005), means "to bring a criminal out of the jail". The information that defendants are regarded as criminals imprisoned in the jail places them in an inferior status, which makes the subject defendants become litigation objects in a status of being interrogated (Bian, 2007).

Meanwhile, this information unit is followed by "*<0, 1, 1, 1, 现在 开庭> (court in session)*", the first one at Level 1, which predicts that the criminal will be tried. From this, we can tell that the concept of the presumption of guilt remains in some judges' minds. Since the knowledge category O, the information contained in the sentence with the contextualization cue "*提 (fetch the defendant to be interrogated)*" is shared by all the parties in the court, so is the connotative meaning the judge presupposes.

Therefore, the judge's discourse information processing reflects the presumption of guilt, which undoubtedly impose influence upon the justice of the whole trial, and which is detrimental to the equality between the prosecution and the defense.

3.3.2.2   Sub-frame Shifting

A primary frame is a relative concept because it cannot be recognized without considering their sub-frames. The primary trial frames boast some corresponding sub-frames. Thus, the observation of shifts between sub-frames or shifts between primary frames and sub-frames may contribute to the exploration of PDJ relationship in criminal trials.

Extract 3-10 (Case 04)

<1，5，2，61，WB，A，释法依据>审判长：根据……，<0，1，1，5，WT，A，判后释法>下面进行判后释法。

Presiding Judge: Based on …, the next stage is interpretation of law after judgment.

<1，5，2，62，WF，P，A，诈骗罪>审判长：诈骗罪是指以非法占有为目的……的行为。

Presiding Judge: Crime of fraud refers to a behavior with a purpose of illegal occupation…

<1，5，2，63，WB，A，刑法依据>审判长：刑法第二百六十六条规定……数额巨大或有其他严重情节的，处三年以上十年以下有期徒刑，并处罚金……<1，5，2，67，WF，A，退款事实>法庭考虑……父母已代其退赔赃款……<1，5，2，68，WP，A，减轻处罚>对你予以减轻处罚。

Presiding Judge: In terms of the relevant regulation of Article 266 of the Criminal Law, regarding the behavior with a large amount of fraud money or other cases of gross violation, the defendant is sentenced to fixed-term imprisonment between three and ten years and with a certain amount of penalty. …Taking it into consideration that… the parents have paid compensation for illicit money on behalf the defendant…, the court will give you mitigated punishment.

<1，5，2，69，WJ，A，判决>审判长：同时考虑……，对你作出了如上判决。<1，5，2，70，WA，A，对判决的态度>这次判决只是对你所做的这件

Presiding Judge: At the same time, considering…, the court has sentenced you as the above-mentioned. The

事情的一个处理，<1，5，2，71，WF，A，鼓励>并不是对你整个人生的否定，<1，5，2，72，WF，A，鼓励>你还年轻，<1，5，2，73，WF，A，鼓励>受过高等教育，<1，5，2，74，WA，A，信任>完全有能力通过自己的劳动过上稳定的生活。<1，5，2，75，WA，A，希望>审判长：希望你从此事中吸取教训，<1，5，2，76，WT，A，鼓励>克服虚荣攀比、好逸恶劳的不良思想，<1，5，2，77，WT，A，鼓励>在服刑期间好好接受改造，<1，5，2，78，WT，A，鼓励>回到社会上做一个遵纪守法、孝敬父母，对家庭、对社会负责任的人。

sentence is only a punishment for what you have done in the case, not the negation of your whole life. Being still young and having received higher education, you are completely able to live a stable life by means of your labor.

Presiding Judge: I hope that you can draw a good lesson from the case and overcome an evil idea of excessive vanity, upward comparison, loving ease and detesting work. While serving a prison sentence, you should receive a good reformation and be a person who observes disciplines and obeys laws, respects parents, and holds responsibility for the family and the society after your being released.

The information units in Extract 3-10 have triggered a primary trial frame "判后释法 (interpretation of law after judgment)" in that such variables as Level 1 (<0, 1, 1, 5>), information knot (WT) and knowledge category (A) are combined in the trial setting. The primary frame also rests on its subordinate WB information "<1, 5, 2, 61, 释法依据> (interpretation by law)", which indicates that an information chunk will develop centering on the Level 1 information "<判后释法> (interpretation of law after judgment)".

In the primary frame, a sequence of conversation has taken shape as expected. The judge makes full use of the cross-transmission of a variety of types of information to realize the rational construction of JD relationship with the shifting between the sub-frames.

Firstly, the judge transmits kinds of information, such as WF, WB,

WP and WJ, to activate the sub-frame "判决依据 *(legal basis of judgment)*" in that these four information knots have formed a coherent constructive core of the frame. The WB information "<刑法依据> *(basis of criminal law)*" provides the relevant law, the WF "<退款事实> *(the fact of compensation paid)*" offers specific legal facts, the WP "<减轻处罚> *(mitigated punishment)*" shows mitigation of punishment and the WJ "<判决> *(judgment)*" presents the final judgment. These information knots "… hold together and give coherence to a diverse array of symbols and idea elements (Creed, Langstraat & Scully, 2008)." Thus, the sub-frame has sufficiently supported its superordinate frame, i.e. the primary frame "判后释法 *(interpretation of law after judgment)*".

Surely, the defendant and the other parties involved can be more aware of the judgment of the collegial panel. In accordance with the recognition of legal facts in trial, the accused did commit a crime and has been sentenced according to the relevant law. However, to evaluate whether conviction and measurement of penalty is fair and rational or not is closely relevant to the information units about legal basis and results produced by the judge based on the context of "判后释法 *(interpretation of law after judgment)*". Thus, these information units seem more important than ever in the courtroom setting.

Then, the judge conducts the sub-frame shifting by the change of topics, which reflects the instructive legislative spirit of curing the sickness to saving the patient in the current China's legal system. The topic change has been achieved in the judge's transmission of WA information "<1, 5, 2, 70, 对判决的态度> *(attitude towards the judgment)*" to express his attitude towards the judgment. Then, the judge's first WF information "<1, 5, 2, 71, 鼓励> *(encouragement)*" stands for the collegial panel's opinion of dealing with the case, namely, not denying the defendant's life. The judge also uses two WF information knots "<1, 5, 2, 71, 鼓励> *(encouragement)*" to express his own opinion on the defendant, and one WA information knot "<1, 5, 2, 74, 信任>" to express his trust in the defendant. These four information units are filled with encouragement and consolation.

The presiding judge processes the discourse information in the linear structure "WA—WF—WF—WF—WA", which has activated the second subordinate frame the primary one "判后释法 (interpretation of law after judgment)". Therefore, the sequence of conversation consisting of WF and WA information at Level 2 forms the education core of the sub-frame of "教育被告人 (educating the defendant)" in the trial setting.

Lastly, the judge uses the catchphrase "希望 (hope)" as contextualization cue to activate and shift into another sub-frame. The sub-frame "希望(hope)" has been constructed based on the linear structure of information knots "WA—WT—WT—WT" at Level 2.

In particular, the judge uses the last information unit "<1, 5, 2, 78, 鼓励> (encouragement)" to put forwards the hope from the angle of Chinese ideology—traditional virtues, which universally exists in the ordinary Chinese's social cognition and ideology. It has been a knowledge schema that a person should observe disciplines and obeys laws, respect the parents and hold himself/herself responsible for the family and the society. It is the judge's words that can achieve the agreement of knowledge schema between the defendant and the judge, even between the defendant and all the other parties. The function and effect of this agreement may not be notified but it embodies the judge's responsible attitude towards the defendant because curing the sickness, saving the patient and cultivation according to the relevant law are the best judicial results although the behavior of the defendant is hateful. Maybe the soul of the defendant in the case can receive baptism in the primary frame "判后释法 (interpretation of law after judgment)".

On all accounts, the sub-frame shifts in Extract 3-10 demonstrates that the members in the collegial panel have constructed JD relationship conforming to the relevant laws and regulations.

Extract 3-11 (Case 04)

<罪名是否成立>审判长：被告人，起诉书中指控你犯罪的罪名是否成立？

Presiding Judge: Defendant, do you agree with the crime committing charged in the indictment?

<不成立>被告人：不成立。

Defendant: I disagree with it.

<讯问指令>审判长：下面由公诉人对被告人进行讯问。

Presiding Judge: Next, let the prosecutors interrogate the defendant.

<是否认识盛**>公诉人：被告人，你认识被害人盛**吗？

Prosecutor: Defendant, do you know the victim Sheng**?

The judge uses the catchphrase "讯问 (interrogate)" to direct the prosecutor to investigate the defendant, but the application of the word is against the spirit of criminal suit—equality between the prosecution and the defense. In the trial, judges and prosecutors have the rights to interrogate defendants. The catchphrase "讯问 (interrogate)", namely "审问罪犯 (pump a prisoner)" or "责问 (bring someone who does something wrong to account)", conveys the fact that the judge's declarative information frames the defendant's guilt, which consolidates the defendant's status of being tried. The shift of judge's frame to the prosecutor's conveys the information that it is hard for the defendant to escape the identity of guilt except for being tried. From the data corresponding with the audio and the video, it can be found that the judge usually interrogates the defendant in loud voices and stern expressions, with the presumption of guilt implied throughout the trial.

Extract 3-12

<WT，宣读起诉书>审判长：……首先由公诉人宣读起诉书。
……
<WT，被告法庭供述>审判长：下面由

Presiding Judge: ...Firstly, let the prosecutor read out the indictment.
...

被告人对起诉书指控的犯罪事实向法庭进行供述。

Presiding Judge: Next, let the defendant confess the criminal facts charged in the indictment to the court.

Here the judge uses the catchphrase "*供述 (confess)*" to frame the defendant's guilt. From the syntactic and grammatical perspective, the judge directs the defendant to admit his guilt as the logical object of "*供述 (confess)*" is "*犯罪事实 (criminal facts)*". Meanwhile, WT information represents the speaker's original stance in the discourse processing (Du, 2009a), so it can be seen obviously that the judge wants the defendant's confession in the shift of his frame to the defendant's. Consequently, the frame that a criminal is being tried will be activated by means of the combination of "WT + catchphrase". The frame will take shape in all the other parties' minds due to the common sense of "to confess the criminal facts". It also means what the defendant is required to articulate a chunk of information about his crime.

The discourse information in Extract 3-11 and Extract 3-12 demonstrates that in the information processing, judges often make use of such contextualization cues as "*犯罪事实 (criminal facts)*", "*供述 (confess)*", "*讯问 (interrogate)*", "*提 (fetch the defendant to be interrogated)*" and so on to deliver a certain direction. Moreover, judges' choice of words keeps relatively stable except for the difference in use of certain words. Generally, these WT information units manifest the judge's presumption of the defendant's guilt by the framing device of "information implication or information presupposition" because the information units lead to the frame of defendants' guilt before final verdicts.

3.4 PDJ Relationship Manifested in Questioning

In the courtroom interaction, judges will also question the other participants to investigate the facts in a certain case. Judges' confirmative or expressive information are produced in the criminal courtroom in that "there may be two objectives of legal questioning. One is a genuine process of elicitation of information. The other is to obtain confirmation of a particular version of events that the question has in mind. (Gibbons, 2003: 95)".

3.4.1 Questioning in Judges' Discourse

The advancement of a trial must broadly have to do with ensuring that the interaction works smoothly at an organizational level. It indicates that turns at talking are distributed, that topics are selected and changed, questions are raised and answered, and so forth (Fairclough, 1992). Since courtroom questioning and answering constitute the essential part of a trial, the explication of judges' questioning in the criminal courtroom is expected to uncover the PDJ relationship.

Confirmative information can take on various information knots for the confirmation of legal facts in trials such as WT, WA, WF, WN and so forth. These kinds of information are generally produced in the interaction between judges and the other two parties.

Extract 3-13 (Case 04)

<WF，询问被告人姓名>审判长：被告人你的姓名？……

Presiding Judge: Defendant, what's your name? ...

<WF，生日>审判长：出生年、月、日？……

Presiding Judge: The exact birth date? ...

<WN，逮捕时间>审判长：被告人，你何时被逮捕？……

Presiding Judge: Defendant, when were you arrested? ...

<WA，是否有意见>审判长：被告人是否有意见？……

Presiding Judge: Defendant, is there anything you want to state? ...

<WA，是否听清>审判长：公诉人是否听清？……

Presiding Judge: Prosecutor, have you heard clearly? ...

To associate with the procedural justice, various information units function respectively in the different primary frames in trials. These information units are transmitted for verifying the identity of a defendant, confirming time, places and so on, confirming the attitude towards something (e.g. to interrogate whether defendants agree with some evidence, to examine whether prosecutors or defenders have any questions to ask about some evidence), or confirming whether defendants agree with the application of summary procedure.

3.4.2 PDJ Relationship in the Questioning and Answering

Different from those in the courtroom interaction dominated by judges' monologue and dialogue, the interactive frames may take on distinctive characteristics in the question-and-answer process between judges and the other parties in court.

3.4.2.1 Frame Consistency

Frame consistency means that a speaker or a listener always holds the firm opinion that during the whole interactive process of a trial there must be a certain frame, based on which his/her discourse information is formed and transmitted; or that a speaker or a listener does not achieve the communicative goal by means of a certain frame which is not in accordance with the situation.

Extract 3-14 (Case 17)

1 <1, 12, 2, 33, HW>审判长：被告人蓝**，这个八万元你们是怎么分的？

Presiding Judge: Defendant Lan**, how did you distribute RMB 80,000?

2 <1, 12, 2, 33, HW>被告人：一人四万块。

Defendant: Each for RMB 40,000.

3 <1, 12, 2, 34, WY>审判长：一人四万块，这么短的时间里，这四万块哪里去了？

Presiding Judge: Each for RMB 40,000? How could you spend RMB 40,000 in such a short period of time?

4 <1, 12, 2, 34, HW>被告人：我回

Defendant: I came back to

绵阳，当天晚上就输掉三万五。

Mianyang and lost RMB 35,000 that night.

5 <1，12，2，35，WT>审判长：赌博？

Presiding Judge: Gambling?

6 <1，12，2，35，WT>被告人：是。

Defendant: Yes.

7 <1，12，2，36，WF>审判长：当时你取钱的时候，那银行卡里有多少钱？

Presiding Judge: While you were drawing money, how much was left in the bank card?

8 <1，12，2，36，WF>被告人：总共十五万多。

Defendant: Over RMB 150,000 in total.

9 <1，12，2，37，WF>审判长：十五万多？

Presiding Judge: Over RMB 150,000?

10 <1，12，2，37，WF>被告人：对。

Defendant: Yes.

11 <1，12，2，38，WY>审判长：为什么你就拿八万？

Presiding Judge: Why did you only get RMB 80,000?

12 <1，12，2，38，WF>被告人：我(.)我总共取了八万块钱(0.8)<1，12，2，38，WY>我给朋友陈**一点，<1，12，2，38，WF>我说这个女孩是陕西的，<1，12，2，38，WY>大概也是比较仗义比较贫困的，<1，12，2，38，WP>钱不应全取完，<1，12，2，38，WE>取完了要是有严重后果，<1，12，2，38，WF>我说我心里不安，<1，12，2，38，WF>陈**说回去取，<1，12，2，38，WF>把这钱全部取完，<1，12，2，38，WF>换点金子、搞点名表，<1，12，2，38，WF>我说不要，<1，12，2，38，WF>然后在我走之前，陈**去取了。

Defendant: I(.)I drew RMB 80,000 in total. (0.8) I gave some to my friend, Chen**. I said that the girl was from Shanxi, probably generous and poor. The money shouldn't be drawn out otherwise the result would be serious. I said that I was nervous. Chen** wanted to get it back, drawing it out to buy some gold and luxurious watch. I disagreed with him and Chen** drew the money before I left.

13 <1，12，2，39，WP>审判员：那么你对被害人这八万块的损失，有

Judge: Then, how do you plan to deal with the victim's loss

什么打算?

14 <1, 12, 2, 39, WP>被告人：我分了的四万块我愿意赔。

15 <1, 12, 2, 40, WP>审判员：你愿意退多少?

16 <1, 12, 2, 40, WP>被告人：我愿意退四万。

17 <1, 12, 2, 41, WF>审判员：你有能力退吗?

18 <1, 12, 2, 41, WF>被告人：我现在没。

19 <1, 12, 2, 42, WF>审判员：被告，这两张卡你取了八万以后，你说你不用了?

20 <1, 12, 2, 42, WF>被告人：不用取了。

21 <1, 12, 2, 43, WP>审判员：那么这两张卡你后来怎么处理?

22 <1, 12, 2, 43, WP>被告人：后来把卡扔掉了。

23 <1, 12, 2, 44, WF>审判员：扔掉了? <1, 12, 2, 44, WR>扔在什么地方?

24 <1, 12, 2, 44, WR>被告人：扔在垃圾桶里了。

of RMB 80,000?

Defendant: I got RMB 40,000 and I would like to pay back.

Judge: How much will you pay back?

Defendant: I will pay RMB 40,000.

Judge: Are you able to pay back?

Defendant: I can't right now.

Judge: Defendant, you said that you would discard these two bank cards after you drew RMB 80,000?

Defendant: There was no need to draw.

Judge: Then how did you deal with these two cards?

Defendant: I threw them away later.

Judge: Did you throw them away? Where did you throw them?

Defendant: I threw them into a dustbin.

In Extract 3-14, frame consistency reflects that the two judges aim to investigate the truth and make clear where the money drawn from the bank is and where the bankcard is.

The judges do not use a certain preconceived frame to induce the defendant to give the answers to the questions in the same way as what they desire. By means of the information knots HW in Turn 1, WY in Turn 3, WT in Turn 5 and WF in Turn 7, the presiding judge has detected the amount of money in the bank card, the distribution of the money drawn from the bank, the whereabouts of the money the defendant has got and the reason why he has not drawn all the money in the card. Based on the Criminal Law, the judge wants to investigate thoroughly the truth of the case. In consequence, despite that more information knots are in use, the judge's aim lies in the fact that the criminal event can be reconstructed from various angles so that it is easier to recover the victim's loss after the final judgment.

After that, the judge asks several supplementary questions utilizing the information knots WP in Turns 13 and 15, and WF in Turn 17 for the sake of detecting how the defendant has tackled RMB 80,000 drawn from the bank. During the investigating stage, a judge always makes use of substantive discourse information to communicate with the defendant in order to confirm the truth of the case and to reconstruct the criminal event.

The two judges have produced many information units at Level 2 during the investigating process to make the confirmation of some important facts in the case for the realization of the justice between the prosecution and the defense. Meanwhile, throughout the whole trial, the judges have not made a presumption of guilt or determined the truth subjectively.

As a result, a multiple of information units are combined in the judges' discourse in the case and a frame of "fact confirmation" has been formed. All the judges' information units transmitted center on the same topic, which is beneficial to construct PDJ relationship in a reasonable way.

In fact, a judge usually combines WF information with other types of information in trial so as to investigate the truth of a case.

Consequently, the role of WF information is irreplaceable in the whole discourse. The other types of information such as WN, WH, and WY mostly serve for WF information. In light of the above-mentioned analysis and the following discourse of truth investigation, it can be proved whether judges deal with a case in a fair way with strong responsibility in his mind.

Extract 3-15 (Case 34)

<WN，b>审判长：你们是何时开始这种非法集资的，持续了多久？

Presiding Judge: When did you start the illegal capital raising and how long did it last?

<WN，b>被告人：嗯::2002年到2006年4月。

Defendant: Um::from the year 2002 to April, 2006.

<WF，b>审判长：你们通过这种非法吸收公众存款方式共集得多少钱？

Presiding Judge: How much money in total did you raise by illegally taking deposits in this way?

<WF，b>被告人：3亿多，具体数字要问我老婆。

Defendant: More than RMB 300,000,000? I have to ask my wife for the exact statistics.

In Extract 3-15, although the final judgment is not declared, the judge has framed the defendant's illegal behavior, namely, has activated the frame "*非法集资 (illegal capital raising)*". Consequently, the problems concerned with the defendant's illegal behavior has been presented.

It seems to be reasonable that the judge uses WF information and WN information to interrogate the defendant "*持续时间 (duration of raising capital)*" and "*多少钱 (sum of money raised)*", but the way to interrogate the defendant presupposes an important fact that the defendant's behavior is illegal. From the perspective of pragmatic presupposition, the knowledge categories in these two information knots are both b, which means the information that the judge does not know but the defendant knows. The judge wants to gain such new information as the sum of money raised and the duration of raising capital, but his questions imply the information (illegal capital raising) known to both the parties. The existential presupposition indicates the fact in the judge's mind that the defendant is law-breaking person or a criminal is undoubted, and the priority now is to make clear the seriousness of the defendant's crime. As the question mode of presupposition confines the defendant's concern within WF information (sum of money raised) and WN information (duration of raising capital), the defendant has paid no attention to the WF information "非法集资 *(illegal capital raising)*" while answering the judge.

According to the overall trial data, the presiding judge of the case always frames the defendant's illegal behavior before the final judgment. The frame consistency of guilt presumption has seriously destroyed the relationship between the judge and the other two sides, resulting in the doubt about the judges' neutrality in trial.

Extract 3-16 (Case 11)

1 <WT>审判长：被告人李**，你现在可以对起诉书所涉及的犯罪事实进行陈述。

Presiding Judge: Defendant Li**, now state the criminal facts charged in the indictment to the court.

2 <WF>被告人：仓库是三个人一起去租的，<WF>并不是我一个人去租的。

Defendant: The warehouse was rented by us three together, not by me alone.

3 <WT>审判长：你是不是辩解的意思？<WF>就是说，你这些事实是伙同其他一些人共同犯罪的，<WA>是这个意思吗？

Presiding Judge: Are you trying to excuse your crime? That's to say, you mean the fact is that you have committed the crime in collusion with other persons, right?

4 <WA, b>被告人：嗯。

Defendant: Yes.

In Extract 3-16, the judge consistently applies presupposed information to frame the defendant's guilt.

Firstly, he uses the procedural information, a WT information knot in Turn 1, to direct the defendant to state the criminal fact. Although the presumption of guilt exists in the WT information, the defendant still gains the chance to defend himself.

Then, the presiding judge uses the WT, WF and WA information knots in Turn 3. It seems that the defendant has been treated impartially because the presiding judge has accepted the statement that the defendant does work with the other persons. Actually, the presiding judge has been always framing the defendant's guilt in the investigating extract.

Above all, the WT information in Turn 3 *"你是不是辩解的意思? (Are you trying to excuse your crime?)"* implies that the judge is condemning the defendant, which means that the defendant's behavior is not to defend himself but to find an excuse, or even to quibble. Being in an inferior position, the defendant undoubtedly bears a certain pressure in his mind while hearing the criticism from the judge in a superior position.

And then, the presiding judge uses WF information in Turn 3 to explain the condemning sentence to the defendant, but his explanation is in a qualitative mood and with the use of such contextualization cues as *"伙同 (in collusion with)"* and *"共同犯罪 (fellowship in crime)"* to conduct a presumption of guilt.

At last, the judge's WA information in Turn 3 seems to ask for the defendant's agreement and give the defendant some advantage because the presiding judge's explanation shows that the crime has not been committed by him alone. But as a matter of fact, the information is to reinforce the presumption of guilt because the defendant may be ignorant with the catchphrases such as *"伙同 (in collusion with)"* and *"共同犯罪 (fellowship in crime)"* and may be highly possible to agree with the judge. Then, the defendant's answer proves everything. That is to say, even if the defendant has different ideas, the presiding judge's information of framing his guilt has already been in existence.

It is proved from the analysis of the above three extracts that the frame consistency in the judge's discourse has still led to the grading of JD relationship—the judge is high in a superior position while the defendant is guilty to be tried. To some extent, frame consistency consequently imposes direct influence both upon the construction of PDJ relationship and upon the trial justice of the case as well.

3.4.2.2 Frame Agreement

Frame agreement means that a frame activated by a questioner or a questioner's framing process is in agreement with that of a replier and no conflict arises therein. Moreover, frame agreement conduces to making the questions and answers go smoothly.

Extract 3-17 (Case 17)

1 <WA> 审判长：被告人，刚才公诉人宣读被害人的陈述内容是不是事实？ <WA> 他讲的是不是事实？

Presiding Judge: Defendant, the prosecutor reads out the facts that the victim states. Are they the truth?

2 <WF> 被告人：▬▬总共是十五万，<WF> 我们取了八万。

Defendant: ▬▬ RMB 150,000 in total, we drew RMB 80,000.

3 <WF> 审判长：你们**取了八万**是不是？

Presiding Judge: You **drew RMB 80,000**, right?

4 <WF> 被告人：是。

Defendant: Yes.

5 <WA> 审判长：他讲的过程对不对？

Presiding Judge: Is the course of the crime committing in his statement true?

6 <WA> 被告人：过程对。

Defendant: Yes.

7 <WT> 审判长：公诉人，把这个辨认照片向被告人出示一下，

Presiding Judge: Prosecutor, show the defendant the identifying photo

<WT> 把这个照片让被告人辨认一下，<WT> 被告人仔细看一下，<WF> 你在这些辨认照片里是几号？<WF> 有没有你的照片？<WF> 几号？

and let the defendant recognize the photo. Defendant, which number is your photo in it? Is there your photo in it? Which number is it?

8 <WF> 被告人：3 号。

Defendant: Number 3.

The discourse in Extract 3-17 represents the transition from the procedural discourse information into substantive discourse information, during which the trial has been advancing smoothly because the frame in the judge's discourse is in accordance with that in the defendant's discourse and there is no conflict between each other.

At first, the judge does not frame the presumption of the defendant's guilt. In this extract, the judge performs his duty to manipulate the trial procedures and to ask for the defendant's opinion on the victim's statement. During the whole course, no discourse information is used to presume the defendant's guilt.

Secondly, the judge makes use of the repetitive information to confirm the truth. The first repetitive information "……是不是事实? (…the truth?)" is WA in Turn 1, which makes it prominent that the defendant has the chance to make a defense against the content of suit or the evidence closely related with his own interests. The second repetitive information "……取了八万…… (…drew RMB 80,000…)" is WF in Turn 3, which does something good to exactly confirm the defendant's behavior.

In addition, there is no discourse information inducing the defendant's active confession of his crime. In the final part of this extract, the judge asks the defendant to identify the photos to confirm whether he is involved in the case. The judge does not use any inductive discourse information to manipulate the defendant's discourse so as to achieve the goal of making the defendant confess the crime actively.

In sum, there is no conflict between the frame of the judge's confirmation and that of the defendant's answers in this extract from the beginning to the end. Frame agreement consistently exists between the two parties, which is helpful to advance the fair trial smoothly.

Extract 3-18 (Case 08)

1 <1，2，2，18，WT>审判长：Presiding Judge: Do you have any 你对起诉书指控你的犯罪事 objections to the criminal facts and the 实及罪名有意见吗？ accusation charged in the indictment?

2 <1，2，2，18，WT>被告人：Defendant: Yes. 没有。

3 <1，2，2，19，WA>审判长：Presiding Judge: Are you voluntary 你是否自愿认罪？ to confess the crime committing?

4 <1，2，2，19，WT>被告人：Defendant: I confess my guilt. 我认罪。

The first information unit in this extract gives rise to the violation of the retributive justice, as the final verdict has not been made to confirm the defendant's guilt. The judge wants to know whether the defendant agrees with the prosecutor's charge, but the judge has actually used the WT information in Turn 1 to presuppose the content of charge as a criminal fact, i.e. no matter whether he has different opinions; the fact of the defendant's guilt has been presumed. According to Case 08, the WT information is procedural discourse, with its father information "<法庭调查> (court investigation)" and the previous information at the same level only the prosecutor's "<宣读起诉书> (reading out the Bill of Indictment)". Therefore, there is no evidence to confirm the content of charge to be a criminal fact. No previous context supports the defendant's guilt, either.

The judge's information knot WA in Turn 3 here is against

procedural justice. Defendants have no obligation to confess to be guilty according to CPL, but the judge seeks the defendant's attitude towards the confession. It is repeatedly emphasized that everyone has instinct of self-protection, as a result, from the point of morality and ethics, he is unwilling to speak out the fact unfavorable to himself, even has no obligation of proving himself guilty or not (Bian & Yang, 2006). Since the level "<*1, 2, 2, 18*>" is high in this information knot, once the defendant does confirm his own crime, summary procedure will be applied. The application is easy for the judge to manipulate and beneficial to the prosecution, which might damage the judicial justice in court.

Extract 3-19 (Case 06)

1 <3, 82, 4, 61, WF, 看病条件> 审判长：在这种情况下私自给人看病，<3, 82, 4, 62, WG, 造成被害人死亡>造成被害人商**死亡，<2, 27, 3, 82, WA, 什么行为>你这是什么行为？ Presiding Judge: Under such a condition, you made a diagnosis and treatment of patients without legal approval, which led to the victim Shang**'s death. **What kind of behavior is it?**

2 <2, 27, 3, 82, WA, 违法行为> 被告人：属于违法，<3, 82, 4, 63, WA, 非法行医>非法行医。 Defendant: It is an illegal behavior, illegal practice of medicine.

3 <1, 2, 2, 28, WT, 举证质证> 审判长：现在由控辩双方举证、质证。 Presiding Judge: It's time for the prosecutor and the defender to present and challenge the evidence.

In Extract 3-19, the judge uses the inductive discourse information to frame the defendant's guilt, which does not conform to the identity of being a judge to try a case impartially.

By means of WF and WG information, the judge firstly frames that the victim's death related with the defendant's treatment, and then produces the WA information "<什么行为> (*what kind of behavior*)" loudly to make the defendant frame his own behavior. It is obvious that the frame agreement is obtained by the judge's inductive information rather than supported by legal basis. The practice of inducing the defendant to confess the crime voluntarily has violated the relevant regulation in CPL that no one can be forced to confess the crime voluntarily.

From the perspective of the information level, the discourse information in this extract is transferred from a lower level in Turn 2 into a higher level in Turn 3. The turn-taking here imposes rather a deep influence upon judicial justice. For one thing, the judge makes use of inductive discourse information to deceive the defendant into confessing his behavior illegal voluntarily. And for another, the judge then conducts a turn-taking immediately to produce a declarative procedural information unit on a higher level which makes the trial step into the stage of "*举证质证 (presenting and challenging the evidence)*". It is equal to say that the judge has framed the defendant's guilt before presenting and challenging the evidence.

In sum, the judge's information processing in Extract 3-19 has presumed the defendant's guilt, which exerts the negative influence on the rational PDJ relationship constructed.

3.4.2.3 Frame Conflict

Frame conflict refers to the phenomenon that different frames about the same issues are constructed in the interaction due to speakers' different interest-orientations, knowledge structures, or cognitive abilities. Frame conflict always leads to the unsmooth communication, which is one of distinctive characteristics among the interactive frames in trials.

Extract 3-20 (Case 17)

1 <WB>公诉人: 公诉人接下来
向法庭出示的是上海市公安
局火车站派出所的一份工作

Prosecutor: Next, the prosecutor will show a fact sheet of working from the local police station of ** to the court,

情况，<WJ>这份工作情况证明了 2008 年 5 月 14 日，在上海市火车站发现被告人蓝**，<WJ>将其带到警务室进行排查并将其抓获的经过。<WT>请法庭质证。

which proves that the police found the defendant Lan** in the Station of ** on May 14th, 2008 and took him to the police station to examine. The whole process is clearly described in the sheet. Please challenge the evidence.

2 <WT>审判长：公诉人稍微详细一点，<WT>你介绍下，<WR>在什么地方，<HW>怎么会被抓获？

Presiding Judge: Prosecutor, state it in a bit more details. Where and how was the defendant arrested?

3 <WA>公诉人：好的。<WN>这份工作记录记载 2008 年 5 月 14 日 12 时 15 分许，民警张**在地铁一号线上海火车站警务所使用监控设施进行巡查时，<WT>在站厅近一号出口的进站栅梯处发现一名身高一米五左右的携带一只白色红纹拎包的男子，<WF>其体貌特征与 2008 年 4 月 17 日实施诈骗案的作案人之时⊥之一相符。<WT>民警遂将其带至警务站，<WT>也就是说民警发现了被告人蓝**与前期实施一系列犯罪案件的蓝**体貌特征相符，<WT>然后将蓝**抓获的经过。<WT>请法庭质证。

Prosecutor: Ok. The working record notes that the policeman Zhang** inspected the Subway Route One with help of monitoring aids in the local police station at a quarter past twelve, May 14th, 2008. Near the Exit No.1 in the hall, the policeman found a man with height of about 150cm carrying a suitcase with white and red stripes, whose figure style was close to that of the suspect who committed crime of fraud on April 17th, 2008. Then the policeman took him to the police station, that's to say, the policeman found that the figure style of the defendant Lan** was in accordance with that of Lan** who had committed a series of crime in the previous period of time. And then, Lan ** was arrested. Please challenge the evidence.

4 <WT>审判长：被告人听清楚了吗？<WA>你被抓获的过

Presiding Judge: Defendant, are you clear about it? Is the process of

程是不是这样的？   arresting like this?
5 <WA>被告人：是。   Defendant: Yes.

In Extract 3-20, frame conflict results from lack of the amount of discourse information.

At first, the prosecutor only puts forward three information knots in Turn 1 (WB, WJ and WJ) which cannot give a sufficient narration of the course of arresting the defendant. Although the WB information only shows some records, the prosecutor has conveyed the conclusion to the court with the other two WJ knots. Thus, the three knots provide insufficient information and it is hard for a listener to establish a complete frame in his mind. Therefore, a conflict comes into being between the prosecutor's frame and the judge's one. Owing to insufficiency of the prosecutor's discourse information, the judge directs the prosecutor to state in details and uses four information knots (WT, WT, WR and HW) to tell the prosecutor how to narrate the whole course in details.

Then, the prosecutor puts eight information knots (WA, WN, WT, WF, WT, WT, WT and WT) in use to give a detailed description of the whole course of the defendant's arrest. The prosecutor applies a variety of information knots to strengthen the narration in order to construct a frame of the arresting course. The frame conflict between the judge and the prosecutor indicates that in trial the judge conducts a trace of the details in the case so that he can treat the prosecution and the defense impartially. His practice can be beneficial to the final judgment of the collegial panel as well.

Moreover, after his resolution of the frame conflict, the judge's interrogation in Turn 4 guarantees the defendant's full awareness of the prosecutor's description.

Only thus can the defendant enjoy the equal opportunity to accept or reject the prosecutor's opinion in the process of the rational

PDJ relationship construction.

Extract 3-21 (Case 27)

1 <WA, b>审判长：辩护人对公诉人指控何**的犯罪事实有无异议？

Presiding Judge: Defender, do you have any objections to He**'s criminal facts charged in the indictment?

2 <WF, a>辩护人：何**只是跟被害人住在同一房间，并不能说明他拘禁被害人。

Defender: He** only lived in the same room with the victim, which can't prove that he imprisoned the victim.

3 <WF, T>审判长：他跟其他被告人都是该传销组织成员，并负责看守被害人。

Presiding Judge: Like other defendants he also worked in the organization of pyramid selling and he was in charge of keeping watch the victim.

4 <WF, R>辩护人：但是▀

Defender: But▀

5 <WT, R>审判长：好了，你不用说了！

Presiding Judge: Ok, you needn't say anything more.

In Extract 3-21, frame conflict has been resulted from the judge and the defender's disagreement on whether the defendant's behavior is a crime.

Originally, the defender wants to give an answer to the judge's question in Turn 1. Therefore, he uses the WF information to describe the fact that the defendant has not imprisoned the victim and not committed the crime of illegal confinement, which is the frame of non-criminal behavior. But the judge conducts a description to determine the nature of the defendant's behavior and interrupts the defender's utterance by transmitting WF information "<被告人行为> (the defendant's behavior)" in Turn 3 and WT information "<制止辩护发言> (preventing the defender's utterance)" in Turn 5 to frame the defendant's guilt. The frame conflict thus grows between the judge and the defender.

With the knowledge categories T (known to both parties) in Turn 3 and R (known to himself) in Turn 5, the judge obviously helps the prosecutor debate with the defender. The judge transmits the shared information to the defender to frame the defendant's crime. As a matter of fact, the information cannot be recognized by the counterpart, which results in frame conflict cognitively. In consequence, the defender wants to defend his client. However, the judge wants to prevent and interrupt the defender's utterance by use of information R. The judge uses the shared fact, WF information to characterize the defendant's behavior by use of the catchphrases "好了, 你不用再说了! (OK, you needn't say anything more!)" in Turn 5. The aim of the dominant WT information for preventing defending is to make the defender accept his opinion. It can be seen easily that the judge has deviated from his neutral position.

Finally, the defender has to give up defending because of the judge's interruption. Actually, the defendant in the case is a victim himself who is forced to participate in pyramid selling and has to watch over the victim. Nevertheless, the judge in neutral position frames the defendant's guilt from the initial stage of the trial. Meanwhile, the judge prevents the defender's defending because the frame conflict exists in their cognition, which undoubtedly weakens the subsequent defending discourse information against the defendant's innocence or punishment relief.

In fact, the defender has no chance to defend the defendant in the subsequent discourse so that it is hard to guarantee the defendant's rights of defending. Here, the frame conflict thereby leads to the defender's inferior status resulted from the JD relationship of controlling and being controlled.

Extract 3-22 (Case 26)

1 <2, 21, 3, 1, WA, b>审判长: 被告人是否申请回避? Presiding Judge: Defendant, have you applied for withdrawals?

2 <2, 21, 3, 1, WA, b>被告人: …… 嗯? Defendant: ...Umm?

Presiding Judge: That's to say, do

3 <2，21，3，2，WA，b>审判长： you demand to <u>replace the judges</u>
就是是否要求<u>换人审你</u>? <u>or the prosecutors to try you?</u>
4 <2，21，3，2，WA，b>被告人： Defendant: Oh, (0.5) no.
哦(0.5)不换人。

In this extract, the use of "*换人审你 (replace the judges or the prosecutors to try you)*" for the explanation of what "*回避 (withdrawals)*" has framed a disadvantaged defendant.

The reason for the judge's explanation is the conflict between the judge's knowledge schema and the defendant's one in the interaction. The defendant cannot comprehend the term "*回避 (withdrawals)*" in Turn 1 and has to express his bewilderment with "*……嗯? (Umm?)*" in Turn 2. But the judge's explanation "*审 (try)*" in Turn 3 reminds us of an association with "criminal" and the token of judgment "*审 (try)*" degrades the defendant's social esteem and the alignment taken by the judge implies the judge's powerful social status and the defendant's powerless social one. This should be the information shared by both sides. However, the last two information knots in Turns 3 and 4 are both WAs and the knowledge categories are both b, known to the defendant. It means that the judge's information processing mode has concealed the connotation of "*审 (try)*" because the WA information "*哦……不换人 (oh, ... no)*" is the defendant's concern but the connotative meaning of "*审 (try)*" is completely ignored by him. Owing to the defendant's disadvantage at the legal level and discursive level, his lack of mutual knowledge with the judge leads to the difficulty in achieving the goal of communication (van Dijk, 2006), i.e. the professional knowledge results in inequality of power (Cotterill, 2003).

Despite the judge's use of the shared information "*换人审你 (replace the judges or the prosecutors to try you)*" to explain the term "*申请回避 (apply for withdrawals)*" to the defendant, the realization of the communicative purpose has imposed the psychological pressure upon the defendant. Hence, as a non-professional in court, the defendant can only be disempowered while confronting with laws (Gibbons, 1994c). Although the turn-taking between discourse information units appears at the same level, the first two knots at Level 3 in the initial stage of the trial definitely influences the fair transmission of the subsequent information.

Therefore, even though the judge's use of "*换人审你 (replace the judges or the prosecutors to try you)*" cannot reflect the judge's mentality to conduct the presumption of guilt, it is evident enough to reflect the defendant's disadvantageous situation.

3.4.2.4   Frame Conflict to Frame Agreement

Due to manipulating trial procedures in criminal court, judges might solve some frame conflict by means of his discourse information processing. Judges' shift from frame conflict to frame agreement seems important in the construction of PDJ relationship.

Extract 3-23 (Case 21)

1 <WY, b>审判长：那么为何要刺被害人啊？

Presiding Judge: Then why did you want to stab the victim?

2 <WF, b>被告人：不是刺，是他又要打我，我就用刀在挡，<WF, b>具体刺到了什么位置我也不知道。<WF, c>我一个手捂着耳朵低着头，对吧？

Defendant: I didn't stab him but he wanted to beat me. I had to block with the knife. I even didn't know the exact part at which I had stabbed him. I covered the ear with one hand and lowered my head at the same time, right?

3 <WF, b>审判长：就是被害人对你拳脚相加，是不是啊？

Presiding Judge: You mean the victim beat you with boxing and kicking, right?

4 <WF, b>被告人：是。

Defendant: Yes.

5 <WF, c>审判长：然后你向他刺

Presiding Judge: Then you stabbed

了一刀，<WF，c>刺在肩部！ <WF，b>左肩还是右肩啊？

6 <WF，b>被告人：我也不知是哪个肩膀。

him with the knife once again in the shoulder. **On the left side or the right side?**

Defendant: I don't know, either.

In Extract 3-23, owing to the frame conflict with the defendant, the judge uses the inductive words to solve the conflict and achieves the frame agreement.

The defendant holds the fact: he is bullied by the victim when he is unlocking the bike; after being beaten heavily, he covers his injured ear with the left hand and takes out the fruit knife conveniently from the key chain with the right hand, accidentally injuring the victim. The frame produced in his cognition is "用刀挡 (to block with the fruit knife)" in Turn 3. However, from the very beginning, the judge frames the defendant's stabbing the victim with knife. Hence, frame conflict comes into being.

To force the defendant to accept the frame of "刺 (stabbing)" and confess the crime of stabbing the victim on purpose, the judge pays no attention to the defendant's explanation. Instead, he puts in use one WY information knot in Turn 1 and three WF information knots in Turn 5 to define the defendant's behavior as stabbing, finally forces the defendant to confess the crime. Among them, the knowledge in the two questions in Turns 1 and 5 can be categorized into b, which belongs to the counterpart's known information. Nevertheless, the defendant's behavior is presupposed as stabbing rather than blocking. The knowledge category in the other two information knots in Turn 5 is c, which has demonstrated that stabbing is the shared fact by both the parties. Thus, the defendant does not need to defend whether his behavior is stabbing, but needs to admit which of the victim's arm is stabbed by him.

According to the procedural criminal law[11], judicial personnel must, in accordance with the legally prescribed process, collect various kinds of evidence that can prove the guilt or innocence of the accused and the gravity of his/her crime; it shall be strictly forbidden to collect evidence by enticement. Based on the data, it can be proved that the judge combines WF information with other kinds of information, utilize the questions in form of the presumption of guilt to induce the defendant' information of active confession or admission what the judge wants to know, and force the defendant to accept the judge's opinion passively. At last, it changes potential presumption of guilt in the judge's discourse information into factual presumption of guilt.

Consequently, the judge's forcible discursive manipulation to shift frame conflict to agreement might lead to an irrational PDJ relationship and the defendant might be in a more disadvantageous position in the courtroom.

Extract 3-24 (Case 26)

1 <WA，b>审判长：被告人是否有意见？

Presiding Judge: Defendant, do you have any objections?

2 <WF，b>被告人：这不是事实。

Defendant: It's not the fact.

3 <WA，b>审判长：(*逼问*)被告人是否有意见？

Presiding Judge: (*asking more coercively*) **Defendant, do you have any objections?**

4 <WA，b>被告人：--没意见。

Defendant: --No.

The conflict appears between judge's expectation of negative answer and the defendant's positive one. However, the solution to the conflict is attributed to the judge's two WA information knots in Turns 1 and 3, which have limited the defendant's answer.

---

11. Article 43 in Criminal Procedure Law of the People's Republic of China (CPL) (1996)

It seems that the defendant can give an affirmative or negative answer because the judge's knowledge category in the two information knots is b, which implies that the defendant knows the answer while the judge does not. This kind of yes-no answer influences the nature of the answer in particular (Levi & Walker 1990: 158), let alone the defendant is always placed in an inferior status in criminal trials (Long, 2001: 130). Here, the judge does not permit the defendant to defend but rather force him to give an answer, which means that the defendant cannot give a "yes" answer but a "no" one. Otherwise, it is unnecessary for the judge not to permit the defendant to defend himself. It can be seen that the aim of the judge's question does not agree with its mode. Consequently, the answer does not do anything good to the defendant himself but contributes to the prosecutor's charge, which makes his answer easily controlled by the judge and the prosecutor.

Therefore, the judge's use of coercive yes/no question to achieve frame agreement has actually led to the inequality towards the defendant.

Extract 3-25 (Case 26)

1 <1, 2, 2, 1, WA, b, 指控是否属实>审判长：被告人，你对起诉书指控你的犯罪事实有没有意见，<1, 2, 2, 1, WA, b, 有无意见>有没有意见啊？

Presiding Judge: Defendant, do you have any objections to the criminal facts charged in the indictment? **Do you have any objections?**

2 <1, 2, 2, 1, WF, b, 打我>被告人：当时是他们几个人先打我，<1, 2, 2, 2, WF, b, 没办法>我没办法，<1, 2, 2, 3, WF, b, 残疾人>我还是个残疾人▬

Defendant: At that moment, they firstly beat me and I had no way because I'm a disabled person▬

3 <1, 2, 2, 4, WT, R, 不要说别的>审判长：被告人，你不要说别的，

Presiding Judge: **Defendant, don't say anything else but just give a "yes" or "no" reply to**

<1，2，2，5，WT，R，要求承认> 你现在只能回答是与不是！ <1，2，2，6，WA，b，是否属实>公诉人指控你故意用刀砍伤受害人，这是不是事实？

4 <1，2，2，6，WA，b，承认>被告人：--是。

the question. The prosecutor charges you against that you cut up the victim with knife on purpose, **is that the truth?**

Defendant: --Yes.

The judge's three WA information knots and two WT ones in the extract reflect the judge's intention by which he asks the three questions in the information units.

The judge firstly employs two WA information knots "<有无意见> *(any objections or not)*" repetitively in Turn 1 with the expectation of the defendant's negative reaction, which is the judge's expectation rather than the opposite of his will (Du, 2009b). The intentional repetition undoubtedly exerts mental pressure on the defendant in that the judge wants to know whether the defendant makes an objection or not. Here in fact the judge manipulates WF information "犯罪 *(commit a crime)*" covertly whereas he wants to obtain his expected reaction from the defendant by means of WA information "有没有意见 *(any objections or not)*". Such dialogic contraction has presupposed that the fact in the indictment must be "犯罪事实 *(criminal facts)*", that is to say, no matter whether the defendant makes an objection, the frame of "criminal facts" has been constructed.

In the extract above, the discourse contains three WF information knots in Turn 2, through which the defendant wants to expand the information to explain why he hurt the victim in the case rather than answer the judge directly. The account for not telling here is a common sense psychological avowal, not wanting (Edwards & Potter, 2005) as the defendant expects the judge's sympathy. In order to downgrade or eliminate the seriousness of his behavior, the defendant wants to frame a kind of social injustice in the case, in which he himself was in an unfavorable situation because more than one man beat a handicapped one. However, it results in the conflicts between the defendant's frame and the judge's one, between the defendant's expectation and the judge's one. Therefore, the judge has ignored the WF information in Turn 2, but used WT information in Turn 3 to interrupt the defendant and frame the defendant as a criminal instead. He limits the defendant's discourse production by means of dialogic contraction with the expressions "不要说别的 (don't say anything else)" and "只能…… (but just...)". Subsequently, he employs the two WT information knots in Turn 3 to ask the defendant to answer a closing yes/no question. The framing process undoubtedly influences the judicial justice because of the defendant has missed the opportunity to defend himself.

The judge's last question with a WA knot in this extract, which is the subsequent information of the judge's WT knots, frames the defendant's illegal behavior of intentionally injuring the victim. The WA information shows the judge's purpose to trace the defendant's attitude, but betrays the judge's intention virtually. In the procedural discourse, the judge uses dialogic contraction "故意 (on purpose)" to control the defendant's expansion of information and limit the defendant's way to reply. Thus, the defendant has to react positively. Although the defendant hurt someone in the case, it is undetermined to say whether the defendant's behavior was intentional or not. Nonetheless, the judge's asymmetric discourse distribution has framed the intentional crime.

Although this kind of information knots differ in some way, they all appear in the judges' interrogating the defendants' identity in the initial stage of courtroom discourse according to the information levels "<1, 2, 2, 1>". In fact, they belong to the information of fact confirming. The information always starts to impose pressure upon defendants from the initial stage, for instance, judges' interrogating defendants' previous experience, forcing defendants to express no doubt on evidence, taking no account of the defendants' different opinions, or inducing defendants to agree with the application of summary procedure. Eventually, the information manifests "PD inequality" or a relationship of "adversarial inequality" through the framing device of "information contraction".

3.5   Results and Discussions

The above analysis gives us the first impression: on one hand, in the criminal trial, judges try to construct a rational PDJ relationship in terms with the requirement of the relevant laws and regulations. Thus, judges aim to achieve the requirement of judicial justice as much as possible to manifest PDJ relationship by means of procedural monologue, dialogue and questioning in accordance with the relevant laws and regulations. During the course, judges usually form the specific frames in their cognition and boost the advancement of trial under the guidance of the frames. These frames are reasonably established based on the requirement of the relevant laws and regulations. On the other hand, a reasonable PDJ relationship may not be constructed as what is desired in trial. Generally speaking, it is always presented by means of the discourse information of presupposition of guilt conveyed by judges in trial, such as the frame consistency of judges' presumption of guilt, the frame conflicts between the judges' frames and the defendants'. Judges always make use of the power to monitor trial procedures forcibly or end frame conflicts coercively. As a result, judges' achievement of frame agreement is not beneficial to the defendant. The analysis on these extracts can actually make PDJ relationship be presented in a clearer way under the support of information distribution and information development.

3.5.1 Distribution of Discourse Information

3.5.1.1 Distribution of Discourse Information Units

The ideal structure of criminal trial should take on the shape of a regular triangle, in which a judge is located in vertex angle while a prosecutor and a defender are put in the other two base angles respectively (Bian & Li, 2004). The structure basically means that the prosecution and the defense enjoy equal litigation status, on which the litigation opposition can be carried out. A judge should keep a neutral attitude towards the prosecution and the defense and make a fair judgment on the neutral prerequisite (Bian, 2007). Therefore, it can be found whether discursive power of each side is equal or the prosecution and the defense is balanced or not by means of investigating the information distribution of interrogation and examination in trial. The following table provides the statistics from 34 courtroom texts.

Table 3-2   Information Distribution of Interrogation and Examination

Information Units				Total
IN to D by P	IN to D by J	EX to D by DE	EX to W by DE	
1115	932	244	9	2300

Note: IN=interrogation, EX=examination, D=defendants, P=prosecutors, J=judges, DE=defenders, W=witnesses

Based on the statistics in Table 3-2, it is illustrated that discourse information varies a lot when judges or prosecutors interrogate defendants, and defenders examine defendants. In the 34 trials, the information units on prosecutors' interrogating defendants amount to 1115, which covers 48.5% of all; the information units on judges' interrogating defendants come to 932, which accounts for 40.5%; the information units on defenders' examining defendants sums up to only 244, which takes up 10.6%. From the statistics above, it is true that functions of the prosecution and the judge have been obscure to some extent in the current stage of trial in China. The relationship of the prosecution and the judge leads to the impossibility of judges' neutrality, and the deserved regular-triangled structure of criminal justice has been distorted. The role of judges is transformed from a neutral and passive "umpire" into an active interrogator similar to that of prosecutors, with the intention of punishing defendants (Bian & Li, 2004).

The statistics conform to Bian and Li's analysis of China's current criminal trial structure (ibid). The structure not only inherits the ancient style of judicial work known as "三司会审 *(the joint trial by the Ministry of Punishments, the Court of Censors and Dali Court)*" and "坐堂问案 *(to sit on the judgment seat to interrogate criminals)*" to make the defendant's position of being trialed stand out, but also vividly depicts in China's court the cooperative relation between judges and prosecutors, and the defendant's embarrassed situation in trial. Prosecutors, defenders and judges construct a net of law, among which the defendant is taken as a target of public attack or covered under a big umbrella. The defendant's situation provides food for thoughts and such a kind of court trial is an interrogation in essence.

Meanwhile, it is shown that the discourse information on defenders' interrogating witnesses is extremely deficient due to the low rate of witnesses' appearance in court. In the stage of presenting and challenging evidence, the witnesses' testimony is mainly read out by prosecutors and quite few or no witnesses appear in court. In the 34 trials, there are only 2 witnesses in the two trials. One appears in court only in Case No. 5, who is a scout from the police; the other appears in the second instance of Case No. 33. There is no witness on the side of the defense appearing in court in all the 34 trials, which is seen as the current situation of witness appearance in court. According to Xu (2004), judges usually ignore the trial procedure of challenging evidence or do not expect witness to be in court, with an intention of being afraid of difficulty in mind; and they intend to take the existing written form of testimony, which can be mutually proved, as the evidence of deciding on a verdict. In consequence, it is really common that prosecutors and defenders' interrogating witness is replaced by reading out testimony in judicial practice (ibid). It is investigated that the rate of witness appearance in court in trial of criminal justice in China is only 5%-7%, even 2% in some places, and the severe situation results in the impossibility of cross examination by defenders in the stage of court debate, which influences the judicial justice to a large extent (Gong, 2003).

3.5.1.2 Distribution of Discourse Information Knots

According to the data analysis in this chapter, judges' inappropriate processing of discourse information always leads to the irrational construction of PDJ relationship. The types of information can be represented and featured in Table 3-3.

Table 3-3 Information Knots of Judges' Violation of Procedures

Case	Information Knot	Property	Case	Information Knot	Property
Case 34	WN WF	presumption of illegal capital raising	Case 06	WT WA	Lack of legal basis for summary procedure
Case 07	WF	Presumption of dividing loot	Case 08	WT WA	Lack of legal basis for summary procedure
Case 21	WF	Presumption of stabbing	Case 20	WT WA	Lack of legal basis for summary procedure
Case 26	WA	Presumption of guilt	Case 27	WA WF WT	Interruption of the defender
Case 02	WT	Presupposition of crime committed	Case 20	WT	Interruption of the defendant's statement
	WT				
Case 11	WT WF WA	Presumption of guilt	Case 21	WT WF	Interruption of the defendant's statement and confirmation of criminal facts
	HW	Presumption of guilt	Case 26	WT	Interruption of the defendant's statement
				WA	Asking for the agreement forcibly

Based on the description of discourse information knots in Table 3-3, the properties of judges' discourse processing in the irrational construction of PDJ relationship can be inducted as follows.

Judges' presumption of guilt constitutes a major part in the irrational PDJ relationship construction. Presumption of guilt can be caused by judges' overt use of catchphrases in their WT directive information, e.g. "审你 *(to try you)*" in Case 26 and "提被告人 *(to fetch the defendant)*" in Case 02. It also results more frequently from judges' presupposition, which has been implied in some WT directive information or various confirmative information, e.g. "非法集资 *(illegal capital raising)*" in Case 34, "犯罪事实 *(criminal facts)*" in Case 02 and so on. No matter whether it results from WT directive information or various confirmative information knots, defendants' guilt has been presumed by judges without the support of WB information (indicating certain legal basis) or confirmed WF information (indicating certain confirmed legal facts).

Judges provide insufficient information to explain legal terms to defendants. Judges utilize the information processing model of "WT—WA" to declare the start of a new stage in trials. For example, in Cases 06, 08 and 20, the judges declare the application of summary procedure with a WT information knot and then immediately ask for the defendants' agreement. Judges' discourse processing has demonstrated the insufficient explanation of legal terms, which leads to the violation of criminal procedures. Without certain legal basis (WB information) in the process of judges' declaration, judges' yes/no question for agreement can be construed that they force the defendants to accept certain procedures.

Judges' forcible interruption with WT information knot can end defendants' statements or defenders' defense. The interruption (in Cases 20, 26 and 27) may appear without the support of legal basis, i.e. violating criminal procedures. Sometimes, judges use a WT information knot to interrupt the defendant for the immediate confirmation of legal facts. However, the confirmation has always been made based on insufficient basis, i.e. lacking of WB information in Case 21.

Meanwhile, judges may use repetitive WA information to interrogate defendants or seek defendants' answers forcibly. For example, the judge's repetitive WA information knot in Case 26 can be regarded as the violation of criminal procedures since the forcible interrogation is made without the support of legal basis (WB) information.

On the whole, the lack of WB information constitutes the major manifestation of judges' deviation from neutrality. The tendency of imposing penalty makes judges degrade from a neutral pessimistic referee into an active interrogator (Bian & Li, 2004).

3.5.2 Discourse Information Levels

The realization of the judge's judicial power depends on the cross transmission of courtroom discourse information. In the course of trial, the information levels of judges' discourse and all the other parties' imposes a certain influence upon the establishment of inter-relationship in between. Hereby, we make a statistic analysis of information levels as shown in Table 3-4, which illustrates the features of judges' discourse information levels.

Table 3-4   Levels and Development of Judges' Discourse Information

Numbers Knots \ Levels	Level 1	Level 2	Level 3	Level 4	Level 5	Level 6	Level 7	Total
Judges' Knots	146	891	1030	350	483	54	14	2968
Total Knots	146	1190	3241	2785	1952	887	690	10891

According to Table 3-4, there are totally 10891 information knots in the 34 discourses, among which 146 information knots at Level 1 belong to the judges'. Meanwhile, the information knots at Level 2 and Level 3 amount to 1921, covering 17.6% of the total and 64.7 percentage of the judges'. It is shown from the statistics that judges' highly leveled discourse information is in accordance with the regulations in Procedural Criminal Law, in which judges are in charge of the trial. Namely, it is judges' discursive practice that realizes the transition and transference of all the main stages in a trial. Information knots at Level 4 and Level 5 add up to 833, coming to 7.6% of all and 28.1% of the judges'.

The reason for the relative rich information lies in the fact that judges can be active to interrogate defendants, to examine witnesses and expert witnesses according to the relevant regulations in Procedural Criminal Law to investigate and verify the evidence (Bian & Li, 2004). Consequently, judges usually conduct a deeper courtroom interaction in order to accomplish the trial task. However, there are only 68 information knots at Level 6 and Level 7, taking up less than 0.6% of all and 2.3% of the judges'. It indicates that implementing the investigation of the case details does not depend on the interaction between judges and all the other parties but rather on the interaction between the prosecution and the defense at the stages of presenting evidence, challenging evidence and court debate.

Based on the statistics in Table 3-5, judges' discourse information boasts higher levels or holds the position forward at the same levels, which exerts further influence upon the subordinate information or the subsequent information. For example, in Cases 06, 08 and 20, the judges declare the application of summary procedure with WT information at Level 2 ("<1, 1, 2, 19>", "<1, 1, 2, 14>" and "<1, 1, 2, 13>"). The information is at stage of opening the court, so the lack of legal basis for summary procedure will lead to the injustice of the follow-up court investigation and final judgment, which develop based on the summary procedure. The defendants' right cannot be guaranteed. In Cases 21, 26 and 02, the judges' presumption of guilt appears at the

Table 3-5 Information Levels of Judges' Violation of Procedures

Case	Information Level	Property	Case	Information Level	Property
Case 34	1,15,2,29	presumption of illegal capital raising	Case 06	1,1,2,19	Lack of legal basis for summary procedure
	1,15,2,20			2,19,3,21	
Case 07	2, 8,3,9	Presumption of dividing loot	Case 08	1,1,2,14	Lack of legal basis for summary procedure
				2,14,3,1	
Case 21	2,16,3,7	Presumption of stabbing	Case 20	1,1,2,13	Lack of legal basis for summary procedure
	2,16,3,7				
	2,16,3,7			1,1,2,13	
Case 26	2,21,3,2	Presumption of guilt	Case 27	1,7,2,15	Interruption of the defender
				1,7,2,16	
				1,7,2,18	
Case 02	1,2,2,7	Presupposition of crime committed	Case 20	2,9,3,14	Interruption of the defendant's statement
				2,9,3,17	
	2,2,3,9			2,9,3,20	
Case 11	1,2,2,19	Presumption of guilt	Case 21	2,10,3,21	Interruption of the defendant's statement and confirmation of criminal facts
	1,2,2,19			2,16,3,7	
				2,16,3,7	
	1,2,2,19			2,16,3,7	
	2,24,3,15	Presumption of guilt	Case 26	1,2,2,4	Interruption of the defendant's statement
				1,6,2,39	Asking for the agreement forcibly

anterior position at Level 3 ("<2, 16, 3, 7>", "<2, 21, 3, 2>" and "<2, 2, 3, 9>"). The information is at the beginning of judges' interrogation, so the presumption of guilt must result in the judges' deviation from neutrality in the subsequent investigation.

In a word, the higher or the more anterior position information levels hold, the more subordinate or subsequent information units will be influenced. Therefore, the analysis above demonstrates that information levels of judges' violation of procedures will exercise negative influence upon the rational construction of PDJ relationship to some extent.

3.5.3   Current PDJ Relationship Constructed

According to the above analysis, the judges' discourse processing in criminal court may lead to the difficulty of the rational construction of PDJ relationship. Actually, the PDJ relationship has sometimes been presented in an inverted triangle, in which the prosecutor and the judge are on the top while the defense is at the bottom.

Firstly, defendants do not enjoy the right of keeping silent in the course of trial and become the target interrogated by judges and prosecutors (Bian & Li, 2004). In addition, defendants may be in a helpless situation even without the guidance of and the consultation with defenders. As a result, they cannot perform their defending function actively and effectively to form an equal fight against prosecutors. Consequently, they are consistently in a situation of being attacked passively. Meanwhile, defenders have sometimes been interrupted in the courtroom by judges' discourse while prosecutors have never been done. Thus, the defendant, as a subject in a suit, is virtually degraded into an object (ibid).

In the current stage, the improper links between the prosecution and the judge have not been completely cut out and it is possible for the judge to keep the prior idea of "guilt of the defendant" in the mind (ibid). As a result, the linguistic analysis of the judge's courtroom discourse information helps to prove the existence of such kind of possibility.

3.6 Summary

The data analysis in this chapter reveals various manifestations of PDJ relationship framed through judges' discourse processing in the criminal courtroom. Integrated with discourse information analysis and context analysis, frame theory has facilitated our interpretation of the current PDJ relationship in court. The general findings in this regard are summarized as follows:

1) Primary frames formulated by judges' monologue have taken on the main procedures in the criminal courtroom, which can never be disarranged to violate relevant laws and regulations. The data analysis embodies that PDJ relationship should be constructed in the interactive process of primary trial frames.

2) In the interactive process, judges' monologue can also activate sub-frames. Although some sub-frames manifest judges' rational manipulation of trials, the shifts between sub-frames and primary frames or between sub-frames themselves might have reflected the inequality resulted from "PJ cooperation" in court.

3) Judges' dialogue with the other participants in court sometimes violates procedural justice and frames defendants' guilt, which leads to the irrational PDJ relationship constructed.

4) Judges' questioning, especially their interrogation of defendants, may frame defendant's guilt, or frame PD adversarial inequality. Consequently, defendants as litigation subjects have been changed into litigation objects.

5) Irrational manifestations of PDJ relationship have also been supported by the jurisprudential analysis and discourse information statistics. The present PDJ relationship has sometimes been

manifested as an inverted triangle, in which it is difficult to maintain defendants' legal rights.

These findings are substantiated and supported by a set of framing features or through specific devices of information processing as follows:

a) Information omission or information shifting has been used by judges' as framing devices to construct the relationship as "PJ cooperation".

b) Information implication or information presupposition has been applied to frame defendants' guilt.

c) Information contraction has been utilized to frame PD adversarial inequality.

d) Frame consistency, frame agreement, frame conflict, and frame conflict to frame agreement boast the main framing characteristics in the process of the current PDJ relationship constructed through judges' questioning processing.

All in all, both rational and irrational manifestations of PDJ relationship have been embodied by the discourse analysis, which can be supported by the jurisprudential analysis and discourse information statistics. Specifically speaking, the present PDJ relationship has sometimes been manifested as an inverted triangle, in which the prosecutor and the judge are on the top while the defense is at the bottom. We conclude that the fortuitous irrational PDJ relationship will violate judicial justice in China's criminal courtroom.

Since PDJ relationship has been manifested as what we have analyzed above, it is indispensable to explore what factors affect the construction in the courtroom interactive process. Chapter 4, therefore, is to focus on the causes that lead to the present PDJ relationship.

Factors Affecting Judges' Construction of PDJ Relationship

4.1 Introduction

PDJ relationship has been constructed via judges' discourse information, which keeps in touch with judicial justice from the very beginning to the end of a criminal trial. In criminal courts, judges may shift their footings to help framing some manifestations of PDJ relationship which are embodied through social cognitive factors. Sanders and Hamilton (2000) argue that the justice dimensions relate to one another, in which the most important for law is the relationship of perceptions of procedural justice, distributive justice and retributive justice and whether the last two are observed actually reflects whether procedural justice is abided by. Thus, we will take the three dimensions of judicial justice as the principle for analyzing the factors which influence PDJ relationship constructed by judges' courtroom discourse information.

Data analysis will begin with frame analysis of judges' discourse information, focus on the specific factors on the three dimensions of judicial justice, and explain structures of PDJ relationship concerning the perception of judicial justice.

4.2　Factors on the Dimension of Procedural Justice

In terms of Sanders and Hamilton's opinion (2000), there are three relational factors surrounding the interaction between decision makers and the recipients. The theory points to three factors that are important to the belief that procedures are fair: standing, neutrality, and trust (ibid: 8).

Standing—the authority treats one politely, with dignity, and with respect for one's rights and opinions.

Neutrality—the authority engages in evenhanded treatment.

Trust—the authority tries to be fair. (Sanders: 371)

The three variables influencing procedural justice can be seen as "judgments concerning one's relationship with authorities" (ibid: 76). In court, procedural justice is generally embodied by judges' processing of procedural discourse information in which declarative information, directive information and confirmative information have framed different manifestations of PDJ relationship.

4.2.1　Standing in the Framing Process

Standing or status recognition is concerned with whether the authority treats individuals with dignity and respect and people's perceptions of their status within a group (Sanders & Hamilton, 2000: 8). "When an authoritative third party treats the disputing person with politeness, dignity and respect, it gives the disputant a feeling of positive social status" (Howeison, 2002).

Extract 4-1 (Case 23)
1 <WF，Z，故意伤人>审判长：　Presiding Judge: Wang** intentionally
王**于今年 5 月 13 日，在我　hurt An** in a hotel in the ** Town

区**镇一家客店内，故意伤害安**，<WF，Z，致轻伤>致其轻伤…… <WF，Z，主动申请和解>并且被害人主动提出和解申请，<WF，Z，被告接受和解>被告方亦接受和解…… <WY，R，和解的基础>我院认为双方存在刑事和解的基础，<WE，R，和解的决定>故此今天我们组织双方当事人开展刑事和解会谈。……

2 <WF，R，证据的提交>审判长：……(被害人)提交了医疗费单据、误工证明等证据，<WT，R，指令辨认>被告方辨认一下，<WT，R，谈意见>说说你们的意见。

……(受害方和被告方因赔偿款额而产生分歧后，先劝被告人。)

3 <WY，Z，邻居>审判长：你们双方都是乡里乡亲的，<WY，Z，一起生活>以后还要在一起生活，<WC，R，协商解决>能够协商解决这个问题，<WE，Z，有利于共处>有利于你们双方之后的和平共处。

……(再劝受害人)

4 <WY，Z，老朋友>审判长：安**，你跟王**毕竟还是老朋友，<WY，Z，被告人是个孩子>现在刑事被告人是小王，

in our district on May 13th this year and resulted in An**'s slight injury… The defendant took the initiative in applying for reconciliation and he received reconciliation as well… The court believes that a foundation of criminal reconciliation exists between both the parties. In consequence, we organize both the parties involved to conduct a criminal reconciliation. …

Presiding Judge: … *(The victim) has presented some evidence, such as receipts of hospital bills, a proof of loss of working time. Defendant, identify them and put forward your opinions about them.*

… (When there is difference between the victim and the defendant, the defendant is persuaded first.)

Presiding Judge: Since both of you are neighbors living in the same town, solving the problem by friendly negotiation is beneficial to your future life in peace together.

… (persuades the victim again)

Presiding Judge: An**, Wang** and you are old friends after all. Now, the criminal defendant, Xiao Wang is a child, if you can reach an agreement

他还是个孩子…… <WC，R，today，Wang** and Xiao Wang 和解>如果你们今天达成了和 undoubtedly appreciate you for the 解，<WE，Z，感激>王**和小 whole life. 王肯定会感激你一辈子。

……(赔偿协议达成)　　　　　　… (The agreement has been reached.)

The judge in Extract 4-1 is presiding over a victim-offender-reconciliation (VOR), in which his standing embodies his respect for both the victim and the defendant.

In order that all the other parties in the trial know the reasons for VOR and both the victim and the defendant accept the reconciliation, the presiding judge utilizes four information units with WF knots in Turn 1, that is, "<WF, Z, 故意伤人> (hurt the victim intentionally)", "<WF, Z, 致轻伤> (slight injury resulted)", "<WF, Z, 主动申请和解> (apply for VOR voluntarily)" and "<WF, Z, 被告接受和解> (The defendant accepts the VOR)". The knowledge categories of the four are all the information known to all, i.e. Z. As the four WFs show that all the information takes on clear facts and all the Zs demonstrate that all the information are plain to everyone, the presiding judge produces the information that the VOR has some solid foundation with the WY information in Turn 1 "<WY, R, 和解的基础> (the foundation for the VOR)", then declares the decision of the VOR made by the collegial panel. Therefore, with the WF information known to all as the foundation in the interaction, participants in criminal proceedings can accept the court's requirements or decisions more easily.

In Turn 2, to have the defendant accept the victim's claim for compensation, the presiding judge, based on the former WF information, presents another information unit "<WF, R, 证据的提交> (the evidence presented)" indicating some fact. In the interaction the information (R) is only known to the presiding judge, so the defendant's recognition is needed to pave a smooth road for the deep communication between the judge and the defendant. Thus, the presiding judge's other two directive information units "<WT, R, 指令辨认> *(to direct to identify)*" and "<WT, R, 谈意见>" *(to give some opinions)*" appear to be extremely necessary.

In order to achieve the successful reconciliation in spite of the divergence of the victim's and the defendant's opinions on the amount of the compensation, the presiding judge, based on his presented facts, begins to reason things out. In the same way to processing discourse information, the presiding judge firstly persuades the defendant and the victim with two information units of reasons respectively, that is, "<WY, Z, 邻居> *(neighbors)*" in Turn 3 or "<WY, Z, 老朋友> *(old friends)*" in Turn 4 and "<WY, Z, 一起生活> *(live in the same community)*" in Turn 3 or "<WY, Z, 被告人是个孩子> *(The defendant is young.)*" in Turn 4. From the perspective of social relations, the four information units, known to all (Z), are utilized to bring the two families closer and make the two intimate again.

Then the presiding judge proposes the court's assumptions with the WC information "<WC, R, 协商解决> *(to solve the dispute by negotiation)*" in Turn 3 or "<WC, R, 和解> *(reconciliation)*" in Turn 4, which are known to the judge rather than to the defendant or the victim. The two information units indicating conditions have laid a solid foundation for the following two information units "<WE, Z, 有利于共处> *(beneficial to live as neighbors)*" in Turn 3 or "<WE, Z, 感激> *(to show his appreciation)*" in Turn 4. The two information units, with information knot WE indicating the effects and knowledge category Z expressing that the effects are known to all, provide the victim and the defendant with the meaning of the successful VOR because the future harmonious living keeps with the common interests of the two families.

In a word, the judge in Extract 4-1 keeps his standing clear with the appropriate discourse processing, in which he sets forth facts and reasons things out. His full utilization of the functions of various discourse information knots represents his respect for both the victim and the defendant in the process of the VOR. Therefore, the judge's discursive practice eventually maintains the procedural justice resulted from the successful reconciliation.

Extract 4-2 (Case 07)

1 <WN，出生日期>审判长：出生日期?

Presiding Judge: What's your birth date?

2 <WN，2007 年 8 月 23 日>被告人：07 年 8 月 23 号。

Defendant: August 23rd, 07.

3 <WN，几几年啊>审判长：几几年啊?

Presiding Judge: In which year?

4 <WN，07 年>被告人：07 年，<WN，1907 年 8 月 23 号>1907 年 8 月 23 号。

Defendant: 07, August 23rd, 1907.

5 <WN，强调是出生日期>审判长：法庭现在问你的出生日期(声音提高)!

Presiding Judge: The court now asks for your birth date! (*in a louder voice*)

6 <WN，出生年>被告人：1907 年嘛。

Defendant: In the year 1907.

7 <WN，19>审判长：一九::?

Presiding Judge: Nineteen::?

8 <WN，出生年>被告人：1970 年。

Defendant: In the year 1970.

9 <WN，出生年>审判长：1970 年啊。<WF，1970>**1970 年?** <WI，评论年龄>这个岁数，这人好像没这么年轻啊?

Presiding Judge: In the year 1970. **In the year 1970?** The person doesn't seem so young at this age.

In Extract 4-2, the presiding judge firstly makes use of confirmative procedural discourse information to confirm the defendant's date of birth, and then his footing shift in the end leads to the appearance of unjust JD relationship. The presiding judge initially puts three WN information knots to inquire the defendant's date of birth, but the defendant makes slip of tongue three times because of nervousness or unconsciousness. He mistakes the year 1970 for the year 1907 and doesn't give the correct answer until the presiding judge asks him in a remindful question " 一九······? (19...?)" in Turn 7 for the fourth time. Among these questions, the judge plays the role of a truth confirmer. It is equal to say that the defendant is placed in the position of litigation subject. But finally the judge's confirmative information "<WF,1970>" and expressive information "<WI, 评论年龄> (to comment the age)" in Turn 9 seem to be a joke with evaluation, in which the judge plays the role of a commentator. In a serious criminal trial, it is the joke in the role shift that leads to the inclining of the judicial justice. In this way, the defendant's inferior position has become prominent.

In Chinese social cognition, this kind of discourse information similar to joke is actually a satire on the defendant's slip of tongue resulting from nervousness or carelessness. The judge can play such a joke on the defendant in a serious trial, whereas the defendant absolutely cannot. According to the judge's view on the defendant's standing, "undignified, disrespectful, or impolite treatment by an authority carries the implications that one is not a full member of the group" (Tyler & Lind, 1992: 76). As a result, this joke embodies that the judge plays down or looks down upon the defendant and takes him as a target of being interrogated or an inferior role while he himself is considered to be put in a higher position and controls the whole process of the trial. From the angle of the defendant's perception of his own standing, he stays in such an inferior position and feels so nervous that he makes slip of tongue several times. After being corrected, he has become the target for the judge's satire, his esteem suffers from the judge's damage and he has no respect at all. Meanwhile, even if he was a criminal, the defendant's position of litigation subject should be guaranteed in court. Undoubtedly, his sense of being impartial comes into being.

One way, therefore, in which legal procedures can foster dignity and respect, and thus promote perceptions of fairness, is by giving people opportunities to express their views and feel that legal authorities listen to and consider their concerns (voice). Thus, for relational theorists, voice forms part of this relational variable and are not a separate effect (Howeison, 2002).

4.2.2　Neutrality in the Framing Process

Neutrality refers to whether the authority acts in an unbiased manner (Sanders & Hamilton, 2000: 8). Prejudice, the idea of discrimination based on group membership, is perhaps the strongest evidence of a lack of neutrality, since people are not given an equal opportunity to have access to social resources (Tyler & Lind, 1992: 76).

Extract 4-3 (Case 11)

1 <WF>审判长：你直接跟付＊＊联系过没有？	Presiding Judge: Had you ever contacted with Fu** directly?
2 <WF>被告人：没有。	Defendant: No.
3 <WF>审判长：没有任何的联系是吧？	Presiding Judge: You had never contacted with him, have you?
4 <WF>被告人：没有。	Defendant: Never.
5 <WF>审判长：那么你刚才说的是你给老板打工，<HW>那在这件犯罪事实当中，你是怎么样做的呢？	Presiding Judge: Then, you said just now that you worked for the boss. **What had you done** in the **criminal fact**?
6 <WF>被告人：我讲不了，<WT>让我的辩护律师来说。	Defendant: I can't say anything. Let my defense counsel do it for me.
7 <WF>审判长：这是基本事实，<WT>你必须自己回答。	Presiding Judge: This is the basic fact. **You must give an answer to it by yourself.**
8 <WF>被告人：哦。	Defendant: Oh.

The case, to which summary procedure does not apply, indicates that the defendant has not confessed his crime voluntarily. Therefore, in Extract 4-3, the judge's discourse information is not in a neutral position to treat the defendant, which results in the occurrence of the interrogative discourse adverse to the defendant. Undoubtedly, it is not in accordance with the requirement of a courtroom trial and it violates the procedural justice.

Above all, the presiding judge frames the defendant's guilt by means of processing discourse information. In the information unit "<HW>那在这件犯罪事实当中，你是怎么样做的呢? (What had you done in the criminal fact of this case?)" in Turn 5, the presiding judge's information knot is HW with the focus on the defendant's mode of the participation in the crime committing. However, "这件犯罪事实 (the criminal fact)" in this information unit has firstly makes a presumption of guilt so that the defendant has to give his reply to the mode of the crime committing rather than need to explain whether he is guilty.

Then, the presiding judge makes use of dominant discourse information to force the defendant to give up a reasonable request. Nondiscriminatory treatments (termed "neutrality") are crucial to judgments of procedural fairness (Tyler & Lind, 1992: 75). In these interrogative turns, the defendant put in use the WF information "<WF>我讲不了 (I can't give an answer to it.)" and WT information "<WT>让我的辩护律师来说 (Let my defence counsel do it for me)" in Turn 6 to express his reasonable request. But the presiding judge gives responses respectively to WF information and WT information in Turn 7 with the aid of his dominant identity—being in charge of the trial. Namely, he uses the following "<WF>这是基本事实 (This is a basic fact.)" and "<WT>你必须自己回答 (You must give an answer by yourself.)" to refuse the defendant's request flatly. In essence, this response is a kind of discriminatory treatment or decision-making for the reason that the presiding judge has regarded the defendant's "如何参与犯罪 (how to participate in the crime?)" as "基本事实 (a basic fact)", which renders the presumption of guilt more apparent. It is just the frame of "被告人即是罪犯 (The defendant is a criminal.)" in the presiding judge's mind that leads to the deviation from neutrality in his mode of processing discourse information.

Obviously, the presiding judge acts in a biased manner in the process of interrogation. Accordingly, the defendant has lost his right that his defense lawyer will defend him on this topic in this extract.

Extract 4-4 (Case 22)

1 <WB，A>审判员：根据**区人民检察院的建议，<WF，A>本案适用普通程序简化审。<WN，R>被告人，本院对本案适用普通程序简化审理后，<WP，R>将依法对你作出有罪判决，<WP，R>并酌情从轻处罚，<WA，b>你对此有没有异议？

Judge: Based on the proposal from the People's Procuratorate of …, summary procedure is applied in the case. Defendant, you will be sentenced according to the relevant laws and a lesser punishment will be taken into account at discretion after summary procedure. Do you have any objections to it?

2 <WP，b>被告人：没有。

Defendant: No.

The judge applies the mode of information omission in this extract to simplify the procedure that causes the defendant to lose his own right of expressing his opinions and violates the principle of judges' neutrality.

Here, let us not go into the question whether "<WB, A>根据……检察院的建议，<WF, A>本案适用普通程序简化审。(Based on …the proposal from the People's Procuratorate, the summary procedure is applied in the present case.)" in Turn 1 is reasonable and whether it is possible to bring about the doubt of convicting the defendant before the trial or not. As far as the cases applicable to the summary procedure are concerned, judges need to direct prosecutors "<WT>宣读起诉书 (to read out the indictment)" firstly, then interrogate defendants "<WA>对指控有无异议 (any objections to the accusation or not)". If defendants do not have, judges can ask defendants for their agreement with the application of the summary procedure in trials. According to the jurisprudential analysis above, it is obvious that the judge has omitted two information knots (WT and WA) at least in Extract 4-4. Since the summary procedure is actually quite simple, the omission of information knots that should not be omitted will definitely result in more negative influence upon the justice of the trial.

From the angle of knowledge categories, the first five information units are known to the judge himself (A or R) in the six information units produced by the judge, which indicates that the defendant is not aware of the legal basis and the fact of the summary procedure, and the disposal resulting from the trial. Only the last information unit makes use of the knowledge category b, which means that the question is raised to aim at the preceding information. Too little information known to the hearer can force the defendant to give the replies to the application of the summary procedure under the condition of his ignorance of the content of the indictment. Therefore, the judge's mode of omitting the discourse information apparently deviates from the neutrality and violates the procedural justice.

However, neutrality captures only part of what makes authority legitimate to the disputants whose problems they are trying to handle, people are also interested in the authorities' trustworthiness (Tyler & Lind, 1992: 84).

4.2.3 Trust in the Framing Process

Trust focuses on whether the authority considers the views of individuals and attempts to act fairly (Sanders & Hamilton, 2000: 8). In court, the manipulation of information levels can help construct some specific PDJ relationship, which reflects whether judges trust or distrust some party and will lead to procedural justice or injustice. The next example shows that the presiding judge limits the appearance of the subordinate information and the expansion of the sister information (the information at the same level), which will lead to the injustice.

Extract 4-5 (Case 26)

1 <1，2，2，6>审判长：公诉人指控你故意用刀砍伤受害人，这是不是事实？

Presiding Judge: The prosecutor charges you against the fact that you cut the victim with knife on purpose. Is that true?

2 <1，2，2，1>被告人：当时是他们几个人先打我，<1，2，2，2>我没办法，<1，2，2，3>我还是个残疾人━

Defendant: At that moment, they beat me first and then I had no choice because I'm a disabled person ━

3 <1，2，2，4>审判长：=被告人，你不要说别的，<1，2，2，5>你现在只能回答是与不是！

Presiding Judge: = Defendant, don't mention anything irrelevant. Now, you have to give a "yes" or "no" answer to it.

Without trusting the defendant's response, the judge produces the discourse information to interrupt the defendant, which is articulated as subordinate information of a Level 1 information knot before the stage of presenting and challenging evidence in court. In the data above, just after the prosecutor reads out the bill of the prosecution, the judge asks the question in Turn 1 and interrupts the defendant in Turn 3. The information at this stage and the subsequent information of the prosecutor's question are at the same level, i.e. the subordinate information of Level 1 information "<法庭调查> (court investigation)". The distrustful information of the defendant's response articulated at the higher level or such anterior information will destroy the trial process unjustly.

Extract 4-6 (Case 12)

1 <WT，S，证言和笔录>公诉人：审判长，宣读证人狄某某的证言及辨认笔录。

Prosecutor: Presiding judge, let me read out the witness Di**'s testimony and the identification record.

2 <WT，R，出示身份证号码请求>辩护人：请公诉人出示他的身份证号码，<WT，R，明确身份>明确他的身份。

Defender: Prosecutor, please show the number of his ID card to confirm his identity.

3 <WA，R，没必要>公诉人：我认为没有必要。

Prosecutor: I think it unnecessary to do so.

4 <WP，R，公安机关核实>审判长：关于证人的身份问题，公安机关在找他们作证言的时候会核实的，<WT，R，发表质证意见>请辩护人就质证问题发表意见。

Presiding Judge: With regard to the issue of the witness' identity, the public security organ will confirm it when they ask them to give the testimony. Defender, please state your opinion on the evidence-challenging.

5 <WI，R，合理怀疑>辩护人：我们对尸检报告有一个合理的怀疑…… <WF，R，是否救助不当>这里面是否有救助不当的问题。

Defender: We have a reasonable doubt that the report of postmortem examination reflects the victim's left vein. … Is there any improper treatment?

6 <WP，R，庭后咨询专家>审判长：关于这个问题，辩护人可以在庭后咨询专家，<WF，Z，公诉人非法医专家>公诉人不是法医学专家。

Presiding Judge: As for this issue, the defender can consult the relevant expert after trial because the prosecutors are not legal medical experts.

According to the analysis of Extract 4-6, at the stage of presenting and challenging the evidence the judge trusts the prosecution rather than the defense.

When the frame conflict appears, the judge's WP information in Turn 4 is contradictory to his preceding WT information in Turn 1 as he rejects the defender's requirement for the reason that it does not belong to the evidence-challenging. The defender's information units "<WT, R, 出示证件请求> (the request for the number of the witness' ID *card)"* and *"<WT, R, 明确身份> (to identify the witness' identity)"* in Turn 2 have framed the issue on recognizing the witness' identity while the prosecutor's WA information in Turn 3 shows his objection to the recognition. This leads to the frame conflict, which requires the judge to dissolve.

As for the judge's treatment, even though the WP information *"<公安机关核实> (to be verified by the People's Public Organs)"* in Turn 4 is beyond reproach, his WT information *"<发表质证意见> (to present the opinion on challenging the evidence)"* in Turn 4 means the defender's question on the identification of the witness' identity does not belong to the scope of challenging the evidence. The judge's treatment is against the common sense and does not conform to the law as he has failed to trust the defender. Meanwhile, after the defender expresses the doubt on the autopsy, the judge has also rejected the defender's opinion by means of producing WP information in Turn 6, that is, he pushes the defender's opinion out of the court for the settlement with the information unit *"<庭后咨询专家> (to consult the relevant experts after the trial)"*, and supports the prosecutor's opinion with the WF information *"<公诉人非法医专家> (The prosecutors are not legal medical experts.)"* in Turn 6.

Obviously, the use of WP information knots will embody whether judges trust the prosecution or the defense and will influence judges' manipulation of trial procedures.

4.3   Factors on the Dimension of Distributive Justice

Based on allocation research by Hegtvedt and Cook (2000: 93-132), various factors affect allocation decisions which include the goals and motivations, individual-level characteristics and non-individual factors. All the factors interact with each other in that individuals can assess whether a particular distribution rule will fulfill their goals, and relational and situational factors will also be involved. The allocation in criminal courts is mainly realized through the discourse distribution to each party by judges, which reflects whether distributive justice exists or not. In addition, discourse distribution consists of procedural discourse distribution and substantive discourse distribution.

4.3.1 Goals and Motivations in the Framing Process

The pursuit of various goals, each constituting a form of motivation, results in different types of distributions (Hegtvedt & Cook, 2000: 93-132). In criminal courts, the distribution of discourse power will take on the inequality between the prosecution and the defense due to judges' goals and motivations while manipulating trials. The judge's discourse control exerts much mental pressure on the defendant. Just as Fairclough (2001) says, in discursive and social struggle, the powerful control and restrain the powerless.

Extract 4-7 (Case 21)

1 <WT>审判长：……汪**先是骂了一句，<WT>又一拳打在了你的耳朵。<WF>你有没有还手？

Presiding Judge: …firstly, Wang** hurled abuse at you, and then blew your ear with fist. Did you strike back?

2 <WF>被告人：我反应都没有反应过来▀

Defendant: It was hardly too late for me to give any response ▀

3 <WT>审判长：**>直接回答我的问题<**。<WF>**还，还是没还？**

Presiding Judge: >**Give a direct answer to my question**<, **yes or no?**

4 <WF>被告人：没(.) 没有。

Defendant: No (.) no.

……

5 <WF>审判长：这个刀，刺了几刀？

Presiding Judge: How many times did you stab the victim with it?

6 <WF>被告人：两刀。<WT>我用这把刀▀

Defendant: Twice. With this knife, I ▀.

7 <WF>审判长：=>两刀↑。<WF> Presiding Judge: = >Twice ↑ . In 哪两刀啊<? which parts did you stab him twice<?

According to Extract 4-7, the judge's goal is to manipulate the trial and control the defendant's answer with the motivation of advancing the trial smoothly, which violates distributive justice.

For one thing, the judge uses different information knots to manipulate the turn-taking, which influences the judicial justice in court.

The first interruption is articulated by the judge for the purpose of wanting to obtain the defendant's immediate answer. With high pitch and quick tone, the WT information "*直接回答我的问题。(Give a direct answer to my question)*" in Turn 3 forces the defendant to answer the yes/no question without delay, which is a WF information knot "*还，还是没还? (…yes or no?)*" in the same turn. Here the judge utilizes the yes/no question as a more controlling and coercive method with the expectation of a positive response (Tiersma, 1999). The first interruption thus places the defendant in an inferior position.

As for the second interruption "*两刀。(Twice.)*" in Turn 7, the judge's goal lies in the grasp of the WF information in Turn 6 or the answer given by the defendant, which is positive to the declaration of the guilt due to the active confession. Therefore, the judge immediately shifts her turn to the WF information "*哪两刀啊? (In which parts did you stab him twice?)*" in Turn 7, which represents that the defendant's behavior "*刺了两刀 (stab twice)*" does not need to be doubted. The judge's second interruption and her subsequent question thereby activate the frame of "the defendant's active assault". The judge's framing eventually leads to presumption of guilt.

And for another, the defendant enjoys less speech privilege resulting from the two interruptions by the judge in this extract. The first interruption prevents the defendant from describing his disadvantageous situation while being hit in the ear by the victim Wang** in this case. The discourse "<WF>我反应都没有反应过来······ *(It was hardly too late for me to give any response…)*" interrupted in Turn 2 has demonstrated the fact that the victim assaults the defendant rather than both the two men assault each other at the moment. Nevertheless, the judge wants to obtain the answer that the defendant has also assaulted the victim actively here, so the interruption has been produced, which leads to the defendant's insufficient description of the fact. The second interruption has also stopped the defendant from describing the fact how he uses the fruit knife at the scene. The WF information "我用这把刀······ *(With this knife, I…)*" interrupted in Turn 6 has shown that the defendant desires to express his behavior clearly during the interrogation. However, to frame the defendant's guilt, the judge has deprived the defendant of his right to defend himself.

The analysis of the extract has told us the flexible use of different information knots can help the judge realize his goal in the trial on the one hand, but sometimes will lead to the violation of the discourse distributive justice on the other hand.

Extract 4-8 (Case 12)

1 <WF，b>审判员：你作案的时候穿的衣服上有血迹吗？ Judge: Was there any bloodstain on your clothes while you were committing the crime?

2 <WF，b>被告人：没有。 Defendant: No.

In Extract 4-8, the judge' goal or motivation to advance the trial smoothly has firstly led to the misuse of knowledge category.

The judge's WF information in Turn 1 is ostensibly articulated for the defendant's answer about bloodstain because of the knowledge category b, but another important fact "作案 *(commit the crime)*" has actually been implied in the information unit. "作案 *(commit the crime)*" is the information about the defendant's guilt known to all the parties. Consequently, no matter whether it is "yes" or "no", the defendant's answer cannot shake off the chains of information in that his subsequent answers will center around the fact "作案 *(commit the crime)*" (Du, 2009c).

The defendant's guilt has been framed by the judge's discourse information although summary procedure is not applicable to this case. Thus, the judge's misuse of knowledge category induces the defendant to give the expected answer and frame the nature of the defendant's behavior by means of discourse information employed.

4.3.2   Individual Factors in the Framing Process

"The nature of goals or motivations in the distributive justice may stem from individual-level factors, which include personal attitudes, cognitive elements and so on (Hegtvedt & Cook, 2000: 93-132)". Therefore, the factors concerning judges' attitude, perception and ideology will be explored in this section.

4.3.2.1   Attitudinal Factors

Social identity theory posits that people are strongly motivated to develop a positive or negative social identity, in which positive attitudes are taken towards their own group and negative attitudes or prejudice against others (Tajfel & Turner, 1986).

Extract 4-9 (Case 31)

1 <R，指令讯问>审判长：控方可以向被告人黄**进行发问。……

Presiding Judge: The prosecutor can ask the defendant Huang** questions. …

2 <R，讯问结束>公诉人：审判长，对这个被告人黄**的发问暂时到此。

Prosecutor: Presiding judge, it's time to end questioning the defendant Huang** for the time being. …

3 <b, 有无补充发问>审判长：黄** 的 辩 护 人 对 此 有 什 么 补 充 发 问？……

Presiding Judge: Defender of Huang**, do you have anything more to ask? ...

4 <b, 有无补充发问>审判长：被 告人蔡**的辩护人有什么补充 发问？……

Presiding Judge: Defender of Cai**, do you have anything more to ask? ...

Different ways to process discourse information embody the judge's different attitudes towards the prosecution and the defense.

The directive discourse information in Extract 4-9 is produced by the judge just after the prosecutor reads out the indictment and interrogates the defendants. The judge directs the prosecutor to interrogate one of the defendants with the WP information "<指令讯问> (to direct to interrogate)" in Turn 1. Since the knowledge category is R, the information is known to the judge himself. The characteristics of the information units and the declarative sentence show that the prosecutor's interrogation is the key part of the trial and the indispensable process in the court investigation.

After the prosecutor's interrogation, the judge does not use a declarative sentence to direct the defenders. Instead he raises two yes/no questions to learn whether the two defenders have "补充发问 (supplementary questions)" in Turns 3 and 4. As the information is known just to the defenders (b), the two yes/no questions mean that the defenders' examination can be regarded by the judge as supplement to the prosecutor's interrogation. The yes/no questions further demonstrate that the defenders' examination is not indispensable in court investigation and prove again that the prosecutor's interrogation is the key part in the trial.

Accordingly, judges' different attitudes towards the prosecution and the defense will have led to the inequality in trials in that one of the two parties is not regarded as the equal subject in litigation.

Extract 4-10 (Case 19)

1 <HW，b>审判长: 那你怎么知道 Presiding Judge: How did you
用烘干机进行诈骗的过程的？ know to engage in fraud with the
aid of a dryer?

2 <HW，b>被告人: 我是感觉到 Defendant: I felt it and I was with
的，<WF，b>取钱的时候我与 Lü** while drawing money.
吕**在一起。

3 <WF，b>审判长: 你们一起骗到 Presiding Judge: Did you share any
的 25000 元，你分到了吗？ of RMB 250,000 gained by means
of cheating?

4 <WF，b>被告人: 没有，<WF，Defendant: No, he only gave me
b>他只给了我1500元和那张卡，RMB 1,500 and that card. He told
<WT，b>说以后再汇款给我。 me to remit some more later on.

Although Extract 4-10 is not the case involved in the summary procedure, the presiding judge's negative attitude towards the defendant results from the utilization of discourse information transmission to presume the guilt in the judge's interrogation before the defendant's voluntary confession of his crime and the complete investigation of the facts. Here the information such as an HW information knot (indicating the way) and a WF information knot (indicating the fact) used by the judge superficially belongs to knowledge category as b (indicating the information known to the hearer). However, the two information units actually contain the information known to all "诈骗 (fraud)" and "骗到的钱数 (the sum of money obtained by fraud)", which presuppose the defendant's illegal behavior. Due to the situation in which the judge maintains the negative attitude that the defendant must be guilty to investigate the facts, the defendant always ignores the information with the presumption of guilt. Consequently, the defendant must fall into the judge's trap if he answers the questions following the judge's expectation.

Since such an interrogation has actually framed the defendant in

"*诈骗过程 (the process of engaging a fraud)*", the judge's negative attitude towards the defendant results in distributive injustice which prevents the rational PDJ relationship from being constructed in the criminal court.

4.3.2.2 Perceptional Factors

To understand distribution justice, it is necessary to examine "allocator's perceptions of the situation which affects resulting distribution decisions" (Hegtvedt & Cook, 2000: 101).

Extract 4-11 (Case 14)

1 <WA>审判长：你对检察院指控你犯有诈骗罪有何看法啊？

Presiding Judge: Do you have any opinions on your crime of fraud accused by the People's Procuratorate?

2 <WF>被告人：我根本就没有诈骗。

Defendant: I haven't committed a fraud at all.

3 <WF>审判长：你在预审中向刑警供述过诈骗吗？

Presiding Judge: Have you made a confession of your fraud to the police in the preliminary trial?

4 <WF>被告人：在刑警做的口供做的笔录，不是我说的。

Defendant: The statement in the police's record isn't my words.

5 <WF>审判长：在预审阶段的口供你签过字吗？

Presiding Judge: Have you signed on the record in the preliminary trial?

6 <WF>被告人：签过字。

Defendant: Yes.

7 <WI>审判长：知道什么意义吗？

Presiding Judge: Do you know what the signature means?

8 <WE>被告人：要负法律责任，<WF>我没有开坛设法。

Defendant: It means that I should bear a legal liability, but I haven't established a religious forum to conduct the superstitious activity.

9 <WT>审判长：公诉人有无补充讯问？

Presiding Judge: Prosecutor, do you have any supplementary questions?

In Extract 4-11, the judge seems to offer the defendant enough speech opportunities, but his perception of the defendant's behavior of signing determines that the discursive distribution is actually his control over the defendant's transmission of discourse information. As the transmission goes on following the step of the judge's information control, the discursive distribution is essentially adverse to the defendant.

When the defendant uses the first WF information "*我根本就没有诈骗。(I haven't committed a fraud at all.)*" in Turn 2 to answer the judge's question, the judge gives no response to the defendant's viewpoint. Neither does the judge use WY information (indicating the reason) or WB information (indicating the basis) to interrogate the defendant why he gives such an answer to the judge's question or the evidence for not considering himself as a fraud at all.

The turn taking in the extract embodies that the judge's perception is put on the truth information (WF) that the defendant's signature exists in the record. As a result, the judge concentrates on this WF information all the time. The judge utilizes two WF information knots (indicating the facts) in Turns 3 and 5 and a WI information knot (indicating the induction) in turn 7 to manipulate the interrogation and the defendant has to give his answers to these questions as what the judge expects.

The defendant has used a WF information knot in Turn 6 to confess he has signed and then used a WE information knot in Turn 8 to explain the meaning of his signature. The cause-effect relationship has consequently been developed, which provides enough information to frame the fact of his fraud. At last, the defendant makes use of a WF information knot "*我没有开坛设法。(I haven't established a religious forum to conduct the superstitious activity.)*" in Turn 8 to try to defend himself. However, the judge gives no response to the defendant's last answer and does not use WY information (indicating the reason) or WB information (indicating the base) to continue interrogating the defendant, either. The reason for this is that the judge has formed a fixed perception of the defendant's behavior and cannot change the mode and tendency of his distribution of discourse information.

Consequently, the judge's perception in trial will impose a certain influence upon discursive distribution relevant to judicial justice.

4.3.2.3　Ideological Factors

There is certain overarching "dominant ideology' in a society that determines the structure of the judicial justice beliefs (Hegtvedt & Cook, 2000).

Extract 4-12 (Case 26)

1 <WA，b>审判长：就是是否要求换人<u>审你</u>？

Presiding Judge: That's to say, do you demand to replace the members in the collegial panel or the prosecutors to <u>try you</u>?

2 <WA，b>被告人：不要求。

……

Defendant: No, I don't.

…

3 <WA，b>审判长：被告人，你对起诉书指控你的<u>犯罪事实</u>有没有意见，<WA，b>有没有意见啊？

Presiding Judge: Defendant, do you have any objections to <u>the criminal facts</u> charged in the indictment? Do you have any objections?

In the trial, the judge intensifies the defendant's guilt with WA information. The first information knot offers knowledge category b, which conceals the implication of the word "审 (try)". In fact, the word "审 (try)" is often followed by "犯人 (a criminal)" which implies the defendant is a criminal. It is the information that is shared by all the parties in court. However, in Turn 2 the information knot WA and knowledge category b demonstrate that the defendant concerns the information WA but has ignored the collocative meaning of "审 (try)" completely. As the first line of defense for the criminal litigants, the system of withdrawals is one of the basic requirements in the process of criminal procedures (Yang, 2007). Therefore, the insufficient discourse information offered by the judge violates both distributive justice and procedural justice in the maintenance of the defendant's legal rights.

The judge also controls the defendant's reply with the help of WA information in the trial. Actually the judge's questions, especially yes/no questions greatly affect the nature of the answers that those questions will elicit (Levi & Walker, 1990). In Turn 3, the judge raises two yes/no questions with WA information to control the defendant's reply. It is obvious that the judge's purpose contradicts the way of questioning because the defendant is forced to react negatively.

It is important to note that socio-historically motivated language consciousness tends to persist and grow even as literacy in a single national language increases and isolated social groups disappear (Gumperz, 1982a). The judge ideologically views the defendant as a criminal and ignores the equality between all the parties in court as he plays an institutional role, and his discourse is backed by the institutional power (van Dijk, 1989). The inequality is also demonstrated by the judge's professional legal language. The defendant, a lay participant in the trial process, is typically unaccustomed to such an environment and is at a disadvantage, both legally and linguistically (Cotterill, 2003). Lack of mutual knowledge will prevent communicative aim from being realized (van Dijk, 2006), so the judge uses "换人审你 (change the judges or the prosecutors to try you)" to explain the term "申请回避 (apply for withdrawals)". Nevertheless, the mental pressure on the defendant exerted by the judge's explanation shows the lay participant is disempowered before the law (Gibbons, 1994b).

Extract 4-13

1 <WT, 指令陈述>审判长：被 Presiding Judge: Defendant Chen**, 告人陈**, 有没有最后陈述啊？   do you have any final statement?

2 <WA, 认罪>被告人：我认罪，<WT, 请求法官>我请求法官大人，<WF, 80 岁老人>我们家上有八十岁的老人需要照顾，<WF, 两个读书的孩子>下有两个孩子读书，<WA, 希望宽大处理>希望能对我们的案子宽大处理，谢谢! (Case 07)

Defendant: I confess my guilt. I beg the judge, my Lord. I have an 80-year-old man to be looked after and two children to be educated in my family. Thus, I hope I can gain lenity. Thanks! (Case 07)

1 <WA, 供述是否正确>审判长：被告人黄**，刚才公诉人向本庭宣读的你的供述对不对啊？

Presiding Judge: Defendant Huang**, do you agree with the confession that the prosecutor reads out in court just now?

2 <WA, 认罪>黄**：法官大人，我认罪，<WA, 认罪>我认罪。

Defendant: My Lord, I confess my guilt. I confess.

3 <WT, 记录在案>审判长：记录在案。<WT, 有无检举揭发>被告人黄**，你有没有检举揭发？

Presiding Judge: I keep it on record. Defendant Huang**, do you have anything to accuse and expose?

4 <WT, 有一点>黄**：法官大人，我还有一点……

Defendant: My Lord, I have one point to…

5 <WT, 对着话筒>审判长：**对着话筒！** <WT, 对着话筒>**对着话筒！**

Presiding Judge: Speak facing to the microphone! Speak facing to the microphone!

<WT, 作何辩护>审判长：被告人蔡**，有什么要辩护的吗？

Presiding Judge: Defendant Cai**, do you have anything to defend?

6 <HW, 罪名定义>蔡**：法官大人，我想问一下刚才公诉人提到就是说非法制造爆炸物品罪的定义怎么定的？<WY, 没听清>就是刚才没听清楚。

Defendant: My Lord, I want to know how to define the crime of illegal manufacture of explosive that the prosecutor mentions just now. I can't catch just now.

7 <WF, 已经讲清>审判长：控方已经讲得很明白了……
(Case 31)

Presiding Judge: The prosecutor has made it very clear… (Case 31)

Through the analysis of the conversation between the judges and the defendants in Extract 4-13, the authority-based thoughts can be reflected in the people's cognition, and even the ideology will affect distributive justice in criminal trials.

The defendants from different trials look on the judges as "*法官 (law official)*" rather than "*judges*", that is, judges have always been the "*官 (officials)*" and "*法官 (law official)*" is definitely called as "*大人 (Lord)*" in the Chinese people's cognition. People also think that the law officials have power of life and death over the defendants in criminal courts because in their ideology "*官 (official)*" dominates "*法 (law)*". Therefore, in the final statement in Turn 2 of Case 07, the defendant expresses her honest attitude towards the trial with the WA information "*<认罪> (confess my guilt)*", and hopes to win the judge's sympathy with the WT information "*<请求法官> (beg the judge)*", the WF information "*<80 岁老人> (80-year-old woman)*" and the WA information "*<认罪> (confess guilt)*". Therefore, the ideological factor is especially important for the judge to deal with the case justly. Whether the judge values the demand of ruling by law in the modern society or still believes in the traditional feudal idea of ruling by man will exert its enormous influence on the just judgment of the case.

Once they accepts the defendants' call like this, judges may feel superior enough to distribute turns unequally and even reproach defendants in trials. In Case 31, the implied acceptance of the defendant's call "*法官大人 (My Lord)*" shows the judge cannot shake off the feudal ideology "officials dominate the law" (Zhong, 2009: 135). In the turn distribution, the judge interrupts the first defendant Huang with the two WT information knots "*对着话筒 (speak to the microphone)*". The WT information represents the judge's order, which embodies his power over the defendant. In a loud voice, the repetitive information understandably influences the defendant's own defense more or less. While responding to the second defendant's rational request, the judge orders to stop the defendant's enquiry with the WF information "<已经讲清> (*have explained clearly*)". The WF information means that legal facts are clear and the defendant's request has been refused. Without distributing the turns to the prosecutor to explain again, the judge will not have given any opportunities to the defendant for the knowledge of "<罪名定义> (*the definition of the crime*)".

4.3.3 Non-individual Factors in the Framing Process

4.3.3.1 Relational Factors

"Relational influences on distributive justice include individuals' relative standings on reward-relevant factors as well as the nature of the relationship between the individuals involved (Hegtvedt & Cook, 2000: 101)". Social relations determine the basis of the information structure of legal discourse, in which participants generally have their own roles and position themselves in a definite network of social relations. Discourse articulated by each person, linguistic description or prescription of the discourse will directly influence the discourse information processing and the arrangement of information structures (Du, 2007). In a trial, a judge's neutrality for trial justice is based on the established social relations between all the parties because power, legal facts and neutrality inevitably exert a force on judges' speaking (Solan, 1993). Consequently, the manifestations of PDJ relationship framed in the criminal court is caused by the judge's rational or irrational use of his power and realized through his discourse information processing.

Extract 4-14 (Case 07)

1 <HW, 如何想到偷>公诉人：你是如 何会想到去偷这套红木家具的呢？   Prosecutor: How did you think of stealing this set of mahogany furniture?

2 <WA, 没想偷>被告人：这个，其实   Defendant: As for it, in fact, I

我也不是想偷。

3 <HW，怎么叫不想偷>公诉人：怎么叫不想去偷？

4 <HW，沉默>被告人：……

……

5 <WY，为何给他打电话>公诉人：你为什么打电话给李**？ <WY，就是想偷>**就是想偷嘛**，<WY，确认是否就是想偷>**就是想偷？**

6 <WF，确认>被告人：啊::?

……

7 <HW，按起诉书上说>公诉人：**你说，你说的，起诉书上怎么说就怎么说吧**，<WA，征求同意>**好不好？**

……

8 <WT，报告法庭>公诉人：报告审判长，<WT，问话完毕>公诉人对被告人倪**的问话暂时到此。

9 <WT，讯问被告人>审判员：这个被告人倪**啊，<WT，今天是法庭审理>今天是法庭审理啊，<WT，请如实回答>希望你实事求是地回答法庭的提问。

was unwilling to steal it.

Prosecutor: What do you mean by "was unwilling to steal it"?

Defendant: …

……

Prosecutor: Why did you call Li**? **It means that you just wanted to steal. You mean you just wanted to steal?**

Defendant: Ah::?

……

Prosecutor: **Tell the court… tell the court the facts written on the indictment, Ok?**

……

Prosecutor: Presiding judge, the prosecutor has finished interrogating Defendant Ni** for the time being.

Judge: Defendant Ni**, it is court trial today. I hope you can give your answer to the questions in court based on the facts.

PJ relationship can result in the fact that a judge neglects a prosecutors' suppression against a defendant with the power in criminal trials.

In Extract 4-14, a large amount of the prosecutor's discourse information presuming the defendant's guilt or combining threats with inducement can be advanced in a smooth way mainly because the presiding judge has not interrupted or stopped the prosecutor's unreasonable interrogation in time.

To frame the defendant's guilt in this extract, the prosecutor makes use of two HW information knots—"<如何想到偷> (how did you think of stealing)" in Turn 1 and "<怎么叫不想偷> (what do you mean by "was unwilling to steal it")" in Turn 3, and two WY information knots in Turn 5—"<就是想偷> (just wanted to steal)" and "<就是想偷> (just wanted to steal)". Especially these two WY information knots demonstrates that the prosecutor raises questions based on the truth being framed by himself and gives the replies as his own will. Hence, it has induced the defendant to give an answer to the interrogation towards an unfavorable direction to himself.

Meanwhile, the prosecutor's follow-up HW information "<按起诉书上说> (to answer as what's in the Indictment)" and WA information "<征求同意> (asking for permission)" in Turn 7 are employed to force the defendant to answer the questions according to the content in the indictment. The HW information determines that the defendant will lose the opportunity to defend himself in this turn-taking because the prosecutor's leading question—the WA information has induced the defendant to give a positive answer. To accomplish his objective to frame the defendant's guilt, the prosecutor utilizes the more controlling and coercive question (Tiersma, 1999). Thus, the prosecutor's discourse is apparently not in agreement with the relevant regulations of the criminal procedural law. Based on Lin (2009), it is the most intensive reflection of leading to disharmony between the prosecution and the defense that the prosecution uses the dominant power to suppress the defense in judicial practice. Hereby, the judge does not stop the prosecutor's unreasonable interrogation, but rather helps the prosecutor by intimidating the defendant following the prosecutor's discourse information.

The judge's neutral position cannot be maintained and the judge tends to be line with the prosecutor. In this way, an unharmonious and partial relationship can be formed between the prosecution and the defendant.

Extract 4-15 (Case 20)

1 <WF, R>被告人：第一个，那个绰号，是我的网名，<WF, R>他们把它定为绰号。<WF, R>马**是在 2008 年的 11 月份，蒲**说跟山东的一家铁通公司要签合同➡

Defendant: Firstly, the nickname is my Internet name. They defined it as a nickname. In November, 2008, Ma**… Pu** said that he had signed a contract with a branch of China Railcom in Shandong Province ➡

2 <WT, R, 陈述犯罪事实>审判长：被告人，你应当将你的犯罪事实向法庭供述……

Presiding Judge: Defendant, you should make a confession of your criminal facts in court…

3 <WT, b>审判长：就本案的事实，被告人有没有证据要向法庭出示?

Presiding Judge: As for the facts in the case, Defendant, do you have any evidence to show in court?

4 <WF, b>被告人：我想说的是他里面做的证据里面➡

Defendant: What I want to say is that the evidence he has made ➡

5 <WT, A>审判长：现在问你有没有证据要向法庭出示……

Presiding Judge: The court asks you now whether you have any evidence to present to the court…

6 <WT, b>审判长：被告人杨**，你有什么要为自己辩护的?

Presiding Judge: Defendant Yang**, do you have anything to defend for yourself?

7 <HW, b>被告人：……在我羁押期间，曾有两次他们用诱骗的手段，<WT, b>让我去做**节目的采访，<WT, b>还有**节目也是以诱骗的手段来让[我去做采访]➡。

Defendant: …during the period when I was detained, they beguiled me twice into making the interview program**. What's more, in the program** [the interview was also made] by means of beguilement ➡

8 <WA, R>审判长：[被告人

Presiding Judge: [Defendant Yang**,

杨**，你]在法庭上的用词你要注意啊！ — you] should pay attention to the choice of words in court!

9 <WF，R>被告人：这些都是事实，<WN，R>包括**节目当时采访我的时间，我第一次采访完了，<WF，R>他说你这样说是不行的，<WF，R>然后那个主持人▄ — Defendant: These are all truth including the fact that he said my words were unsuitable after my first interview was over, then the host ▄

10 <WT，R>审判长：被告人杨**，你仅仅围绕本案指控的犯罪事实来为自己辩护。<WT，R>超出部分不要说了！…… — Presiding Judge: Defendant Yang**, you can only defend for yourself focusing on your criminal facts charged in the case. You can't say anything beyond this. …

According to the analysis of the judge's four interruptions of the defendant's reply in Extract 4-15, distributive justice has been violated by the judge's discourse information processing.

Here the defendant's guilt has been presumed by the judge's interruption of the defendant's statement with the WT information "<陈述犯罪事实> (to state your criminal facts)" in Turn 2. Before the judge's first interruption, the defendant wants to clarify the facts in the case. Although all the information knots are WF (indicating the facts) in Turn 1, the defendant's statement is interrupted when the judge has not gained the information concerned with the circumstances of the crime in the defendant's first three information units. Instead of directing the defendant to continue, the judge forces the defendant to confess his criminal facts with the WT directive discourse information. Despite the fact that summary procedure is inapplicable to the case, the judge has framed the defendant as a criminal, with the presumption of guilt demonstrated by the judge's unequal distribution of turns in this extract. The interruption in Turn 2 thereby supports the prosecution impliedly, which leads to the inequality between the defense and the prosecution.

When the defendant's defense concerns such focuses as sources of the evidence and the record, the judge prevents the defendant's discourse articulation that is against the authenticity of the prosecutor's evidence-presenting. Before these interruptions, the defendant challenges the prosecutor's evidence-presenting because he wants to explain to the court with various information knots (WF, WT, WA, HW and WN) that the source of the record is doubtful. During the interactive process, the judge's discourse information typically represents his personalized language, which is closely relevant to the interactive social background and courtroom settings (Chen & Huang, 2009). For example, the judge orders the defendant to reply to the prosecutor's and the judge's questions implied guilt presumption through the two interruptions in Turns 5 and 10. Another interruption embodies the judge's different attitudes towards the defendant and the prosecutor, that is, he stops the defendant from using such harsh words as "诱骗 (beguile)" in Turn 8 to question the authenticity of the prosecutor's evidence-presenting. However, the judge ignores his own discourse information with the presumption of the defendant's guilt in the trial. It is obvious that the judge's discourse information processing actually maintains the interest of the prosecution.

In this extract, whether to interrupt the defendant's statement or the defendant's defense, the judge always frames the defendant's guilt with his personalized discourse information processing. Burge holds that personalized meaning of language is dependent on the social interactions that the individual engages in and social factors access the individual minds or the semantic structures of the individual discourse in a complex way (Baghramian, 1999). Accordingly, the nature of some mental structures can be ascertained based on the relations between the individual and the environment (Chen & Huang, 2009). The relationship shown in Extract 4-15 is actually the prosecution and the judge as two members in the same family, but the judge and the defense as two parties in unequal positions.

Lin (2009) holds the view that both the prosecution and the judge possess the natural affinity in China's criminal procedural process, which can lead to the fact that the judge favors the prosecution and suppresses the defense, and even cooperates with the prosecution to fight against the defense in some cases. The judge unconsciously becomes a secondary prosecutor resulting in the misplacement of the judge's role, which is proved in this case. The cooperative relationship between the prosecution and the judge is in fact the feudalist inquisitory model that is considerably disadvantageous to protecting the defendant's rights.

4.3.3.2   Situational Factors

Actually, PJ cooperation appears based on both objective circumstance and subjective circumstance (Rawls, 1999: 109-110). The former includes circumstances "which make human cooperation both possible and necessary." The latter refers to "the relevant aspects of the subjects of cooperation, that is, of the persons working together."

Extract 4-16 (Case 07)

1 <WF, 有无事先告诉他>审判员：那么，是不是你事先告诉他的，<WF，告诉他再叫两个人>告诉李**再叫两个人过来？

Judge: Then, **you told him beforehand, didn't you?** You told Li** to ask two more persons to come over, right?

2 <WF, 没有>被告人：没有。

Defendant: No.

3 <WA, 没有么>审判员：没有？

Judge: No?

......

......

4 <WT, 接着公诉人问话问>审判员：那么，我接着公诉人的提问，接着问你，<WF，公诉人问及分赃情况>

Defendant: Then, following the prosecutor's questions, I want to ask you something about the

刚刚公诉人问你的具体的这个分赃情况，<WF，事先有无作案分工>那么你们事先有没有谈这个具体的作案分工情况。<WF，确定所问问题>就是分工情况是吧？

specific loot-dividing that the prosecutor just asked you. Then, have you ever talked of the specific assignment of crime committing in the case in advance?

......

...

5 <HW，他们如何进去>审判长：他们三个人具体怎么样进去，<HW，如何把东西搬出>怎样把东西搬出来，<WF，事先有无商量>**事先商量过没有？**

Presiding Judge: How did they three go into and move out the properties? **Had you ever consulted in advance?**

6 <WF，没>被告人：这我没有。

Defendant: I hadn't done that.

7 <WA，确认有无>审判员：没有？

Judge: You hadn't?

......

...

8 <WF，知道分赃情况否>审判员：**怎么分赃的**，知道么？

Defendant: Do you know **how they divided the loot?**

9 <WF，不知道>被告人：不知道，<WA，不知道>不知道。

Judge: I don't know. I don't know.

10 <WA，确认不知道>审判员：不知道？

Defendant: You don't know?

The cooperative relationship between the judge and the prosecutor is reflected in the way of the judge's interrogation following the prosecutor's in Extract 4-16. The judge aims to make certain whether the defendant takes part in the concrete division of the conspiring stealing. In fact, it is to proceed with the presumption of the defendant's guilt.

The litigious relations between the people's courts, the people's procuratorates and public security organs as "to divide their work according to law, cooperate with and moderate one another to ensure correct and effective enforcement of law" (Bian & Li, 2004) are embodied as the judge's being as a cooperative partner of the prosecutor in criminal trial. As a result, similar to the prosecutor's in

Extract 4-14, the judge's interrogation in Extract 4-16 makes a presumption of the defendant's guilt. The information in this extract is actually the successive discourse information in Extract 4-14, in which the judge does not prevent or interrupt the prosecutor's unreasonable interrogation. Instead, he utters a WT information knot "那么，我接着公诉人的提问，接着问你……(*Then, following the prosecutor's interrogation, I ask you some more questions…*)" in Turn 4. The judge has deviated from his neutral position, playing the role of a secondary prosecutor.

The judge utilizes the power of trial to conduct presumption of the defendant's guilt with the aid of the techniques of discourse information processing. In the articulation of the three WF information knots in Turn 4—"<公诉人问及分赃情况> (*the prosecutor's interrogation about loot-dividing*)", "<事先有无作案分工> (*specific assignment of crime committing beforehand or not*)" and "<确定所问问题> (*confirming all the questions being asked*)", the judge still plays the role of a secondary prosecutor. His role-play is not fit for his identity since he aims to force the defendant to confess his intention of the participation in the specific assignment of cooperative stealing and loot-dividing. This kind of practice enables the trial of this case to go and end in a very smooth way. Actually, it is possible to result in the construction of some unreasonable PDJ relationship, which is unfavorable to the defendant.

The subjective circumstances lie in the judge's flexible discourse processing while interrogating the defendant. We can observe that three parts in this extract belong to the same interrogative mode in the judge's utterance.

Firstly, the judge carries on the interrogation aiming at a certain fact. All the discourse information belongs to WF information and the defendant give the negative answers to all these questions in Turns 2, 6 and 9, namely, "没有。(*No.*)", "这我没有。(*No, I don't.*)" and "不知道。

(I don't know.)".

Then, the judge asks three rhetorical questions with WA information in Turns 3, 7 and 10, namely, *"没有? (No?)"*, *"没有? (You don't?)"* and *"不知道? (You don't know?)"*, which are full of distrust of the defendant. The judge utilizes WF information in form of yes/no question in Turn 1—*"有无事先让李某再叫两个人过来 (Had you ever asked Li to send for two more persons to come beforehand?)"* to conduct presumption of guilt because this question, to which the defendant has given a negative reply, has been asked by the prosecutor. This indicates that the judge virtually helps the prosecutor interrogate the defendant. The presiding judge uses a yes/no question—*"事先商量过没有 (Had you consulted with others in advance?)"* as well to interrogate the defendant, which is also the same question being asked by the prosecutor.

At last, the judge applies another WF information knot in Turn 8—a yes/no question *" 知道分赃情况否 (Do you know the loot-dividing?)"* to presuppose the defendant's guilt. The catchphrase *"分赃 (loot-dividing)"*, a contextualization cue, is sufficient to frame the defendant's guilt in that it is until the moment of pronouncing the final judgment that whether the money is illicit money and the behavior is melon-cutting can be decided.

The two judges' distrustful mode of processing information in form of presumption of guilt can impose subtle influence upon the collegial panel's attitude towards the case and the final verdict. It will frequently result in or even has resulted in the construction of some unreasonable PDJ relationship unfavorable to the defendant.

Power in discourse is concerned with discourse as a place where relations of power are actually exercised and enacted (Fairclough, 2001). In the stage of court investigation, the judge's use of his power in the footing shifts and his wording of injustice to identify crime and to control the trial will result in the intensification of the defendant's guilt, the negative impact on the judgment and the damage to judicial justice.

The analysis above shows that distributive justice might have been influenced by many factors in the PDJ relationship constructed. However, considered as one type of justice, distributive justice serves procedural justice in essence because it is closely linked to the concepts of human dignity, the common good, and human rights[12].

4.4   Factors on the Dimension of Retributive Justice

Most research on retribution has taken place within the context of formal legal processes, especially those involving criminal justice issues (Sanders & Hamilton, 2000: 6-7). Typically, retribution, which concerns the desire for retribution and revenge, is an important concept in the development of meanings of criminal responsibility (Umphrey, 1999), so criminal law or criminal procedural law falls under retributive justice, another dimension of justice that considers proportionate punishment a morally acceptable response to crime.

Coleman (Coleman, 1992: 348-354) suggests that retributive justice is concerned with punishment. "To the degree this is the case, retributive justice is more concerned with what happens to a wrongdoer (Sanders & Hamilton, 2000: 6)". "Within court and correctional systems, proportionality is concerned with factors such as the severity of the wrong, the wrongdoer's responsibility and remorse, equity across wrongdoers, and sometimes, the needs of the wrongdoer (Sanders & Hamilton, 2000: 7)". Therefore, discourse processing of final judgments or judges' other decisions made in criminal courts will be focused on as follows: whether to be punished or not, the person who should be

---

12. http://www.ascensionhealth.org/ethics/public/key_principles/distributive_justice.asp

punished, and the severity of punishment.

4.4.1　Deserving Punishment in the Framing Process

Punishment is not justified by any good results, but simply by the criminal's guilt; criminals must pay for their crimes, or an injustice has occurred (Kant, 1887).

Extract 4-17 (Case 20)

<WT>审判长：**区人民法院今天依法组成合议庭公开开庭审理**区人民检察院提起公诉的被告人徐**信用卡诈骗一案，<WP>本案适用普通程序简化审，<WO>由……依法组成合议庭，……**区人民检察院指派代理检察员孙**出庭支持公诉。……<WT>法庭调查开始。

Presiding Judge: Today, the People's Court of ** constitute the collegial panel based on the relevant law to hear the case of credit card fraud committed by Defendant Xu**, which is prosecuted by the People's Procuratorate... The summary procedure is applied in the case. The collegial panel is made up in terms of the relevant law. An acting prosecutor, Sun** is assigned to appear in court for the support of the public prosecution by the People's Procuratorate**. ... Now we proceed to court investigation.

In Extract 4-17, the presiding judge prematurely declares "<WP, A> 本案适用普通程序简化审 (the summary procedure is applicable to the present case)", which is equal to presuppose the defendant's guilt. The judge's practice not only violates procedural justice but also is against retributive justice.

The data demonstrates that the presiding judge declares the mode of trial before the prosecutor reads out the indictment and that the defendant is inquired to confess his crime voluntarily and the defender is asked for agreement. Here, there is no WB information in support of the WP information "<WP, A> 本案适用普通程序简化审 (the summary procedure is applicable to the present case)". And subsequently there is no advice being asked for WA information (the defendant's and the defender's attitudes), but immediately after the turn of speech is directly transferred to all the members appearing in court, the presiding judge declares that the trial steps into the stage of court investigation.

Therefore, based on the relevant regulations of the law, the presiding judge omits quite a few information knots in the course of declaration of trial mode. These omitted information knots include the WB information (the legislative basis applicable to the summary procedure), the WA information (whether the defendant confess his crime voluntarily), and the WA information (whether the defendant and the defender agree with the application of the trial mode). The omission of these important information knots will lead to the fact that the defendant is to receive punishment once he steps into the court. His crime committing is undoubted and he deserves to be punished.

As a result, in the course of processing discourse information in criminal trials, the judge's omission of information will result in the serious damage to the defendant's legal rights and the appearance of retributive injustice. It is impossible to form adversarial equality between the prosecution and the defense in court, and then the PDJ relationship will appear increasingly unreasonable.

4.4.2 Criminals Punished in the Framing Process

Punishment can be regarded as a matter of justice in that if the guilty are not punished, justice is not done (Rachels, 2007).

Extract 4-18 (Case 16)

1 <WB>审判长：……本庭认为本案事实已经查清，<WF>证据确实充分，<WT>本案现已审理终结，<WT>下面进行宣判： Presiding Judge: The court holds the view that the facts in the case are clarified and the evidence is fully confirmed. The trial is ended and the court sentences as follows:

2 <WJ>审判长：本院认
为……公诉机关指控被
告人张**的犯罪罪名成
立，<WP>本院予以确
认。……

3 <WY>审判长：关于超载
由他人指使，由于缺乏证
据，<WP>不予采信。……
<WF>被告人在明知其驾
驶的车辆超载且在未确
保安全的情况下从事货
物运输，……<WB>依照
《中华人民共和国刑
法》……之规定，<WT>
判决如下：<WF>被告人
张**犯交通肇事罪，
<WP>判处有期徒刑四年
六个月。

Presiding Judge: The court holds that the accusation against Defendant Zhang** by the prosecutors is found valid and confirmed by the court. ...

Presiding Judge: With regard to the fact that the overfreight was done at the instigation of others, it is not confirmed for lack of evidence. ... The defendant was still engaged in freight under such a condition that he obviously knew his lorry was overloaded and the security was impossible to be guaranteed... Based on the regulations in Criminal Law of the People's Republic of China, the court sentences as follows: Defendant Zhang** commits crime of causing traffic casualties and is sentenced a fixed prison term of four and a half years.

In Extract 4-18, it is impossible to investigate the truck owner's or the truck employer's criminal responsibility for lack of evidence. Consequently, the collegial panel has to sentence the defendant Crime of Causing Traffic Casualties at last.

From the judge's discourse information, the trial is actually the course of reasoning. In this extract, as a pronouncer of the final judgment, the judge frames the defendant's guilt by means of the combination of various information knots indicating certain disposition, which mainly include WB, WF, WP and WJ information. Meanwhile, the judge makes use of WT information in Turn 1 to explain the whole course of the trial in order to achieve the final goal of the sentence. Actually the reasoning of courtroom discourse has gained the powerful support from WF information and WB information in Turn 1, which embodies the judicial principle in China's legislative environment—"以事实为根据，以法律为准绳 (taking facts as the basis and the laws as the criterion)" (Du, 2009b).

In the information knots indicating disposition, the three types of information—WI information (indicating induction), WP information (indicating processing) and WJ information (indicating judgment), are the strongest in subjectivity and the lowest frequency in appearance in discourse (ibid). Generally speaking, these types of information all gain the effective support from a great deal of WF information (indicating fact) or WB information (indicating bases). Furthermore, these types of information are not usually in singular appearance on a certain level, but put forward with other types of information. In this way, a subjective opinion cannot become some isolated statement.

In consequence, the judge here takes WB information and substantial WF information in Turn 1 as the support and arrives at the WJ information (indicating the judgment) of the collegial panel in Turn 2—"本院认为……公诉机关指控被告人张**的犯罪罪名成立 (The court holds that the accusation against Defendant Zhang** by the prosecutors is found valid)". At the same time, the judge utilizes other types of information, such as WY information (indicating the reason for not adopting the defender's opinion). The information above eventually brings about the final judgment, namely the production of WP information.

All in all, whether criminals punished violates retributive justice or not relies on whether information knots indicating disposition have been produced sufficiently.

4.4.3 Punishment Means in the Framing Process

Judicial punishment can never be used merely as a means to promote some other good for the criminal himself, but instead it must in all cases be imposed on him only on the ground that he has committed a crime (Jacqueline, 2005).

Extract 4-19 (Case 31)

1 <WT, R>公诉人：审判长，起诉书宣读完毕。

Prosecutor: Presiding judge, I have finished reading out indictment.

2 <WP, b>审判长：(问公诉人)先审哪一个？<WT, R>(征求意见后)将被告人蔡**带出法庭候审。<WF, S>被告人黄**坐下，你对起诉书指控你的犯罪事实有什么意见没有？

Presiding Judge: (asking the prosecutor) Which defendant should be tried firstly? (after the prosecutor's agreement) Please take out Defendant Cai** to wait for the trial. Defendant Huang**, take a seat, do you have any objections to your criminal facts in the indictment?

In Extract 4-19, the judge's ignorance of identity and his frame of the defendant's guilt have violated retributive justice in the criminal court.

After the indictment is read out, the judge asks the prosecutor for advice with the WP information "先审哪一个被告人 (Which defendant should be tried firstly.)" in Turn 2. The knowledge category b (known to the prosecutor) means that the judge has forgotten his required role of manipulating the trial because he gains the prosecutor's advice rather than the other two judges'. The judge's discourse information processing has also shown obviously that he will try the defendants cooperating with the prosecution. The judge functions as a secondary prosecutor, aligning with the prosecutors in court.

Therefore, like the judge in Extract 3-22, the judge in this extract will substitute "审人 (to try defendants)" for "审案 (to try cases)" to frame the defendant as a criminal. Since handling a case is changed into punishing a defendant, the punishment means have been added. In the modern society, judicial process is required in the context of justice. However, the uncertain factor "权大还是法大 (Which is more dominating, the power or the law?)" in China's judicial environment, the judges' contradictory position between the pursuit of the truth and the hunting for the power will, in a sense, lead to the phenomenon that the judges' courtroom discourse deviates from legal facts and applications of laws (Chen & Huang, 2009).

Thus, in case that their discourse information frames the trial as a means of punishing the defendant, judges will have violated retributive justice.

4.4.4 Punishment Severity in the Framing Process

According to ethics and law in most cultures throughout the world, "Let the punishment fit the crime" is the principle that the severity of penalty might be determined by the amount of harm, unfair advantage or moral imbalance the crime caused (Cavadino & Dignan, 1997).

Extract 4-20 (Case 33)

<WJ, A>审判长：……本院认为，被告人许**以非法占有为目的，<HW, O>伙同同案人采用秘密手段，<WT, A>盗窃金融机构，<WF, A>数额特别巨大，<WJ, A>其行为已构成盗窃罪。……<WF, O>当其发现银行系统出错时即产生恶意占有银行存款的故意，<WF, O>共分171次恶意提款17万多元而非法占有，<WF, O>得手后潜逃并将赃款挥霍花光，<WJ, A>其行为符合盗窃罪的法定构成要件，<WJ, A>当以盗窃罪追究

Presiding Judge: ... the court holds the view that with purpose of illegal possession, Defendant Xu** stole a large amount of money from the financial institution with secret aids in collusion with the accomplice in the case. He is found guilty of crime of theft. ... When he found there was something wrong with the banking system, he immediately formed an evil purpose to occupy the bank deposits maliciously. He maliciously drew money 171 times and the sum came to 170,000 in total. After his drawing from ATM successfully, he absconded and ran out of all the illicit money. His behavior is in accordance with the constitutive requirements of crime of

其刑事责任。<WP，A>辩护人提出的辩护意见，与本案的事实和法律规定不相符，本院不予支持。<WB，A>依照《中华人民共和国刑法》第二百六十四条第（一）项、第五十七条、第五十九条、第六十四条的规定，<WT，A>判决如下：<WJ，A>一、被告人许**犯盗窃罪，<WP，J，A>判处无期徒刑，<WP，J，A>剥夺政治权利终身，<WP，A>并处没收个人全部财产。<WP，A>二、追缴被告人许**的违法所得 175000 元发还**市商业银行。

theft. The defensive view from the defender is not in accordance with the facts of the case and the relevant regulations. The court is not in support of it. According to the relevant regulations in Item 1, Article 264, Article 57, Article 59, Article 64 of Criminal Law of the People's Republic of China, the court sentences as follows:

Firstly, Defendant Xu** has committed crime of theft and **is sentenced a life imprisonment, deprived of political right for life and all his personal property is to be confiscated.**

Secondly, Defendant Xu**'s illegal gains, RMB 175,000, is to be recovered and return to Commercial Bank of …

In Extract 4-20, the court verdict is the presiding judge's discourse information of his pronouncing a judicial sentence, which represents the voice of all the members in the collegial panel. Taking the conviction of crime and measurement of penalty into consideration, the court verdict is far more severe than the treatment in accordance with the objective fact. From the perspective of information processing, it has resulted from the misuse of information knots and the lack of information.

The judge misuses the type of information knots and knowledge categories. For example, the HW information "伙同同案人采用秘密手段 (… *with secret aids in collusion with the accomplice)*" is used to indicate the mode of behavior, which has framed the defendant's behavior as a secret theft. While in terms of Zhong's jurisprudential analysis of the concept of theft (Zhong & Huang, 2009), since the defendant in the case drew money under supervision of outdoor digital camera and the deal was recorded, the behavior was not totally secret and the defendant had not been malicious to destroy the cash dispenser to perform the theft. In addition, Xu** drew the money via his own bankcard and his own password. The way in which he drew money has no difference from that in which money is drawn normally. Hence the judge's determination of crime has obviously broadened or altered the connotations of "秘密 (secrecy)" and "盗窃 (theft)". According to knowledge categories, the judge conveys the known information O to frame the defendant's serious crime committing, which indicates the defendant's secret theft is known to all the parties in the trial.

The misuse of information knots brings about the information (indicating the judgment) "<WJ>其行为已构成盗窃罪 (His behavior has constituted the crime of theft.)", and lays down a foundation for the latter pronouncement of the final judgment.

Furthermore, the deficiency of the judge's information conveying results in an important factor for a severe punishment of the crime. For instance, the appearance of the information knot "<WF>当其发现银行系统出错时即产生恶意占有银行存款的故意 (When he found there was something wrong with the banking system, he immediately formed an evil purpose to occupy the bank deposits maliciously.)" only emphasizes the fact that the defendant is completely responsible for the case. However, there is a lack of the information involved in the problem resulting from the bank itself. What's more, the information "<WB>依照《中华人民共和国刑法》……的规定 (based on the relevant regulations … in Criminal Law of PRC)" is not completely applicable to the case because the information cannot provide sufficient basis for the application, for example, the judgment lacks the basis of "《关于审理盗窃案件具体应用法律若干问题的解释》(Interpretations on Several Specific Problems of Application of Laws in Trial of Theft Cases)" issued by the

Supreme People's Court.

In short, the misuse of information knots and the lack of information lead to the defendant's severe punishment, which violates retributive justice.

4.5 Summary

This chapter has explored the factors influencing judges' construction of PDJ relationship on the three dimensions of judicial justice. Frame analysis of judges' discourse information processing yields the following findings:

1) The dimension of procedural justice has been defined and delimited firstly, which involves such three variables as judges' standing in trials, neutrality towards both the prosecution and the defense, and trust in the defense. Data analysis shows that unreasonable PDJ relationship sometimes results from judges' footing shifts, deviations from their neutral position, or distrust in the defendants' discourse information articulated in the interrogation.

2) On the dimension of distributive justice, the analysis of discourse information reveals that cognitive factors and social factors have influenced judges' equal allocation of opportunities to both the prosecution and the defense. Judges' goals and motivations, individual variables (attitudes, perceptions or ideologies), and non-individual variables (social relations or situational factors) may lead to the violation of distributive justice, and even result in PJ cooperation or PD adversarial inequality.

3) On the dimension of retributive justice, deserving punishment, criminals punished, punishment means and punishment severity in judges' framing process in court have affected the abidance by or the violation of retributive justice.

Meanwhile, we have also obtained some findings regarding judges' discourse information processing.

a) The upgrade of information levels leads to procedural injustice in that the trial procedures might be destroyed.

b) The flexible use of different information knots can help the judge realize his/her goal in the trial on the one hand, but sometimes will lead to the violation of the discourse distributive justice on the other hand.

c) The misuse of knowledge categories, insufficient discourse information, or interruption of defendants' discourse information transmission presumes defendants' guilt, leads to unequal allocation of discourse power or even exerts stress upon defendants.

d) The misuse of information knots or the loss of information in the discourse processing sometimes leads to more severe punishment assigned to a defendant in the final sentence than the degree to which the defendant should be punished reasonably.

The findings above demonstrate that the factors on three dimensions of judicial justice influence the construction of PDJ relationship through judges' discourse information processing. The violation or the observation of procedural justice plays the vital role since whether it is abided by is also reflected by the observation of distributive justice and retributive justice (Sanders & Hamilton, 2000).

However, our ultimate purpose is to solve the problems that irrational PDJ relationship still exists in trials. Hence, next chapter will concentrate on the judges' framing strategies in the reconstruction of rational PDJ relationship by means of analyzing judges' reasonable and efficient discourse information processing in criminal court.

Chapter 5

Judges' Framing Strategies in Reconstruction of PDJ Relationship

5.1 Introduction

The two chapters above have analyzed the current PDJ relationship constructed in court via judges' discourse information processing and the factors influencing the relationship constructed respectively. In the trial, judges' manipulation of discourse information processing and different footings taken at all the stages might have led to the irrational PDJ relationship constructed from the perspective of the three dimensions of judicial justice. In the process, judges' misuse of knowledge category to view the defendant as a criminal violates retributive justice in court; and his misuse of information knots and adding information units at will to limit the defendant's reply infringe on distributive justice. Retributive, procedural justice and distributive justice do not exist independently of each other (Sanders & Hamilton, 2000). Thus, the identification of the defendant's criminal behavior before the final judgment does not conform to the principle of presumption of innocence and violates procedural justice as well. Such violations of judicial justice embodied by judges' discourse information processing have directly influenced whether the rational PDJ relationship can be constructed in court.

Since the justice of judges' discourse is determined by the

importance of judges' presiding over trials and the inevitability of the final judgment (Wu, 2002), judges' footing shifts and discursive devices in reframing process will result in relative rational PDJ relationship constructed in court. Therefore, it is necessary to explore how the judge takes reasonable footings and employs appropriate framing strategies in trial. These forthcoming strategies will be valuable to reconstruct rational PDJ relationship and keep PD balance. Taking into account the perception of judicial justice, role-orientations, social relations and so on, this chapter will concentrate on the judges' reframing strategies at the macro-level and discursive devices at the micro-level.

According to the theoretical framework based on frame analysis, participation framework and interactive frames are the two core elements in frame theory, among which framing process represents the dynamic behavior from the participants in the communication (Duranti, 1997: 295-307; Tannen & Wallat, 1993). Due to the courtroom activities controlled by judges' discourse processing, judges' footing shifts and reframing process will be investigated to see whether footing shifts and reframing can be employed by judges to reconstruct PDJ relationship in criminal court.

5.2 Footing Shifts by Discourse Information

With the advancement of the judicial reform in Mainland China, judges' role in criminal trials tends to be neutral and their duty to make judgments in a neutral position becomes more luminous. However, PDJ relationship has always taken on some unharmonious tones involved in China's current criminal procedures. To alter the status quo, it is judges who play the key role to upgrade judicial concept for the relocation and the reset of their roles, that is, judges should adopt an objective and neutral position (Lin, 2009). Judges' footing shifts via discourse information processing will help reconstruct PDJ relationship in the criminal courtroom. Based on the data analysis below, we will categorize judges' footing patterns and then interpret how judges shift their footings to reconstruct rational PDJ relationship.

5.2.1 Categorization of Judges' Footing Patterns

5.2.1.1 Animator

In criminal courtrooms, presiding judges will transmit some settled discourse information to organize trial procedures or distribute turns to the prosecution and the defense. This type of discourse information always activates various primary frames or sub-frames, in which judges take their footing as animator and they often play the roles of organizer or distributor.

Extract 5-1

1 <1, 2, 2, 18, WT, P, A>审判长：首先由公诉人宣读起诉书。(Case 11)

Presiding Judge: Prosecutor, read out the indictment first.

2 <1, 2, 2, 27, WF, b, 是否一致> 审判长：被告人，公诉人宣读的起诉书与你收到的起诉书副本内容是否一致？(Case 04)

Presiding Judge: Defendant, is the indictment read out by the prosecutor in agreement with the content in the copy of indictment you've received?

3 <1, 3, 2, 16, WT, A, 请被告人自行辩护>审判长：被告人做自行辩护。(Case 05)

Presiding Judge: Defendant, defend yourself.

4 <2, 10, 3, 32, WT, A, 公诉人继续举证>审判长：公诉人继续举证。

Presiding Judge: Prosecutor, go on with presenting evidence.

5 <2, 35, 3, 81, WY, A, 评议结果>审判长：经合议庭评议，辩护人出示的这一证据与本案没有关联性，

Presiding Judge: After the review by the collegial panel, the evidence shown by the defender is proven to be irrelevant to the

6 <2，35，3，82，WJ，A，不再质证 case. Thus, to challenge the
>故当庭不再质证。(Case 04) evidence is unnecessary in court.
7 <0，1，1，4，WT，A，法庭辩论 Presiding Judge: The court debate
结束>审判长：法庭辩论结束。 is over. It's time for the defendant
8 <0，1，1，5，WT，A，指令被告 to make a final statement.
人最后陈述>被告人作最后陈述。

(Case 07)

The judge's role of an organizer in this extract is realized through the trial organized by his utilization of the procedural discourse information on higher level (Levels 1 or 2). For instance, Information Knots 1, 2, 3, 4, 7and 8 are settled discourse in criminal trials, just articulated out of different judges while Information Knots 5 and 6 are the discourse information representing the judgment made by all the members in the collegial panel. It is just "animator" as the footing that the judges take because the judges play the role as the "sounding box" while using the language representing the nation and the court. Accordingly, it is unnecessary for them to become "author" to reorganize the discourse information to declare the judgment by the collegial panels.

Information Knots 1, 3, 4, 7 and 8 are all WT expressing behaviors and known to the judges themselves (A). This shows that the judges manipulate the trial procedures and distribute discourse information to the hearers who need to follow the judges' directions. Information Knots 1, 3 and 4 have directly realized the distribution and the transmission of information in the interaction. In Case 07, the judge articulated two discursive actions "<宣布法庭辩论结束 (declaring the end of court investigation)>" and "<指令被告人最后陈述> (directing the defendant to make the final statement)" to transit the judicial procedure from the court debate to distributing discourse information to the defendant. However, there exists a cause-effect relation between the judge's WY "<评议结果> (the judgment by the collegial panel)" and WJ "<不

再质证> (no need for challenging the evidence)" information knots, which prevents the judge from distributing the information to the prosecutor and accordingly makes the defense's evidence presented legally invalid.

The analysis above shows that judges take the footing as "animator" to achieve the manipulation of trial procedures in accordance with the criminal procedural law. Furthermore, Goffman suggests that interactants do not simply change footing, but rather embed one footing within another (Ribeiro, 2006).

5.2.1.2 Combination of Animator and Author

Different from the footing as animator, the combination of animator and author (animator + author) embodies that speakers employ their own discourse structures to express the standpoints of certain party they represent.

Extract 5-2

1 <WB, 考虑各方意见>审判长: 通过刚才的开庭审理, 本合议庭在合议时认真考虑了公诉人、被告人、辩护人的意见, <WB, 证据材料>公诉人当庭宣读和出示了证据材料, <WB, 举证质证>控辩双方对证据进行了举证、质证, <WB, 观点阐释>在法庭辩论阶段充分阐明了各自的观点, <WJ, 结论>合议庭经评议作出结论, <WT, 宣判>现进行宣判。(Case 10)

Presiding Judge: After the court trial just now, in the panel discussion the collegial panel takes a careful consideration of the opinions from the prosecutor, the defendant and the defender. The prosecutor has read out and shown the materials of evidence in court and both the prosecutor and the defender have conducted presenting and challenging the evidence. They both have fully stated their respective opinions in the process of court debate. After the review by the collegial panel, it's time to pronounce a sentence.

2 <WB, 核实事实>审判员: 通过刚才的法庭审理, 法庭核实了本案的事实, <WB, 质

Judge: Through the court trial just now, the court has confirmed the facts

证>并对本案的证据进行了
质证，<WB，听取意见和陈
述>又听取了公诉人、被告
人、辩护人的意见及被告人
的最后陈述，<WJ，结论>合
议庭经评议认为，……<WT，
判决>判决如下: (Case 22)

in the case, conducted challenging the evidence, listened to the opinions from the prosecutor, the defendant, the defender and the defendant's final statement. After the review by the collegial panel, it's sentenced as follows:

The two paragraphs in Extract 5-2 are discourse information articulated by judges before the final court decision, with similar contents mainly outlining the trial process and indicating the legitimacy and integrity of the trial procedures. However, with their own styles, the judges have output a different number of information units (Paragraph 1 has four WB information knots, while Paragraph 2 has only two), and achieved the combination as "animator + author".

The first information units "<考虑各方意见> (having taken the views from different parties into account)" and "<核实事实> (having verified the facts)" in Paragraph 1 and Paragraph 2 respectively are expressed in different ways with completely different contents. The second information unit "<质证> (having challenged the evidence)" in Paragraph 2 actually contains the contents expressed in the second information unit "<证据材料> (the material of evidence)" and the third one "<举证质证> (presenting and challenging the evidence)" in Paragraph 1. And the link between the fourth information unit "<观点阐释> (having explained their opinions)" and the first one "<考虑各方意见> (having taken the views from different parties into account)" in Paragraph 1 has just enjoyed the fairly similar content with the third information unit "<听取意见和陈述> (having heard opinions and statements)" in Paragraph 2.

It is obvious that procedural discourse information articulated before the pronouncement of final judgments is essential, which represents the views given by all the members in collegial panels, so judges should at least take "animator" as their footings. Nonetheless, because language organization has a relative flexibility, judges can be relatively free to generate discourse information with their own styles, which leads to the realization of their footing as the combination "animator + author".

5.2.1.3 Combination of Animator, Author and Principal

While discussing the interactive process through institutional discourse, one often implies that the individual "speaker" is "formulating his own text and staking out his own position through it: animator, author, and principal are one (Goffman, 1981: 145)".

Extract 5-3 (Case 19)

1 <WO>审判员：包内 55000 元是谁的？

Judge: Whose was RMB 55,000 in the bag?

2 <WO>被告人：25000 元是被害人的，<WF>3 万是假的，<WP>是我们放进去的。

Defendant: 25,000 of it belonged to the victim. The rest 30,000 was forged currency that was put into the bag by us.

3 <WT>审判员：吕**调包时，你在做什么？

Judge: What were you doing when Lü** was changing the bag?

4 <WT>被告人：我在和被害人说话，<WT>分散她的注意力。

Defendant: I was talking with the victim in order to distract her attention.

5 <WF>审判员：被害人知道你们调包了吗？

Judge: Did the victim notice that you had changed the bag?

6 <WF>被告人：她不知道调包了。

Defendant: No.

In the process of substantive discourse information transmitted by judges, a lot of frames may be initiated by judges' own discourse owing to different cases, reflecting their distinctive fact-investigating modes. As a result, their footing is the combination of the three, "animator + author + principal".

In Extract 5-3, the judge plays the role of a fact investigator (Zhong, 2009), on behalf of the collegial panel to carry out an interrogation to clarify the facts. In this extract, the judge produces three information knots to interrogate the defendant about such three closely linked issues as WO (indicating relevant persons) in Turn 1, WT (indicating the defendant's behavior) Turn 3 and WF (indicating some fact) Turn 5.

With the WO information, the judge has obtained the information that the money belongs to the victim in the case. Via the question asked with WT information, the judge has got the information that the defendant cooperates with the other suspects in the crime committing. As for the destination via the WF information, the defendant's answer shows that the sum of money has been stolen without the victim's knowledge.

Eventually, the three information knots have proved the defendant's guilt. The design and the arrangement of the three information knots represent the judge's individual style of discourse organization in the interrogation, showing the judge's personal footing with such impromptu discourse information.

Unquestionably, if he makes a court investigation of another criminal case, the judge will employ different discourse information to frame different legal facts.

Extract 5-4 (Case 24)

<WF，O>审判长：这是一起法治观念淡薄，诚信意识缺失，藐视司法权威，视法院裁判文书为儿戏而引发的案件，<WF，O>案情简单，<WF，A>结果却发人深省。<WO，C>本案的被告人当你有困难的时候，是谁伸出了援助之

Presiding Judge: It is weak understanding of the law, deficiency in faith consciousness, contempt for judicial power and treating adjudicative documents as plaything that results in the happening of the case. Though the case is simple, its result is thought-provoking. Defendant in the case, who

手，帮助你及你的企业度过难关？<WO，C>是你的亲朋好友！<WC，O>如果不到万不得已，<WO，O>有谁会通过诉讼途径来讨债？<WC，A>如果本案的被告人能遵守法律，诚实守信；<WC，A>如果……；<WC，A>如果……，<WE，A>那么，被告人也不会走上犯罪之路。……<WC，A>倘若被告人多一点法制观念；<WC，A>倘若……；<WC，A>倘若……；<WC，A>倘若……；<WE，A>今天的结果是可以避免的……

<WA，A>法官真诚地希望被告人能够从中吸取教训，真心悔罪。<WA，A>更希望与被告人有相似行为的人，以此为戒……

<WB，A>审判长：综上所述，依据……的相关规定……，<WP，A>判决如下：……

<WA，A>庄**回到社区后，应当遵守法律、法规，服从监督管理，接受教育，完成公益劳动，做一名有益社会的公民。

lent you a helping hand, and pulled you and your enterprise through when you were in trouble? It was your relatives and friends! Who wanted to dun for debts via litigation **unless** it was absolutely necessary? **If** the defendant in the case abided by the laws and be honest, **if**..., **if**..., the defendant would not be on the way to the crime committing. **Provided that** the defendant was stronger in the understanding of the law, **provided that**..., **provided that**..., **provided that**..., **provided that**..., the result would be avoidable today. The judge sincerely hopes that the defendant can draw a good lesson from it and be penitent at heart. In addition, the judge hopes that those who have conducted similar behaviors to the defendant can take this as a lesson.

Presiding Judge: In sum, based on the relevant regulations, it is sentenced as follows: ... After Zhuang** returns to the community, you should abide by the laws and relevant regulations, obey management by supervision, receive education, finish labor for public good and try to be a citizen beneficial to the society.

The judge, as a social member in the organization of criminal trial procedures (Zhong, 2009), evaluates the case and educates the defendant in his own way to deliver discourse information at the phase of declaring the final judgment. On behalf of his own view on the case and that of the other members in the collegial panel, the judge in Extract 5-4 takes his footing as "animator + author + principal", acting as an evaluator and an educator.

The judge presents his overall evaluation of the case to the other parties in the trial with three WF information knots, of which the first two with knowledge category O are the information known to all. In the third one, the judge shares his personal view that "结果却发人深省。 (The result of the case is thought-provoking)", so knowledge category A (indicating his own opinion) has been marked. While evaluating the defendant, the judge utilizes "如果 (if)" conditional sentences (4 WC information knots), expressing his regret for the defendant; in addition, he has also used five "倘若 (provided that)" conditional WC information knots to express his regret for the consequence resulting from the case. All the judge's discourse information units are full of individuality, representing his personal feelings, so the footing is taken as "animator + author + principal".

Additionally, the judge's footing is manifested through his role played as an educator. As the information known to the judge (knowledge category A), the last three WA information knots reflect the judge's attitude towards the defendant through his education, among which the first two WA information knots show the judge's hope for the defendant and others, and the last one indicates the judge's requirement for the defendant after the pronouncement of judgment.

5.2.2 Judges' Footing Shifts

Goffman uses quasi-synonyms for describing a change in footing: "participant's alignment, or set, or stance, or posture, or projected self" (1981: 128). In the process of constructing rational PDJ relationship, it is worth exploring judges' footing shift in criminal court through their discourse information processing.

5.2.2.1 Degradation of Information Levels

Information levels constitute the major part of discourse structure in that superordinate information dominates its subordinates and influences the subsequent information. Degradation of information levels refers to the mode of discourse information processing that certain types of information units fall from a higher level down to the one lower than its original father information. Judges' adoption of degradation of information levels in criminal trials may lead to the shifts of their footings. For example,

Extract 5-5 (Case 25)

(简化审中的法官讯问)……	(judges' interrogation based on summary procedure)…
1 <3，31，4，5>审判员：--你们诈骗所得的5600元和银行卡里的 17 万是谁保管的？……	Judge: --who kept the money RMB 5,600 you had gained by cheating and the money RMB 170,000 in the bank card?...
2 <3，35，4，12>审判员：19万多，<3，35，4，13>这里都是赃款吗？……	Judge: More than RMB 190,000. Was it all the illicit money here?...
3 <3，41，4，34>审判员：(被扣留的电脑等)是不是用来网上行骗的？	Judge: (detained properties, such as a computer, etc.) Were they all gained by cheating on line?

In Extract 5-5, the use of the catchphrases "诈骗 (fraud)", "赃款 (money by fraud)" and "行骗 (cheat)" does not presume the defendant's guilt in his interrogation with the judge's footing shift resulting from degradation of information level.

In the case tried through summary procedure, the defendant has confessed his fraud before the court investigation. All the information units here are on Level 4 dominated by Level 3 information "法官讯问 *(the judge's interrogation)*". The father information ensures that the judge's catchphrases represent the standpoint of the collegial panel since summary procedure has been applied. The substantive discourse in this extract is the evidence for the footing taken by the judge as "animator + author".

Unless the support was gained from the information on the higher levels, the judge's question here could have shown the presumption of the defendant's guilt, just representing his individual subjective inference. As a result, the judge would take his footing as "animator + author + principal".

Different from the assumption, the result from degradation of the information level in this extract has brought forth sufficient information on the higher levels to prove the defendant's guilt; therefore the judge has realized his footing shift from "animator + author + principal" to "animator + author", with his questions having appeared fairly reasonable.

The example proves that judges' footing shift via adoption of degradation of information levels in criminal trials may help them avoid presumption of guilt and construct rational PDJ relationship.

5.2.2.2 Displacement of Information Levels

Displacement of information levels refers to the transfer of some information unit between the same levels, including forward move and backward move. Both phenomena in displacement of information levels can help realize footing shift in the interaction. In criminal trials, judges' footing shift may result from displacement of information levels to reconstruct PDJ relationship. For example,

Extract 5-6 (Case 18)

1 <1，2，2，4>审判长：被告人吴**，法庭向你提问，<2，4，3，21>你听清楚法庭问题……<2，4，3，22>根据刚才你的回答，主要是，你们三个人由顾**扮成算命先生，<2，4，3，23>由你们去搭识 KTV 小姐，<2，4，3，24>并借开光之机配合顾**把被害人的银行卡和密码弄到手，……<2，4，3，39>事实描述的对不对啊？

Presiding Judge: Defendant Wu**, the court now asks you some questions; listen to the questions carefully… According to your reply, the most importantly, it was Gu** among you three who dressed up as a fortuneteller to strike up conversation with a lady serving in KTV. Taking the opportunity of introducing the light, you got the victim's bank card and its password with aid of Gu**. Do you agree with the description of the facts?

2 <2，4，3，39>被告人：是。

Defendant: Yes.

3 <1，2，2，5>审判长：这个起诉书上指控的这些窃得和骗得财物的内容，你有没有意见啊？

Presiding Judge: Do you have an objection to the content of properties gained by theft and fraud that is described in the indictment?

4 <1，2，2，5>被告人：没有。

Defendant: Yes.

In Extract 5-6, judge's procedural discourse information has eliminated procedural injustice through displacement of information levels, which is advantageous in the construction of reasonable PDJ relationship.

In the majority of criminal trials, judges often interrogate defendants whether they have an objection to the criminal facts accused immediately after the public prosecutor read out indictments. For example, a judge asks, "被告人对起诉书指控的犯罪事实有意见吗? (The defendant, do you have an objection to the criminal facts accused in the indictment?)". The catchphrase "犯罪事实 (criminal facts)" will help frame the defendant's guilt if the case is not applicable to summary procedure. As an information unit, the question asked by the judge constitutes a subordinate of the father information "<法庭调查> (court investigation)". The judge's footing is "animator + author + principal' because no evidence on the same level dominated by this identical father information has proved the facts in the indictment. Since no preceding discourse information supports the presupposition relevant to the defendant' guilt in advance, the judge's question is of strong subjectivity.

But in Extract 5-6, the judge has realized his footing from "animator + author + principal" to "animator + author" because the judge questions the defendant with the information unit "<对指控内容有无意见> (an objection to the accusation or not)" after the prosecutor's and the judge's interrogation through which the defendant's confession and the confirmation of the facts have made the crime relatively clear. In spite of such catchphrases with presupposition as "窃得 (gained by theft)" and "骗得 (gained by fraud)" in Turn 3, actually there does not exist the presumption of guilt. It is the displacement of information levels that result in the procedural justice.

Certainly, if a judge wants to utilize other procedural discourse reasonably to maintain neutrality to make decisions, s/he may also move some information about some facts from the position dominated by the father information unit "<法庭调查> (court investigation)" to that dominated by "<举证质证> (presenting and challenging evidence)".

It will be obvious that presumption of innocence does not prevent proof of a defendant's criminal facts as long as the confirmation of some fact in court has been strongly supported by sufficient evidence (Bian, 2006: 13). Therefore, displacement of information levels will help confirm some factual information to avoid the emergence of the information presuming guilt.

5.2.2.3　Modification of Knowledge Categories

Modification of knowledge categories refers to the discursive device, by which a speaker carries on in-depth processing to the attribution of knowledge categories in the process of delivering the information in order to achieve some communication goal. The device may change a speaker's footing, with his discourse adapted to his need. Specifically speaking, modification of knowledge categories includes elimination of known information and confirmation of unknown information.

We will firstly explore judges' footing shift for observing the relations between elimination of known information and judicial justice. To illustrate the specific strategy, let us take some implied known information about presumption of guilt and presumption of innocence as an example,

Extract 5-7 (Case 16)

1 <b>审判员：辩护人对起诉书指控被告人行为构成交通肇事罪有无意见？

Judge: Defender, the defendant is accused guilty of Crime of Causing Traffic Casualties in the indictment. Do you have any objections?

2 <b>辩护人：有意见。

Defender: Yes.

3 <b>审判员：有何意见？

Judge: What?

4 <b>辩护人：首先，我不同意公诉人对被告人的指控。<b>其行为不构成交通肇事罪构成要件。<b>从本案来看，……主观上没有过错。<b>第二，超载不是引起本案的直接原因。<b>第三，张**作为雇员，责任应由雇主来承担。<b>此外，

Defender: Firstly, I don't agree on the prosecutor's accusation of the defendant, for his behavior doesn't satisfy the constitutive requirements. In the case, the defendant is subjectively innocent. Secondly, overloading was not the direct reason leading to the case. Thirdly, Zhang** worked as an employee and the responsibility should be born

事发的客观环境无法预见。<b> 综上所述，本案的发生不是行为人的作为和不作为所造成的。<b> 应认定为意外事件。

by the employer. In addition, the objective surrounding leading to the case was unpredictable. All in all, it is not the actor's feasance or nonfeasance that resulted in the occurrence of the case. It should be taken as an incident.

5 <b>审判长: 公诉人有无新的意见？

Presiding Judge: Prosecutor, do you have any new opinions on it?

In Extract 5-7, the judge carries on the substantive information transmission by questioning, which has maintained distributive justice here. The known information (b) has avoided such description of the defendant's guilt by the judge as in Extract 3-21. Since the defender has sufficient opportunities to defend his client, no information known to the judge himself (R) is used to stop the defender from speaking.

In the substantive discourse from Extract 3-21, the judge's footing is "animator + author + principal". In order to make the defendant accept his presupposition of guilt in advance, the judge uses the information "<被告人行为> (the defendant's behavior)" known to both parties (T) firstly, and then transmits the information "<制止辩护发言> (to stop the defender from speaking)" known to himself (R) to interrupt the defendant's words. As "a locus of power" (Conley & O'Barr, 1998: 7), the judge's discourse embodies the misuse of his power in Extract 3-21, which harms the defendant's rights of defense inevitably.

But in Extract 5-7, the judge's footing has been shifted to "animator + author" as he carries on the procedural questioning on behalf of the collegial panel. Having changed the dialogue pattern into the questioning pattern, the judge asks the questions with the information known to the defender (b). When the defender disagrees with the judge's yes/no question in Turn 1, the judge directs the defender to express his opinion rather than interrupts the defender.

Although the discourse information is not beneficial to the prosecution, the judge distributes new turns to the defender in Turn 3. Through such modification of knowledge categories, the presumption of the defendant's guilt resulted from the information known to both parties can be eliminated.

Extract 5-8 (Case 17)

<A>审判长：**区人民法院刑事审判庭现在开庭。<A>传被告人蓝**到庭。   Presiding Judge: The Criminal Court of ... is now in session. Lead Defendant Lan** to be interrogated.

Through footing shift, the judge's discourse information in Extract 5-8 has eliminated the information known to all and avoided the phenomenon that litigation subject becomes litigation object.

Here with the catchphrase "传 (to lead someone to come)", the judge directs the bailiff to lead the defendant to the court, taking the footing as "animator + author". The reasonable procedural discourse information transmission represents the decision made by the collegial panel because "传 (to lead someone to come)" is a neutral word without the presupposed information known to all. The catchphrase used has eliminated the expression "<提被告人入庭> (to fetch the defendant to be interrogated)" in Extract 3-9 that changes the litigation subject into the litigation object (Bian, 2007). The catchphrase "传 (to lead someone to come)" has also avoided the known information "被告人即是犯人 (The defendant must be a criminal.)" produced when the footing is "animator + author + principal".

The modification of knowledge category helps treat the defendant equally, and lay the foundation for the construction of reasonable PDJ relationship.

Confirmation of unknown information refers to one of the discursive devices while shifting the footings, in which speakers need to confirm whether their questioning can gain certain unknown information. When the hearer gives negative response to the questioning, speakers may listen to the hearer's explanation rather than impose the expected information on the hearer. Judges' use of this discursive devices helps avoid the phenomenon that their procedural discourse becomes a mere formality. For example,

Extract 5-9 (Case 16)

（公诉人出示证据证明被告人未打过报警电话）

(The prosecutor shows the evidence to prove the defendant has never called the police.)

<1，5，2，29，WA，b>审判长：被告人对公诉人所出示的证据有无异议？

Presiding Judge: Defendant, do you have any objections to the evidence shown by the prosecutor?

<WA，b>被告人：有异议。

Defendant: Yes.

<WF，b>审判长：有何异议啊？

Presiding Judge: What?

<WF，b>被告人：我坚持自己打过110。

Defendant: I insist that I've called 110.

<WA，b>审判长：辩护人对公诉人所出示的证据有无异议？

Presiding Judge: Defender, do you have any objections to the evidence shown by the prosecutor?

In order to confirm whether the defendant has an objection to the evidence presented and what the objection is if he does, the judge in Extract 5-9 utilizes the unknown information to interrogate the defendant, taking the footing as "animator + author". The judge's discursive device here has avoided the misuse of footing appearing in Extract 3-24 and eliminated unfair treatment of the defendant.

The procedural discourse analyzed in Extract 3-24 demonstrates that the judge's footing is "animator + author + principal" because of the contradiction between the judge's goal of questioning and his way in which the question is asked. Foucault (1978: 101) holds the opinion that discourse not only transmits, produces and strengthens power, but exposes and even destroys the power. The judge in Extract 3-24 wants to obtain the information known to the defendant (b) "被告人是

否有意见？ *(Does the defendant have an objection?)*", namely the information unknown to the judge. But the judge actually uses the repetitive information units "*被告人是否有意见？ (Does the defendant have an objection?)*" to press for the defendant's answer, refusing to listen to the defendant's explanation of the answer "*这不是事实。(This is not the fact.)*", which is unfavorable to the prosecution. The defendant has lost the opportunity by replying "*没意见。(No objection.)*". Obviously the unknown information is actually the judge's known information, which shows that the interrogation is unnecessary and of no use. Presumption of guilt in the judge's mind leads to an abuse of his authority and power.

But in Extract 5-9, the judge's footing has shifted to "animator + author". The knowledge categories in all the questions are b, which means there is no the information known to all or the information known to the judge himself. When the defendant has an objection to some evidence, the judge uses WH-question to ask some thorough questions. Not until the confirmation of the defendant's objection (the unknown information) does the judge carry on the turn-taking to direct to continue presenting evidence. Unlike the judge in Extract 3-24, who by no means lets the defendant explain, the judge's questions in Extract 5-9 conform to the role that a judge should play in criminal court due to no existence of any individual subjective opinions, which is beneficial to the maintenance of distributive justice.

The above three extracts illustrate that the two modes in modifying knowledge categories can be employed effectively by judges to eliminate judicial injustice.

5.3   Reframing with Discourse Information

Reframing designates a communication technique or a conversational practice that helps characterize the interplay of incompatible frames in conflict. Hence it also refers to frame change "involving creating a new frame that fits the situation's same concrete details equally well or better than the original way (Agne, 2007)". In light of its purpose to improve a situation, reframing is typically viewed as a positive or at least constructive activity (ibid). For the purpose of achieving communicative objectives, judges might make reframing practice with some specific discourse information processing devices.

5.3.1 Frame Contraction

Frame contraction refers to the process of specifying some frame, in which speakers reframe discourse references through addition or combination of information units while producing discourse information. Frame contraction will show hearers some clearer frames so that hearers can understand the speakers' intention better, or accept the speakers' opinions more easily.

5.3.1.1 Addition of Information Units

In order to make frames of certain legal procedures clearer and more specific, professionals will add information units to help lay participants (e.g. the defendant) understand the unfamiliar legal procedures.

Extract 5-10 (Case 01)

<WB, 相关规定>审判长：根据《最高人民法院、最高人民检察院、司法部关于适用普通程序审理被告人认罪案件的若干意见》的规定，<WC, 自愿认罪>如果被告人自愿认罪，<WP, 从轻处罚>合议庭在对你量刑时从轻处罚，<WP, 简化审>在庭审中简化程序审理。<WA, 是否同意简化审>被告人，是否同意本庭使

Presiding Judge: Based on the regulations in "Opinions on the cases in which summary procedure is applied to make the defendant confess from Supreme People's Court, Supreme People's Procuratorate and Ministry of Justice", if the defendant confesses to be guilty voluntarily, the collegial panel will give you a lighter punishment while measuring

用上述程序对本案进行审理？ <WA，同意简化审>被告人：同意。

penalty. Defendant, do you agree that the court applies above-mentioned procedure to trial?

Defendant: Yes.

Extract 5-11 (Case 18)

<WB，建议>审判长：根据**区人民检察院相关建议，<WT，简化审>本案适用普通程序简化审，<WB，司法解释>根据中华人民共和国，中华人民共和国最⊥最高人民法院，最高人民检察院相关的司法解释，<WP，有罪判决>合议庭在开庭之后可能对你做出有罪判决，<WP，从轻处罚>并根据你的认罪态度酌情从轻处罚，<WA，有无意见>对此你有没意见？

<WB，规定>被告人：没有。

Presiding Judge: Based on the proposal from the People's Procuratorate of ..., summary procedure is applied in the case. According to the relevant judicial interpretation from Supreme People's Court, Supreme People's Procuratorate, the collegial panel may pronounce you guilty after court trial and a mitigated punishment will be given to you at discretion of your attitude toward admission of guilt. Do you disagree with it?

Defendant: No.

Comparing to the judges' proposal of summary procedure in Extract 3-4 and Extract 3-5, the judges reframe the summary procedure through the addition of 3 information units respectively in Extract 5-10 and Extract 5-11 while explaining the legal terms.

In the special context of criminal trials, adding information units has made the frame clearer and more concrete in the defendants' cognition so that defendants can decide whether they agree to apply summary procedure in their cases. In these two extracts, the judges add the information units "相关规定 (relevant regulations)" or "司法解释 (judicial interpretations)", "自愿认罪 (voluntary confession)" or "有罪判决 (guilty judgment)", and "从轻处罚 (a lighter or mitigated punishment)". These information knots are WB, WC and WP respectively, which provide concrete legal basis and conditions for the processing mode.

The sufficient information in the criminal court has reframed summary procedure so clearly that the defendants can understand the legal terms more easily and will make some choices beneficial to themselves in light of their own concrete realities.

In these two extracts, the judges' addition of information units has avoided the phenomenon that defendants are forced to accept summary procedure without sufficient knowledge of the legal procedure, and has made the trial process more reasonable, with the defendant's status in trials promoted.

Extract 5-12 (Case 28)

1 <WB, R, 规定>审判长：三名被告人，根据法律规定，<WJ, R, 告知权利>你们对合议庭的组成人员、书记员以及公诉人享有申请回避的权利。<WF, R, 有无利害关系>也就是说，对于上述这些人员审理你们这个案件，有没有利害关系或者其他关系，<WF, R, 影响公正>影响到对本案的公正处理的，<WP, R, 可以申请>你们可以提出申请，<WP, R, 调换人员>调换其中的人员。

Presiding Judge: The three defendants, based on the relevant laws and regulations, you have the right to claim to withdraw the members of the collegial panel, the reporter and the prosecutor. That's to say, you may apply for the replacement of any member who is possible to impose certain influence upon the justice of court trial due to a stake or other relations with the case.

2 <WT, b, 是否申请回避>审判长：被告人张**，你是否需要申请回避？

Presiding Judge: Defendant Zhang**, do you apply for it?

3 <WT, b, 不要申请回避>张**：不要。

Defendant: No.

In Extract 5-12, the presiding judge reframes to explain to the defendant what is "*申请回避 (to apply for withdrawals)*" through addition of information units after he informs that the defendant enjoys the right to apply for withdrawals.

The judge's discursive device has untied the defendant's difficulty in understanding because he does not know the legal terms. Among the four added information units in Turn 1, the two WF information knots and two WP information knots explain to the defendant his deserved rights as a litigation subject should enjoy. That is, a defendant can make the decision to apply for the change of the members of the prosecution or the judge if he believes there exist some facts influencing the just trial in court. Moreover, all the knowledge categories of these four information units are R. Therefore, not until the judge's sharing the information with him, does the defendant make the decision of "不要申请回避 *(no need for applying for withdrawals)*".

However, in Extract 3-22, the procedural discourse used by the judge gives priority to framing the defendant's disadvantage rather than reframe the "申请回避 *(apply for withdrawals)*" in that the subjectivity of the judge and the objectivity of the defendant reflect the unbalance of discourse power here, i.e. power relations (Yuan, 2008).

It is the chief meaning of presumption of innocence that the defendant is not equal to a criminal (Bian, 2006), so it is essential to add necessary information units to interpret some difficult legal terms in court. The addition of information units will help avoid the use of the powerful word "审 *(try)*" in Extract 3-22, which exerts mental pressure on the defendant because the discourse produced still represents the stance from CPL rather than the judge's individual opinion. After the defendant shares the meaning of the judge's question about "申请回避 *(apply for withdrawals)*", the judge might use a new turn of yes/no question to get the defendant's attitude. Addition of information units will eliminate shared knowledge of "审 *(try)*", frame presumption of innocence and maintain retributive justice in court.

The judges' personalized discursive practice in Extract 5-12 has obeyed the legal spirit and legal rules. According to the regulations by law, no matter whether a defendant understands the meaning of "申请回避 *(apply for withdrawals)*" in the courtroom interaction, judges should have patience to explain the legal terms in order to guarantee the realization of the social significance of judicial justice, to embody that the guarantee of judicial justice is both the beginning and the end of the linguistic expressions in the courtroom interaction (Chen & Huang, 2009).

5.3.1.2 Combination of Information Units

Combination of information units is reframing practice to contract and specify some frame where necessary.

Extract 5-13 (Case 13)

1 <WN, b>审判长：被告人蔺**，你是几点吸食的冰毒？	Presiding Judge: Defendant Lin**, what time did you take in ice?
2 <WN, b>被告人：当天下午。	Defendant: That afternoon.
3 <HW, b>审判长：你是怎么去的**小区？	Presiding Judge: How did you go to ** Community?
4 <HW, b>被告人：从楼外爬空调爬上去的。	Defendant: I climbed from the air conditioner outside the building.
5 <WY, b>审判长：当时你为什么到被害人家里？	Presiding Judge: Why did you come to the victim's house at that time?
6 <WY, b>被告人：产生幻觉，<WY, b>觉得有人追我。	Defendant: I underwent hallucination that someone was chasing me.
7 <WY, b>审判长：你为什么到**小区 701 室？	Presiding Judge: Why did you come into Room ...?
8 <WY, b>被告人：当时产生幻觉了，<WE, c>记不清楚了。	Defendant: I underwent hallucination. I can't remember it clearly.
9 <WF, b>审判长：你到了 701 室都发现什么了？	Presiding Judge: What did you find after you entered Room 701?

10 <WF，b>被告人：发现一个老
太太和一个老头，<WF，b>我
去了之后他们就走了……

Defendant: I found an old woman
and an old man. They left after I
entered.

In Extract 5-13, the presiding judge combines four information units to interrogate the defendant, laying the groundwork for the confirmation of the fact that the defendant entered other's house without permission. Therefore, the judge achieves the communication goal eventually through the verification of the truth with the WF information "*你到了701室都发现什么了？(What did you find after you entered Room 701?)*" in Turn 9.

Firstly, the use of different information knots can make it more efficient to find out the nature of the defendant's behavior from various angles. The defendant's answer to the WN question in Turn 1 has revealed the time at which the defendant took drugs. The period of the lasting time before the crime being committed is essential for the judge to identify whether the drug effect on the defendant's behavior is directly related to the crime committing. The HW information in Turn 3 can help the judge feel out whether the defendant entered the community in a normal way. But the answer to the question shows that the defendant's behavior was abnormal as he "*从楼外爬空调爬上去的 (entered the community by climbing some air-conditioners on the buildings)*".

The two WY information knots in Turns 5 and 7 represent the repetitive information with different expressions for the purpose of confirming the reason and motivation for which the defendant entered other's house. Through the questioning, the court has mastered enough information on the defendant's abnormal behavior, so the presiding judge asks the WF question in Turn 9 eventually to make sure that the defendant did enter other's house in which he did see the witnesses "*老太太 (the old woman)*" and "*老头 (the old man)*".

Secondly, the same knowledge category b in all the judge's questions is used to receive the defendant's description of his own behavior so that the collegial panel will recognize the defendant's psychological state and factual behavior at the time when the crime was committed. It is obvious that the drug effect resulted in the defendant's illegal entry into other's house.

Thirdly, the combination of information knots and knowledge categories can help all the parties in the court reconstruct the event of the case cognitively, as the combination of various information units has formed an interlocked information chain. This information chain reframes the truth that the defendant did break into other's house in the case.

The analysis shows that the combination of information units in this extract makes turns distributed sufficiently and reasonably in the interrogation, the questioning from various angles specifies the frame of the nature of the defendant's behavior clearly. The combination embodies distributive justice and provides a feasible discursive device to verify the truth of a case objectively in the reconstruction of PDJ relationship.

Extract 5-14 (Case 33)

<WY，O，发现柜员机异常>审判长: 鉴于许**是在发现银行自动柜员机出现异常后产生犯意，<HW，O，持卡取钱>采用持卡窃取金融机构经营资金的手段，<WJ，O，性质差异>其行为与有预谋或者采取破坏手段盗窃金融机构的犯罪有所不同；<WY，O，主观恶性不大>从案发具有一定偶然性看，许**犯罪的主观恶性尚不是很大。<WB，

Presiding Judge: In light of the fact that it was after finding there was something wrong with the ATM that Xu** formed an evil idea to commit the crime. Then he stole business fund of the financial institution by using his bank card. His behavior is different from those who steal the financial institution with premeditation or with a destructive means. Based on a certain occasionality of the case,

A，危害程度>根据本案具体的犯罪事实、犯罪情节和对于社会的危害程度，<WJ，A，判处刑罚>对许**可在法定刑以下判处刑罚。<WB，A，依据法规>依照《中华人民共和国刑法》第二百六十四条、第六十三条第二款、第六十四条和最高人民法院《关于审理盗窃案件具体应用法律若干问题的解释》第三条、第八条的规定，<WT，A，判决>判决如下：

<WJ，A，盗窃罪>一、被告人许**犯盗窃罪，<WP，A，五年徒刑>**判处有期徒刑五年**，<WP，A，罚金>**并处罚金二万元。**……<WP，A，追缴所得>二、追缴被告人许**的犯罪所得173826元，发还受害单位。

Xu** was not strongly subjectively malicious. In accordance with the concrete facts, the plot of the crime and the social harm, Xu** can be punished less seriously than the legally prescribed punishment. Based on Article 264, Item 2, Article 63, Article 64 of Criminal Law of the People's Republic of China and Article 3 and Article 8 in "Interpretations of several issues on specific application of laws in trial of theft cases", the court sentences as follows: Firstly, Defendant Xu** has committed crime of theft. **Thus, he is sentenced a 5-year imprisonment and fined the sum of RMB 20,000.** Secondly, the defendant Xu**'s illegal gains, RMB173, 826, is to be recovered and returned to the victim bank.

Different from that in the first instance of the same case (see Extract 4-20), the judgment in the second instance has been made after the judge integrates 4 different information units.

From the jurisprudential perspective, the defendant must have committed the crime of theft as the constituents of the crime are distinct. However, in spite of the defendant's subjective intention, the malfunction of the automatic teller machine (ATM) should be attributed to the responsibility of the bank, which has been embodied by the combination of three information units (information knots: WY, HW and WJ) in the extract.

The WY information "发现柜员机异常 (find there was something

wrong with the ATM)" indicates that the malfunction of the ATM was the direct reason for which the defendant drew much more money than that he owned. The HW information demonstrates that the defendant did not break into the bank to steal but rather "持卡取钱 *(drew money by using his bank card)"*.

Meanwhile, the WJ information "性质差异 *(different in nature)"* proves that the defendant behaved without premeditated malice and without the ill will to destroy the bank, a financial institution. The knowledge category is O in the three information units, so the combination provides efficient support for the extenuation of the defendant's crime.

Moreover, based on the contingency of the case, the WY information "主观恶性不大 *(without much subjective malice)"* *is* produced to extenuate the crime. The knowledge category of this unit is O (known to all) has also supported the mitigation of the defendant's crime.

Finally, some relevant regulations have been added to the basis of the judgment, which means that the normal crime cannot be the legal basis for the conviction and weighing of Punishment.

The combination of the information units above has reframed the defendant's behavior, bringing forth relative reasonable judgment and maintaining retributive justice.

According to the analysis above, in the process of reconstructing PDJ relationship, judges make full use of frame contraction to give the defendant clear explanation of specialized issues, or pave roads for the confirmation of the facts in a case, so the strategy from generalization to specification is advantageous in the maintenance of procedural justice, distributive justice or retributive justice.

5.3.2 Frame Expansion

Frame expansion refers to a speaker's strategy while articulating discourse information for reframing discourse references. Through deletion of redundant information or assimilation of information units, frame expansion can remove the information which specifies certain frame. Frame expansion will avoid the development of discourse information confined to a specified scope.

5.3.2.1   Deletion of Redundant Information

According to presumption of innocence, unquestionable certainty of evidence guarantees the identification of the defendant's guilt; otherwise, the evidence can only be regarded as the legal fact of the defendant's innocence (Zhang, 2000). Before presenting and challenging evidence, discourse information relevant to presumption of guilt can be eliminated to generalize the frame of the fact in a case to maintain justice towards defendants.

Extract 5-15 (Case 19)

<WF，b>审判长：被告人王**，检察院起诉书所指控的是否是事实？	Presiding Judge: Defendant Wang**, is the content charged in the procuratorate's indictment the fact?

Compared with Extract 3-12, Extract 3-18, Extract 3-25 and Extract 4-3, the judge's interrogation in Extract 5-15 eradicates the redundant information.

As the procedural discourse information is produced by presiding judges just after prosecutors read out indictments, the catchphrase "犯罪事实 (criminal facts)" is often used to interrogate defendants whether they accept the indictments. Since the principle of presumption of innocence cannot definitely hinder the confirmation of a defendant's guilt unless no sufficient evidence is provided in court (Bian & Yang, 2006: 13), it is unnecessary for judges to use such catchphrase with the meaning of presumption of guilt too often. Now that the information before the judges' interrogation cannot confirm the defendant's guilt, why the two Chinese characters "犯罪 (crime)" with the redundant information cannot be eliminated?

In Extract 5-15, the judge has articulated an information unit with the information knot WF and the knowledge category b to expand the frame of the fact in the indictment. Because the deletion of the redundant information from "犯罪 (crime)" has generalized the "事实 (facts)" and made no shared information with presumption of guilt exist. Thus, the frame expansion has avoided presumption of the defendant's guilt and maintained procedural justice and retributive justice in the reconstruction of PDJ relationship.

Except that it is used as a device in procedural discourse, deletion of redundant information can also be employed in judges' substantive discourse to reframe some legal facts. For example,

Extract 5-16 (Case 35)

1 <WF>审判长：被告人，你牵头进行集资前，是否通过中国人民银行审批？

Presiding Judge: Defendant, you took the lead in raising capital, was it permitted by People's Bank of China?

2 <WF>被告人：没有。

Defendant: No.

3 <WY>审判长：那你负责集资是处于什么考虑？

Presiding Judge: Why were you responsible for raising capital?

4 <WY>被告人：看到社会上很多集资的，<WJ>就想着我们也可以做。

Defendant: I found that lots of people had raised capital, so I wanted to do in this way.

While interrogating the defendant in Extract 5-16, the judge avoids some redundant information of presuming guilt, which exists in Extract 3-15.

The two extracts have many similarities: both are substantive discourse extracted from the data in the cases of "illegal capital raising"; both are the discourse information for fact investigation before the stage of presenting and challenging evidence; neither of the cases is heard through summary procedure. According to the principle of presumption of innocence, the identification of a defendant's guilt must reach a certainty degree to which "no doubt" exists in the judges' confirmation; if it does not reach the degree, only can the evidence serve as a legal fact to prove the defendant's innocence (Zhang, 2000). Since presenting and challenging evidence does not start, there is no evidence proving the defendant's guilt.

Through the transmission of the substantive discourse information in Extract 3-15, the judge aims to confirm the two facts: WF information "<钱数> (the sum of money raised)" and WN information "<开始和持续时间> (the time when the capital raising starts and the length of the time)". However, the information " 非法 (illegal)" in the questions has specified the frame of the fact "集资 (capital raising)". Now that no information on the same level before the presenting and challenging the evidence becomes the prerequisite to prove the defendant's guilt, the presupposed information " 非法 (illegal)" is redundant.

However, the judge in Extract 5-16 expands the frame of "集资 (capital raising)", which has become more general than that in Extract 3-15. The judge has deleted the information "非法 (illegal)" in the WF information in Turn 1 and the WY information in Turn 3. The judge has not framed the fact "集资 (capital raising)" as the illegal behavior before the incontestable evidence is presented.

Therefore, deletion of redundant information has been proved to help judges avoid presumption of guilt.

5.3.2.2　Assimilation of Information Units

Assimilation of information units refers to a reframing process, in which speakers integrate the specific and general information.

Extract 5-17 (Case 15)
1 <WT, T, 上车>审判长：那么你这 Presiding Judge: Then, you got

个，就上了那辆车，(0.5)<WF，b，是否带刀>那么你上去的时候，刀带了没有？

2 <WF，b，带刀>被告人：刀带了。

3 <WF，c，带刀上车>审判长：刀带了。<WT，b，何行为>刀带了以后，实施了什么行为吗？

4 <WT，b>被告人：我就上去，上车了就讲，快开车，<WT，b>我讲快开车，不关你的事，<WT，b>我讲现在警察追我，<WF，b>我也讲不清了，<WT，b>把我带到一个没人的地方就够了。

5 <WF，b，是否刀顶司机颈部>审判长：起诉书上描述是用刀顶住了驾驶员的颈部，**这个是不是事实啊？**

6 <WF，b，顶过>被告人：这个，也顶上顶过吧。

7 <WF，b，顶过>审判长：顶过啊？

8 <WF，b>被告人：嗯，对。

9 <WF，b，车速>审判长：那么你们这个开车的速度啊，有多快？

10 <WF，b，车速不快>被告人：速度不快。

11 <WF，c，车速不快>审判长：你们的速度不快，<WF，b，车速码数>大概有几码？

12 <WF，b，不好判断>被告人：这个不好判断。

13 <WA，c，同意>审判长：好。

14 <WF，b，码数>被告人：大概，也就二三十码吧。

into the car; (0.5) did you take the knife when you got into the car?

Defendant: Yes.

Presiding Judge: You took the knife. What did you do after that?

Defendant: I got into the car, then I asked the driver to drive faster and it was none of his business. I said that the police were chasing me. I can't say clearly now, and I asked him to take me to a place where there was nobody else.

Presiding Judge: The indictment describes that you pushed against the driver's neck with the knife. **Is it true?**

Defendant: oh, yes.

Presiding Judge: Yes?

Defendant: Yes.

Presiding Judge: Then, How fast was the car?

Defendant: Not very fast.

Presiding Judge: You didn't drive very fast. How many miles per hour?

Defendant: It was hard to tell.

Presiding Judge: Ok.

Defendant: Maybe 20-30 miles per hour.

15 <WF，c，码数>审判长：二三十码，<WF，b，码数概念>你知道二三十概念是多少吗？

Presiding Judge: 20-30 miles per hour? Do you know what 20-30 miles means?

16 <WF，b，知晓>被告人：这个我知道三四十码的概念是多少，<WB，b，市区车多>毕竟市区，毕竟车辆多嘛。

Defendant: I know it. There was too much traffic in the urban area after all.

17 <WF，b，头脑是否清醒>审判长：你当时的时候，脑子清楚吗？

Presiding Judge: Were you well conscious at that moment?

18 <WF，b，当时不知道>被告人：当时是不知道。

Defendant: I was not clear at that time.

19 <WF，c，不清楚>审判长：不清楚。<WY，b，如何知晓>不清楚，那你怎么知道开得有多快？

Presiding Judge: Not clear? Then, how did you know how fast you drove?

20 <WY，b，凭感觉>被告人：因为感觉是嘛，<WB，b，坐车多>坐车比较多，<WJ，b，凭感觉>感觉有，大概有这么多。

Defendant: Because I often took a car, I could feel how fast it was.

Extract 5-17 involves the case in which the defendant's behavior of carjacking by knife-wielding resulted from his own illusion after taking drugs that someone would injure him. In this extract, the judge has not directly made an interrogation of the defendant's concrete carjacking information but rather expanded the frame through assimilating information units. In the whole interrogating process without presumption of guilt, the judge's carefulness and patience have brought the defendant's voluntary confession his behavior.

The presiding judge assimilates 6 information units in order to find out whether the defendant touched the driver's neck with a kitchen knife. The assimilation has integrated some isolated frames into an expanded whole, which brings the truth of the facts.

The presiding judge firstly uses the WT information "<上车> (got *into the car)"* and the WF information *"<是否带刀> (took a kitchen knife or not)"* in Turn 1 to confirm the defendant's behavior. After the defendant answers, the presiding judge integrates several foregoing information units into a whole. In the process of assimilating information units, the knowledge categories shift from T or C (the information known to both the parties) to b (the information known to the hearer), and then to c (he information known to both the parties). Consequently, a sub-frame *"被告人带刀上车 (The defendant got into a car with a kitchen knife.)"* has been constructed.

Then the presiding judge wants to reframe the fact whether the defendant threatened the driver with a kitchen knife after getting into the car with the WT information *"<何行为> (what behavior)"* in Turn 3 and the WF information *"<是否刀顶司机颈部> (pushed against the driver's neck with a knife or not)"* in Turn 5. The former is a WH-question for the defendant's description of what happened after his getting into the car, so the defendant has articulated some opening responsive discourse information (4 WT information knots and 1 WF information knots). The latter is two yes/no questions used to interrogate the defendant whether he will accept the description in the indictment for the confirmation and the reconfirmation of the facts. In the assimilation of information units, the knowledge category is b (the information known to the hearer) and no information known to both the parties is expressed with declarative sentences so that the judge can reframe after the defendant's cautious identification.

In one word, the integration of the two actions *"带刀上车 (got into the car with a kitchen knife)"* and *"用刀顶司机颈部 (pushed against the driver's neck with the kitchen knife)"* has expanded the frame of the legal fact through the presiding judge's assimilating the information units.

In order to investigate whether the defendant was clear-headed, the presiding judge has expanded the frame by means of assimilation of 9 information units in the last half of Extract 5-17, which protects the defendant's rights.

The presiding judge firstly interrogates the defendant about the car speed with 2 WF information knots with the knowledge category as b (the information known to the hearer) in Turns 9 and 11 so that he can confirm whether the defendant was clear-minded at that time. When the defendant responds with "<车速不快> (low speed)" in Turn 10 and "<不好判断> (unable to tell)" in Turn 12, the presiding judge repeats or accepts the defendant's answers with WF and WA information knots in Turns 11 and 13, with the knowledge category is c (the information known to both parties). Therefore, the defendant's description has been identified.

Then, after the defendant voluntarily speaks out the car speed without being interrogated, the judge immediately makes a confirmation. To maintain judicial justice, the judge then utilizes WF information in Turn 17 and WY information in Turn 19 to investigate whether the defendant was clear-headed and interrogate about the bases on which the defendant can have told the car's speed. Without any subjective comments on the defendant's statement in the whole interaction, the presiding judge makes a confirmation of the information transmitted by the defendant himself with repetitive discourse information.

Hence, in the interaction the information offered by the defendant resulting from the frame expansion has laid the groundwork for the decision made by the collegial panel.

Different from Extract 3-23 in which specific word "刺 (stab)" is always grasped by the presiding judge in order to contract the frame of the defendant's action, the judge in Extract 5-17 integrates the defendant's actions decomposed into a whole framing process. In other words, the presiding judge has not constructed a specific frame of the defendant's actions with such information units of presuming guilt as "持刀劫车 *(carjacking by knife-wielding)*" in the whole interaction. Therefore, the defendant in the position of litigation subject enjoys sufficient discursive power and distributive justice in court has been maintained.

In a word, the strategy from specification to generalization leads to judges' removal of redundant factors that presume defendants' guilt.

5.3.3   Frame Negotiation

Frame negotiation refers to a strategy that a speaker reframes discourse reference by means of alteration of information knots, repetition of information units or sharing of information units in order to create the conformity between the frames in both the speaker's and the hearer's cognition, which brings smooth communication and helps achieve a certain communicative goal. Frame negotiation is typically embodied as a discursive strategy by which a speaker solves some dialectic or conflicts between institutional frames and socio-relational frames for talk (Coupland, Robinson & Coupland, 1994). In the criminal courtroom interaction, judges might try to make their counterparts collaborate in and negotiate the work of entering an apparently rational frame of talk for the realization of communicative goal.

5.3.3.1   Alteration of Information Knots

To solve conflicts between specific frames in the interaction, a speaker takes the device of altering information knots actively to reframe discourse reference in order that a hearer can accept the speaker's frame or actively provide the information needed by the speaker. In criminal trials, judges require the information offered by both the prosecution and the defense to reconstruct the events. Any discourse used to interrogate defendants more intensively or threaten defendants will violate judicial justice and hinder the construction of rational PDJ relationship, while flexible alteration of information knots will provide defendants with sufficient opportunities to speak so that the conflicts between institutional and individual frames can be smoothed.

Extract 5-18 (Case 29)

1 <WA，b>审判长：被告人刘**，你对起诉书指控的事实有没有意见？

Presiding Judge: Defendant Liu**, do you have any objections to the facts in the indictment?

2 <WF，b>刘**：没有打人。

Defendant Liu: I didn't beat others.

3 <WF，c>审判长：没有打人是吧，<WF，b>那同案人有没有打？

Presiding Judge: You didn't beat others? Did your accomplice do?

4 <WF，b>刘**：同案人打了，<WF，b>还有几个跑掉了，<WF，b>他们打了。<WF，b>在车子上，他们抓住我，<WF，b>也打了我。<WY，b>我眼都花了，<WE，b>都看不清有没有打人。

Defendant Liu: My accomplice did. Others ran away and they beat as well. In the car, they caught me and beat me dazzling. I couldn't see clearly. How could I beat others?

5 <WF，b>审判长：那第二被告有没有打？

Presiding Judge: Did the second defendant beat others?

6 <WF，b>刘**：第二被告有没有打我看不见，<WY，b>因为我已经被按在地上了。……

Defendant Liu: I couldn't see it because I was flung to the floor.

7 <WF，c>审判长：那你现在说围过去，<WF，c>你现在说你围过去，<WF，c>刚才我问你你又说没有围，<WF，c>那时候被警察抓住按在地上。<WF，b>那究竟是怎么回事？<WF，c>你现在说自己围过去，是吧？<WF，b>究竟是哪个

Presiding Judge: You say now you pushed forward, but I asked you just now and you said no. Why did the police fling you to the floor? You say now you pushed forward, right? **Which on earth is the fact?** Just now

是事实？<WF, c>你刚才说给人抓住了按在地上。

8 <WF, b>叶**：我是在最后边的，<WE, b>所以我是一个人被抓住了。

9 <WF, b>审判长：围过去被人抓住是吧？<WF，b>**是不是围过去的时候被人抓住？**

10 <WF，b>叶**：是。<WF，b>我正准备过去，<WY, b>因为我走在最后边，<WE, b>所以就把我抓住了，<WE, b>我就没有打他。……

you said you were flung to the floor. ...

Defendant Ye: I was the last one, so I was caught alone.

Presiding Judge: Were you caught by the police when you rushed forward? **Is that right?**

Defendant Ye: Yes. I get ready to go there. Because I was the last one, I was caught. I didn't beat him. ...

The extract can be divided into two parts for analysis, in which the two halves are about the judge's interrogation of the defendant Liu and the defendant Ye respectively. Contrasting to the discourse information in Extract 3-24 and Extract 3-25, Extract 5-18 exemplifies that the judge's alteration of information knots has reframed the defendant's actions as the frame conflict has been ironed out reasonably.

The first frame conflict solved by the judge originates from the different frames constructed respectively by the accusation in the indictment and the defendant's response to the indictment read out. Different from the judge's utilization of WT information knots "你不要说别的，你现在只能回答是与不是。(Don't say anything else. Now you can only answer with "Yes" or "No".)" to interrupt the defendant in Extract 3-25, the judge in Extract 5-18 accepts the defendant's opinion with two WF information knots in Turn 3 immediately after the defendant expresses his objection to the accusation in the indictment. Then he interrogates the defendant about the other defendants' actions at the crime scene with WF information knots in Turns 3 and 5. In the interaction, the defendant has provided several WF information knots, 2 WY information knots and 1 WE information knot. Attributed to the presiding judge's opening questioning, these information units have reframed the defendant's action so clearly that the presiding judge can smooth the first frame conflict by reconstruction of the defendant's action.

The second frame conflict ended by the judge results from the inconsistency in the defendant's description. Different from the judge in Extract 3-24 forces the defendant to accept his framing with WA information knots, the judge in Extract 5-18 firstly uses WF information knots in Turn 7 to describe the defendant's inconsistent frames when the conflict results from the defendant's contradictory fact description. And then he investigates the truth with WF information knots "究竟是哪个是事实? (Which on earth is the fact?)" in Turn 7 and "冲过去被人抓住是吧? (Were you caught by the police when you rushed forward?)" in Turn 9. In the interaction, the judge has not forced the defendant to accept his framing. Consequently, such much information has been gained to frame the defendant's actions that the frame conflict is solved.

Therefore, alteration of information knots can be another discursive strategy to construct rational PDJ relationship. In Extract 3-24 and Extract 3-25, the judge misuses his power to damage the defendant's rights as discourse is a locus of power (Conley & O'Barr, 1998). However, the judge in Extract 5-18 changes WT information knot into WF to accept the facts provided by the defendant and asks questions with WF information knots to make dialogic expansion (Yuan, 2007). That is to say, the defendant enjoys the opportunity to describe the legal facts in detail. This has avoided power relations between the judge and the defendant but realize solidarity relations between them, i.e. the frame of inequality shifts to the one of equality. The shared information of presumption of guilt will be eliminated and distributive justice can be kept.

5.3.3.2 Repetition of Information Units

Repetition of information units is also a feasible discursive device to solve frame conflict in communication. When the frame constructed by judges' institutional discourse information occasionally conflicts with that constructed in the other parties' social or individual cognition, judges who manipulate the trials might adopt repetition of information units to dissolve the contradiction and solve the problem.

Extract 5-19 (Case 17)

1 <WF，b，有无证据>审判长：被告人蓝**关于本案事实部分你有没有证据需要向法庭提供？<WF，b，有无证据>**有没有**？<WT，b，是否听清>蓝** 听清楚了没有？

Presiding Judge: Defendant Lan**, do you have any evidence relevant to the facts in the case to show in court? **Do you have any?** Lan**, are you clear about it?

2 <WF，b，不知道>被告人：我不知道这个事情。

Defendant: I don't know it.

3 <WT，c，指控>审判长：公诉人指控你犯有盗窃罪，<WT，c，控方证据>向法庭出示了被害人的陈述、有关银行的对账单据、有关录像的截图资料等，<WJ，b，是否有罪>**那么你认为你犯罪比较轻或者没有犯罪**？<WF，b，有无证据>**这些证据有没有**？

Presiding Judge: You are accused guilty of crime of theft by the prosecutor. The prosecutor has presented to the court the victim's statement, some relevant bank statements and screenshots from the relevant video recordings. **Then, do you think you have committed a less serious crime or you are innocent? Do you have such evidence?**

4 <WF，b，有罪>被告人：有犯罪。

Defendant: I've really committed a crime.

5 <WA，b，确认是否有罪>审判长：你认为自己犯罪了？

Presiding Judge: You mean you've really committed a crime?

6 <WA，b，是>被告人：是。　　Defendant: Yes.

7 <WF，b，有无证据>审判长：　Presiding Judge: **Do you have any**
有没有证据向法庭举证，　**evidence to present in court? Yes or**
<WF，b，有无证据>有还是没　**no?**
有?

8 <WF，b，无>被告人：没有。　Defendant: No.

Frame conflict in Extract 5-19 arises from the contradiction between the judge's institutional discourse information and the defendant's individual cognitive information. Through three rounds of repeating information units, the judge's strategy of frame negotiation has contributed to the frame agreement and dissolved the frame conflict.

In the first round, when interrogating the defendant about the evidence, the judge uses the WF information "<有无证据> *(any evidence or not)*" in Turn 1 consecutively in order to avoid the frame conflict resulting from the defendant's difficulty in comprehension. However, the frame conflict still exists as the defendant gives an irrelevant answer with the information unit "我不知道这个事情。*(I don't know it.)*" in Turn 2. Both the knowledge categories of the judge's repetition are b (the information known to the hearer), so no discourse information with guilt presumption or forcible tone here conforms to the requirements of procedural questioning and promotes the maintenance of procedural justice.

Facing the defendant who cannot comprehend the interrogation, at the second round the judge repeats the information unit for the second time to ask the defendant patiently whether he has any evidence to prove "犯罪比较轻或者没有犯罪 *(lighter guilt or innocence)*", integrating addition of information units. To make the defendant understand the following questions more easily, the judge adds the accusation of the prosecution and the evidence presented by the prosecutor with 2 WT information knots. Then the judge changes to adopt an alternative question to interrogate about the defendant's opinion on his own actions and repeat the WF information "<有无证据> (any evidence or not)" in Turn 3 once more. Because typical alternative questions have some functional characteristics in cognition (Sun & Xie, 2006), the defendant can choose one from the clear frames constructed by the judge's questions with only two alternatives. As a matter of fact, the defendant immediately answers the alternative question with the WF information "我有罪。 (I am guilty.)" in Turn 4 because the difficulty in answering has been reduce greatly. However, since the defendant has not answered the judge's questioning information "<有无证据> (any evidence or not)" yet, the frame conflict still exists.

Thirdly, in order to iron out the frame conflict successfully, the presiding judge takes the trouble to repeat the WF information "<有无证据> (any evidence or not)" in Turn 7 two more times, which has eventually brought the defendant' answer relevant to the issue. According to Tannen (2007: 58-59), repetition allows a speaker to set up a the frame for the new information which stands ready, rather than having to be newly formulated on the one hand; it also facilitates comprehension by providing semantically less dense discourse on the other hand. So the defendant's comprehension benefit of the judge's repetition of the information unit mirrors his production of the response relevant to the question.

Since it can foreground and intensify the frames needed (ibid, 2007: 60), judges can certainly utilize repetition of information units to reconstruct rational PDJ relationship rather than produce inequality between the defense and the prosecution.

5.3.3.3 Sharing of Information Units

In the interaction, sharing of information units is often adopted by speakers to solicit hearers' opinions while preventing frame conflicts. This discursive device can help judges in criminal trials maintain procedural justice and promote the reconstruction of rational PDJ relationship.

Extract 5-20 (Case 30)

1 <WB，R，相关规定>审判长：根据……的规定，<WC，R，自愿认罪>如果……，<WP，R，从轻处罚>……，<WP，R，简化审>……。<WY，Z，无异议>鉴于被告人车**对基本犯罪事实没有异议，<WY，Z，自愿认罪>且自愿认罪，<WP，R，提议简化审>合议庭将采用普通程序简化审理。<WA，b>**公诉人是否同意**？	Presiding Judge: Based on… regulations, if … Since Defendant Che** has no objections to the basic criminal facts and he is willing to confess his guilt. The collegial panel will apply summary procedure in the trial of the case. **Prosecutor, do you agree with it?**
2 <WA，b>公诉人：同意。	Prosecutor: Yes.
3 <WA，b>审判长：**辩护人是否同意**？	Presiding Judge: **Defender, do you agree with it?**
4 <WA，b>辩护人：同意。	Defender: Yes.
5 <WA，b>审判长：**被告人是否同意**？	Presiding Judge: **Defendant, do you agree with it?**
6 <WA，b>被告人：同意。	Defendant: Yes.
7 <WT，A>审判长：合议庭采用普通程序简化审理……	Presiding Judge: The collegial panel applies summary procedure in the trial of the case.

In Extract 5-20, the judge's sharing of information units has avoided the procedural injustice resulting from the discourse information in Extract 4-17.

Firstly, the presiding judge reframes summary procedure with the WB information "<*相关规定*> (relevant regulations)", the WC information "<*自愿认罪*> (voluntary confession)", and the WP information "<*从轻处罚*> (mitigated punishment)" in Turn 1. Secondly, according to the reframing above and based on certain legal facts, the presiding judge makes a decision to "*<提议简化审> (propose the application of summary procedure)*" in Turn 1. Specifically speaking, this proposal is put forward based on the WY information "*<被告人无异议> (The defendant has no objections.)*" and the WY information "*<被告人自愿认罪> (The defendant confesses his crime voluntarily.)*". Then, with 3 consecutive WA information knots in Turns 1, 3 and 5, the presiding judge seeks all the other parties' opinion on the application of summary procedure by means of sharing information units with them. At last, the presiding judge declares the application after all the other parties agree.

But in Extract 4-17, the judge does not solicit the litigants' opinion in court but rather decides directly to apply summary procedure just based on the suggestion given by the People's Procuratorate, that is, "*<WP, A>本案适用普通程序简化审。(The present case applies summary procedure.)*". Therefore, comparatively speaking, sharing of information units in Extract 5-20 ensures that the litigants can fully exercise their rights and judicial justice can be maintained.

5.4   Summary

Based on the current PDJ relationship constructed and the factors influencing the construction analyzed in the foregoing two chapters, Chapter 5 has suggested some framing strategies via judges' discursive devices for the reconstruction of PDJ relationship in criminal courts. Footing shifts and reframing constitute the strategies developed by judges' discourse information processing.

1) Data analysis shows that judges' footing shifts in a right way at the appropriate time will help construct rational PDJ relationship. Judges' footing can be categorized as "animator", "animator + author", or "animator + author + principal" while judges play quite a few roles

in the criminal courtroom such as organizer, fact investigator, educator and so on.

2) Judges' footing shifts in a right way at the appropriate time will help construct rational PDJ relationship. While articulating procedural discourse to maintain procedural justice, judges should not take their footings as "animator + author + principal" representing their own opinions on cases, their own perception of justice and their own ideology, but rather "animator" of the court, of the law and of the nation without discourse information implying presumption of guilt.

3) As another strategy, reframing involves frame contraction, frame expansion and frame negotiation, which avail to maintain procedural justice, distributive justice or retributive justice in the reconstruction of PDJ relationship.

Both the strategies are developed by means of judges' appropriate discourse information processing, embodied by specific discursive devices as follows:

a) The displacement of information levels or the modification of knowledge categories contributes to the judges' footing shifts to avoid distributive injustice.

b) Addition of information units and combination of information units constitute the specific discursive devices for frame contraction, in which the former device can help follow procedural justice in the reconstruction of PDJ relationship and the latter avails to maintain distributive or retributive justice.

c) Frame can be expanded by deletion of redundant information or assimilation of information units, which are beneficial to avoid procedural injustice or distributive injustice respectively.

d) Frame negotiation can be achieved by alteration of knowledge categories, repetition or sharing of information units, in which the former device can distribute equal discourse power to both the prosecution and the defense and the latter is of great importance in the maintenance of procedural justice.

The findings above display that judges' reconstruction of PDJ relationship based on judicial justice can be accomplished through framing strategies developed by judges' specific discursive devices in criminal courts. The rational relationship can be called a "regular-triangled" PDJ relationship, which is manifested as PD balance with the neutral judge. The relationship is not completely corresponding to the one in western countries because it must be constructed in China's legal context. Data analysis has also demonstrated that such core parts in frame theory as footing shifts and (re)framing can be realized by specific and concrete modes of discourse information transmission in the interactive process.

Chapter 6

Conclusion

This chapter presents a brief summary of the reported research to answer the three research questions raised in Chapter 1. Then it discusses the theoretical and practical implications concerning the bearings that this information-based frame analysis may have on PDJ relationship and judicial justice research for academic interest. Finally it also takes up the limitations of the current research.

6.1   Summary of the Present Study

Our objective is to explore how judges construct PDJ relationship through their discourse processing. The whole process of information-based frame analysis focuses mainly on interpreting the relations between judges' discourse and judicial justice in court proceedings.

The study begins with the definition of the working terms. Based on the research background and the research objective, Chapter 1 has also raised three research questions which necessitate being answered to solve the legal issue we have identified. In Chapter 2, by visiting and integrating frame analysis and relevant analytical tools, we derive a conceptual framework of frame analysis, which provides a theoretical guide for the solutions of the research issue. And we have also configured an analytical framework for exploring PDJ relationship, which guides the subsequent analyses and discussions on the discourse processing and framing strategies employed by judges when they interact with other parties in criminal court. Chapter 3 has made a descriptive analysis of judges' discourse information in the framing process. Special light has been shed on the manifestation of PDJ relationship on different dimensions of judges' discourse information processing. The jurisprudential and information statistical analysis has also made for the discovery of current PDJ relationship. Chapter 4 analyzes various variables affecting the judges' choice of framing strategies and language devices. Those variables have revealed judges' discourse information processing leads to the observation or the violation of judicial justice on the three dimensions, which relate directly to the PDJ relationship. Chapter 5 turns to judges' framing strategies in reconstructing PDJ relationship. Those strategies have been induced mostly from contrastive data analysis, during which concrete discursive devices have been explored in judges' trial framing. In a word, discourse analysis in all the three chapters has been made integrated with the jurisprudential analysis. The final chapter brings the research to a conclusion, summarizing the overview of the research, answering the research questions, presenting the implications and pointing out some limitations.

6.2   Conclusions

With the data analysis and the findings in the foregoing chapters, we are now able to conclude the research by answering the research questions set out at the beginning of this study.

The first research question is: *What manifestations of PDJ relationship are framed by judges' discourse in the criminal courtroom interaction?*

By categorizing judges' discourse as declarative information, directive information, confirmative information and expressive information on such three dimensions as monologue, dialogue and questioning, information-based frame analysis has been conducted integrated with context analysis. Special attention has been paid to interactive frames and framing.

With the jurisprudential and statistic support, data analysis shows that judges construct PDJ relationship in the courtroom interaction. In the interactive process of various frames, PDJ relationship may be manifested by PJ cooperation, PD inequality, judges' presumption of guilt and so forth. Therefore, the irrational PDJ relationship has sometimes been constructed by judges in the criminal courtroom even if the order of main trial procedures has never been destroyed.

The second research question is: *What factors influence the construction of PDJ relationship in judges' courtroom discourse practice?*

In addition to interactive frames and framing, footing shifts are scrutinized in the examination of various factors affecting the construction of PDJ relationship. The study has made at the micro-level (information units, turn-taking and so on), at the meso-level (social relations) and at the macro-level (cognitive factors).

Data analysis reveals that some factors influence procedural justice: judges' standing, judges' neutral position and judges' trust in the litigants; the factors affecting distributive justice consist of judges' goals and motivation, attitudes towards the litigants, perceptions of PDJ relationship, and their ideologies, social relations and situations; and the factors influencing retributive justice contain deserving punishment, criminals punished, punishment means and punishment severity embodied in judges' framing process.

The third research question is: *How are framing strategies employed by judges to construct PDJ relationship?*

To answer the third question, we focus on the exploratory analysis of judges' discourse information. How judges employ framing strategies has been anatomized through analyzing information units, information levels, information knots and knowledge categories. Contrastive analysis shows that specific information processing has become judges' discursive devices to reconstruct PDJ relationship.

Data analysis demonstrates that footing shifts and reframing constitute judges' framing strategies in the reconstruction of PDJ relationship. Footing shifts can be accomplished by degradation or displacement of information levels, and modification of knowledge categories. Footing shifts benefit judges' avoidance of guilt presumption or distributive injustice. In the process of reframing to maintain judicial justice, addition or combination of information units can specify certain frames; deletion of redundant information or assimilation of information units helps to generalize certain frames; while alteration of information knots, and repetition or sharing of information units conduce to frame negotiation.

By answering the above research questions, we have fulfilled the general research objective, i.e. **to study how judges construct rational PDJ relationship in the discursive way while performing their duty in China's courtroom.** With the analytical framework constructed and data analysis guided by this framework, we are now in a position to conclude that judges' appropriate footing shifts and reframing in an appropriate way constitute effective means to avoid the violation of judicial justice in the reconstruction of a "regular-triangled" PDJ relationship in China's legal context.

6.3 Implications

The present research is interdisciplinary in nature, involving the issues of language and law. Therefore, the implications are twofold, i.e. theoretical implications for forensic linguistics and legal studies and practical implications for law practitioners in general and judges in particular.

Theoretically, the analytical framework, constructed on the basis of the established theory and analytical tools, i.e. Frame Theory, Tree Information Structure of Legal Discourse and context analysis, proves to be an effective linguistic analytical framework for the description, analysis, and interpretation of judges' courtroom discourse. It is hoped that this framework makes contributions to the research of forensic linguistics, especially to the analysis of courtroom interactions.

Interactive frames, footing shifts and framing have been integrated, which constitute the three constituents of frame analysis. The identification and characterization of frames, the categorization and shifts of footings, and the process and strategies of framing are all mainly attributed to the analysis of discourse information processing in the courtroom interaction. Generally speaking, just one or two aspects of frame analysis have always been involved in practical adoption. However, we hope that the analytical framework can provide a tool for the comprehensive and tridimensional interactive frame analysis of courtroom discourse since the framework can be introduced to probe deeply into legal issues and be hopefully put forward concrete means to solve legal problems.

In a word, the analytical framework is hoped to be applied in legal studies as a supplement to the legal theories to address some legal issues from the linguistic perspective.

Practically, the present study proposes explicitly judges' reconstruction of PDJ relationship in China's courtroom. This proposal is in line with the undergoing legal reform that aims to achieve three aspects of judicial justice. Meanwhile, judges' courtroom interaction with other participants, featuring presumption of defendants' innocence, neutral attitudes towards the prosecution and the defense, role-orientation based on relevant laws and regulations, and so on, is more apt to achieve PD balance by means of appropriate discourse information processing. The practical implication for legal practitioners and judges is to relinquish the traditional perceptions that defendants are the criminals to be punished and to accept the reality that defendants are litigation subjects according to the current laws.

Apart from the implications for language and the law, the present study also ramifies some pedagogical implications. In the class of criminal procedural laws, discursive training is one of the necessities supplementing the legal theories and the concrete laws. We know that the role judges assume and the duties they perform in trials mainly depend on their discursive actions. In other words, rational PDJ relationship can be achieved through judges' manipulation of trials, more specifically, judges' discourse information processing. Therefore, for the future legal workers, especially for the students or trainees who are determined to be judges, it appears especially important and applicable to learn how to avoid judicial injustice, and construct the legitimate, rational and harmonious relations between the parties in trials by means of framing strategies based on discourse information processing.

The present research, in a broader sense, contributes to the construction of China's "Harmonious Society" by protecting and safeguarding human rights, including the defendants' legitimate rights and interests, upholding and maintaining legal justice and social stability.

6.4 Limitations

Although the present study has obtained some significant

findings, drawn satisfactory conclusions to the research questions, and accomplished the general research objective, it has, undoubtedly, not reached the point of satisfaction in many ways.

Firstly, in spite of all the data from the CLIPS, we have not made sufficient statistical analysis. With the purpose of exploring whether there is irrational PDJ relationship constructed by judges' discourse action, we have paid less attention to the statistical analysis. If possible, what degree and what extent to which PDJ relationship has been constructed irrationally might be explored explicitly.

Secondly, the study has not yet taken into account such paralinguistic features as facial expressions and body language of judges and other participants in court, which might be of significance for judicial justice. Though the data from the CLIPS are verbatim records of criminal trials, some trials have no video materials. Therefore, some paralinguistic features have been overlooked. This limitation renders the present research to rely mainly on the linguistic features that may not be able to reveal the whole picture of criminal trials. Therefore, we cannot claim to be exhaustive on the study of judges' discourse.

Last but not least, there might be some areas neglected, particularly in the process of identifying different factors. For instance, we have overlooked the factors of judges' age, gender and psychological activities, which may affect the construction of PDJ relationship in some trials.

References

白俊华(Bai), 2003.论司法公正与我国法院体制改革. *政法学刊*, 20(2): 21-23.

卞建林、杨诚(Bian & Yang), 2006. *刑事正当程序研究——法理与案例*. 北京: 中国检察出版社.

卞建林、李菁菁(Bian & Li), 2004. 从我国刑事法庭设置看刑事审判构造的完善. *法学研究*, 3: 82-93.

卞建林(Bian), 2007. 刑事诉讼中"诉"之辨析. *人民检察*, 8: 36-40.

陈金诗, 黄永平(Chen & Huang), 2009. 法律语言学研究的哲学思考——从语义外在论谈起. *广东外语外贸大学学报*, 20(3): 20-23.

陈瑞华(Chen), 1997. *刑事审判原理论*. 北京: 北京大学出版社.

杜金榜(Du), 2004. *法律语言学*. 上海: 上海外语教育出版社.

杜金榜(Du), 2007. 法律语篇树状信息结构研究. *现代外语*, 30(1): 40-50.

杜金榜(Du), 2008a. 试论语篇分析的理论与方法. *外语学刊*, 1: 92-98.

杜金榜(Du), 2008b. 庭审交际中法官对信息流动的控制. *广东外语外贸大学学报*, 19(2): 36-40.

杜金榜(Du), 2009a. *法律语篇信息研究*. 待版.

杜金榜(Du), 2009b. 从处置类信息的处理看法庭语篇说理的实现. *待发*.

杜金榜(Du), 2009c. 从法庭问答的功能看庭审各方交际目标的实现. *现代外语*, 32(4): 360-368.

冯春萍(Feng), 1998. 论控辩平等与被控人人权保障. *西北政法学院学报*, 6: 65-72.

宫毅(Gong), 2003. 关于刑事审判中证人出庭问题的思考. *郑州大学学报*(哲学社会科学版), 36(6): 93-95.

谷春德(Gu), 2000. *西方法律思想史*. 北京: 中国人民大学出版社.

韩晓玲, 陈中华(Han & Chen), 2003. 框架理论及其在话语分析中的应用. *外语与外语教学*, 9: 1-3.

胡壮麟, 朱永生, 张德禄, 李战子(Hu et al.), 2005. *系统功能语言学概论*. 北京: 北京大学出版社.

冀祥德(Ji), 2007. 控辩平等之现代内涵解读. *政法论坛*, 25(6): 89-101.

邝少明(Kuang). 2000. 论司法公正与我国司法体制的改革. *中山大学学报(社会科学版)*, 40(2): 119-123.

李昌林(Li), 2006. 论通过法官实现控辩平衡. *法律适用*, 12: 41-45.

李战子(Li), 2001. 学术话语中认知型情态的多重人际意义. *外语教学与研究*, 33(5): 353-358.

廖美珍(Liao), 2004. 国外法律语言研究综述. *当代语言学*, 6(1): 66-76.

廖美珍(Liao), 2006. 中国法庭互动话语 formulation 现象研究. *外语研究*, 2: 1-13.

林国强(Lin), 2009. 和谐司法下的控辩审关系. *重庆科技学院学报(社会科学版)*, 1: 69-70.

龙宗智(Long), 2001. *刑事庭审制度研究*. 北京: 中国政法大学出版社.

吕叔湘, 丁声树(Lü & Ding), 2005. *现代汉语词典(第五版)*. 北京: 商务印书馆.

吕万英(Lü), 2005. 司法调解话语中的冲突性打断. *解放军外国语学院学报*, 28(6): 22-26.

吕万英(Lü), 2006. 法官话语的权力支配. *外语研究*, 2: 9-13.

马贵翔(Ma), 1998. 刑事诉讼对控辩平等的追求. *中国法学*, 2: 96-103.

瞿琨(Qu), 2006. 论法官角色与公正司法. *学术界*, 1: 79-84.

申君贵(Shen), 2001. 论审判程序公正. *西南政法大学学报*, 3: 8-18.

宋英辉(Song), 2003. 论合理诉讼构造与我国刑事程序的完善. *湖南社会科学*, 4: 56-61.

孙韶蓓, 谢之君(Sun & Xie), 2006. 选择疑问句的认知研究. *西南交通大学学报(社会科学版)*, 7(4): 78-81.

孙咏梅(Sun), 2007. 跨文化交际、话语分析与互动社会语言学. *外国语言文学*, 2: 104-107.

王瑞芳(Wang), 2006. 法官角色伦理与司法公正. *经济师*, 6: 87-89.

王振华(Wang), 2004. "硬新闻"的态度研究——评价系统应用研究之二. *外语教学*, 25(5): 31-36.

吴伟平(Wu), 2002. *语言与法律——司法领域的语言学研究*. 上海: 上海外语教育出版社.

夏明贵(Xia), 2000. 论法官的多重角色冲突与司法公正. *湖南省政法管理干部学院学报*, 5: 31-33.

徐章宏, 李冰(Xu & Li), 2006. 法庭应答语信息过量的顺应性研究. *外语研究*, 2: 14-18.

许忠(Xu), 2004. 完善刑事证人出庭作证制度的立法构想. *中国人民公安大学学报*, 4: 88-92.

杨丽娟(Yang), 1999. "控辩平等"制约因素的理性思考. *东北大学学报(社会科学版)*, 1(2): 17-19.

杨立凡(Yang). 2007. 刑事诉讼法应健全申请回避的告知制度. *人民检察*, 21: 63.

袁传有(Yuan), 2008. 警察讯问语言的人际意义——评价理论之"介入系统"视角[J]. *现代外语*, 31(2): 141-149.

詹全旺(Zhan), 2006. 话语分析的哲学基础——建构主义认识论. *外语学刊*, 2: 15-19.

张保生(Zhang), 2000. *法律推理的理论与方法*. 北京: 中国政法大学出版社.

张洪忠(Zhang), 2001. 大众传播学的议程设置理论与框架理论关系探讨. *西南民族学院学报(哲学社会科学版)*, 22(10): 88-91.

张丽萍, 刘蔚铭(Zhang & Liu), 2006. 论法官在审判中立中的困境——来自庭审言语交际的证据. *语言文字应用*, 4: 74-81.

张鲁平(Zhang), 2006. 试论民事审判中的法官打断现象. *修辞学习*, 4: 40-43.

张新红, 何自然(Zhang & He), 2001. 语用学理论在翻译中的应用. *现代外语*, 24(3): 285-293.

钟彩顺, 黄永平(Zhong & Huang). 2009. 基于后维特根斯坦语言哲学的法律语言学研究. *广东外语外贸大学学报*, 20(1): 73-77.

朱永生(Zhu), 2005. 框架理论对语境动态研究的启示. *外语与外语教学*, 2: 1-4.

Agne, R. R. 2007. Reframing practices in moral conflict: interaction problems in the negotiation standoff at Waco. *Discourse & Society*, 18(5): 549-578.

Aldridge, M. & Luchjenbroers, J. 2007. Linguistic manipulations in legal discourse: Framing questions and "smuggling" information. *The International Journal of Speech, Language and the Law*, 14(1): 85-107.

Alvesson, M & Karreman, D. 2000. Varieties of discourse: On the study of organizations through discourse analysis. *Human Relations*, 53(9): 1125-1149.

Appelrouth, S. A. 1999. Shifting frames and rhetorics: a case study of the Christian coalition of New York . *Social Science Journal*, 36(2): 329-340.

Atkinson, J. M. & Drew, P. 1979. *Order in Court: The Organisation of Verbal Interaction in Judicial Settings*. London: Macmillan.

Baghramian, M. 1999. *Modern Philosophy of Language*. Washington D.C: Counterpoint.

Bateson, G. 1955. A Theory of Play and Fantasy. In Bateson, G. (Ed.), 1972, *Steps to An Ecology of Mind*. New York: Ballantine Books.

Baunach, P. J. 1977. Framing the Questions in Criminal Justice Evaluation: Maybe You Can Get there from here if You Ask the "Right" Questions. *The Prison Journal*, 57(1): 19-27.

Benford, R. D. 1994. Review of Talking Politics. *American Journal of Sociology*, 99(4): 1103-1104.

Benford, R. D. 1997. An Insider's Critique of the Social Movement Framing Perspective. *Sociological Inquiry*, 67: 409-430.

Berk-Seligson, S. 1990. The Role of the Court Interpreter. In Levi, J. N. & Walker, A. G. (Eds.), *Language in the Judicial Process* (pp. 155-201). New York: Plenum Press.

Bonito, J. A. & Sanders, R. E. 2002. Speakers' Footing in a Collaborative Writing Task: A Resource for Addressing

Disagreement While Avoiding Conflict. *Research on Language & Social Interaction*, 35(4): 481-514.

Bloor, T. & Bloor, M. 1995. *The Funcitonal Analysis of English: A Hallidayan Approach*. London: Edward Arnold Publisher Ltd.

Brennan, G. 1996. *The Role of the Judge*. http://www.hcourt.gov.au.

Brown, G. & Yule, G. 1983. Discourse Analysis. London, Cambridge University Press.

Cavadino, M. & Dignan, J. 1997. *The Penal System: An Introduction* (2nd edn.). London: Sage.

Chenail, R. J. 1995. Recursive frame Analysis. *The Qualitative Report*, 2(2).

Chreim, S. 2006. Managerial Frames and Institutional Discourse of Change: Employee Appropriation and Resistance. *Organization Studies*, 27(9): 1261-1287.

Clayman, S. & Heritage, J. 2002. *The News Interview*. Cambridge: Cambridge University Press.

Coburn, C. E. 2006. Framing the Problem of Reading Instruction: Using Frame Analysis to Uncover the Microprocesses of Policy Implementation. *American Educational Research Journal*, 43(3): 343-379.

Coleman, J. L. 1992. *Risks and Wrongs*. London: Cambridge University Press.

Conley, J. M. & O'Barr, W. M. 1990. *Rules versus relationships: the ethnography of legal discourse*. Chicago: University of Chicago Press.

Conley, J. M. & O'Barr, W. M. 1998. *Just Words: Law, language, and power*. Chicago: The University of Chicago Press.

Coupland, J., Robinson, J. D. & Coupland, N. 1994. Frame Negotiation in Doctor-Elderly Patient Consultations. *Discourse Society*, 5(1): 89-124.

Cotterill, J. 2003. *Language and Power in Court: A linguistic analysis of the O. J. Simpson Trial*. New York: Palgrave Macmillan.

Creed, W. E. D., Langstraat, J. A. & Scully, M. 2002. A Picture of the

Frame: Frame Analysis as Technique and as Politics. *Organizational Research Methods*, 5(1): 34-55.

Donati, P. R. 1992. Political Discourse Analysis. In Diani, M & Eyerman, R. (Eds.), *Studying Collective Action*. London: Sage Publications Ltd.

Downs, D. 2002. Representing Gun Owners: Frame Identification as Social Responsibility in News Media Discourse. *Written Communication*. 19: 44-75.

Drew, P. 1985. Analyzing the use of language in courtroom interaction. In van Dijk, T. A. (Eds.), *Handbook of Discourse Analysis* (Vol. 3): *Discourse and Dialogue* (pp. 133-147). London: Academic Press.

Drew, P. 1992. Contested evidence in courtroom cross-examination: the case of a trial for rape. In Drew, P. & Heritage, J. (Eds.), *Talk at Work* (pp. 470-520). Cambridge: Cambridge University Press.

Drew, P. 1998. Conversation Analysis. In Mey, J. L. (Eds.), *Concise Encyclopedia of Pragmatics* (pp. 165-170). Oxford: Elsevier Science Ltd.

Duranti, A. 1997. *Linguistic Anthropology*. Cambridge: Cambridge University Press.

Edwards, D. & Potter, J. 2005. Discursive Psychology, mental states and descriptions. In te Molder, H. & Potter, J. (Eds.), *Conversation and Cognition* (pp. 241-259). Cambridge: Cambridge University Press.

Fairclough, N. 1992. *Discourse and Social Change*. Cambridge: Polity Press.

Fairclough, N. 2001. *Language and Power* (2nd edn.). Edinburgh: Pearson Education Limited.

Foucault, M. 1978. *The History of Sexuality* (Vol. 1): *An Introduction*. New York: Random House.

Fauconnier, G. and Turner, M. 2002. *The Way We Think: Conceptual Blending and the Mind's Hidden Complexities*. New York: Basic Books.

Feagin, J. R. 2006. Social Justice and Sociology: Agendas for the Twenty-First Century. *American Sociological Review*, 66: 1-20.

Ferenčík, M. 2004. *A Survey of English Stylistics.* Prešovská univerzita v Prešove.

Fillmore, J. 1982. Frame Semantics. In The Linguistic Society of Korea (Eds.), *Linguistics in the Morning Calm* (pp. 111-137). Seoul: Hanshin Publishing Co.

Firth, A. (Eds.), 1995. *The Discourse of Negotiation* [C]. Oxford: Pergamon Press.

Fisher, K. 1997. Locating Frames in the Discursive Universe. *Sociological Research Online,* 2(3). http://www.socresonline.org.uk/socresonline/2/3/4.html.

Foucault, M. 1972. *Archaeology of knowledge.* New York: Pantheon.

Fauconnier, G. 1994. *Mental spaces: aspects of meaning construction in natural language.* Cambridge: Cambridge university Press.

Frake, C. O. 1977. Plying Frames Can Be Dangerous: Some reflections on methodology in cognitive anthropology. In Cole, M., Engestrom, Y. and Vasquez, O. (Eds.), 1997, *Mind, Culture and Activity: Seminal Papers from the Laboratory of Comparative Human Cognition* (pp. 32-46). Cambridge: Cambridge University Press.

Fraser, N. 2007. Re-framing justice in a globalizing world. In Lovell, T. (Ed.), *(Mis)recognition, Social Inequality and Social Justice* (pp. 17-35). London: Routledge.

Gamson, W. A. & Lasch, K. E. 1983. The political culture of social welfare policy. In S. E. Spiro & E. Yuchtman-Yaar (Eds.), *Evaluating the welfare state: Social and political perspectives* (pp. 397-415). New York: Academic Press.

Gamson, W. A. & Modigliani, A. 1987. The changing culture of affirmative action. In Braungart, R. G. & Braungart, M. M. (Eds.), *Research in political sociology* (Vol. 3) (pp. 137-177). Greenwich, CT: JAI Press.

Gamson, W. A. & Modigliani, A. 1989. Media discourse and public opinion: A constructionist approach. *American Journal of Sociology,*

95: 1-37.

Gibbons, J. 1994a. Language and disadvantage before the law. In Gibbons, J. (Ed.), *Language and the Law* (pp. 195-198). London and New York: Longman.

Gibbons, J. 1994b. Language Constructing Law. In J. Gibbons (Ed.), *Language and the Law* (pp.3-10). London and New York: Longman.

Gibbons, J. (Ed.). 1994c. *Language and the Law*. London and New York: Longman.

Gibbons, J. 2003. *Forensic Linguistics: An Introduction to Language in the Justice System*. Oxford: Blackwell Publishing Ltd.

Gitlin, T. 1980. *The whole world is watching: Mass media in the making and unmaking of the New Left*. Berkeley, CA: University of California Press.

Goffman, E. 1959. *Garden City*. NY: Anchor.

Goffman, E. 1974. *Frame analysis: An essay on the organization of experience*. Boston: Northeastern University Press.

Goffman, E. 1981. *Forms of talk*. Pennsylvania: University of Pennsylvania Press.

Goffman, E. 1983. The Interaction Order: American Sociological Association, 1982 Presidential Address. *American Sociological Review*, 48(1): 1-17.

Gu, Yueguo & Zhu, Weifang. 2002. Chinese officialdom (*Guan*) at work in discourse. In Barron, C., Bruce, N. & Nuna, D. (Eds.), *Knowledge and Discourse: Towards an Ecology of Language* (pp. 97-115). London: Longman.

Gumperz, J. J. 1977. Sociocultural knowledge in conversational inference. In Saville-Troike, M. (Eds.), *Linguistics and anthropology: Georgetown University Round Table on Languages and Linguistics* (pp. 191-211). Washington, DC: Georgetown University Press.

Gumperz, J. J. 1982a. *Discourse Strategies*. Cambridge: Cambridge University Press.

Gumperz, J. J. 1982b. *Language and Social Identity*. Cambridge: Cambridge University Press.

Gumperz, J. J. 1999. On interactional sociolinguistics method. In Sarangi, S. and Roberts, C. (Eds.), *Talk, Work and Institutional Order: Discourse in Medical, Mediation and Managements Settings* (pp. 453-471). Berlin: Gruyter.

Hallahan, K. 1999. Seven Models of Framing: Implications for Public Relations. *Journal of Public Relations Research*, 11(3): 205-242.

Hammersley, M. 2003. Conversation Analysis and Discourse Analysis: Methods or Paradigms?. *Discourse Society*, 14(6): 751-781.

Hegtvedt, K. A. & Cook, K. S. 2000. Distributive Justice: Recent Theoretical Developments and Applications. In Sanders, J. & Hamilton, V. L. (Eds.), *Handbook of Justice Research in Law* (pp. 93-132). New York: Kluwer Academic / Plenum Publishers.

Heritage, J. 1998. Conversation Analysis and Institutional Talk: Analyzing Distinctive Turn-Taking Systems. In Cmejrková, S. et al (Eds.), *Proceedings of the 6th International Congress of IADA* (pp. 3-17). Tubingen: Niemeyer.

Heritage, J. & Maynard, D. W. (Eds.). 2006. *Communication in Medical Care: Interactions between Primary Care Physicians and Patients*. Cambridge: Cambridge University Press.

Howeison, J. 2002. Perceptions of Procedural Justice and Legitimacy in Local Court Mediation. *Murdoch University Electronic law Journal*, 9(2). Retrieved April 16, 2007, from http://www.murdoch.edu.au/elaw/issues/v9n2/howeison92.txt.

Hoyle, S. M. 1993. Participation Frameworks in Sportscasting Play: Imaginary and Literal Footings. In Tannen, D. (Ed.), *Framing in Discourse* (pp. 114-145). New York: Oxford University Press, 114-145.

Jacqueline, M. 2005. *The English Legal System* (4th edn.). London: Hodder Arnold.

Johnston, H. 1995. A Methodology for Frame Analysis: From Discourse to Cognitive Schema. In Johnston and Klandermans (Eds.), *Social Movements and Culture* (pp. 217-246).

Kant, I. 1887. *The Philosophy of Law: An Exposition of the Fundamental Principles of Jurisprudence as the Science of Right*. trans. W. Hastie. Edinburgh: Clark.

Kinney, C. J. 1998. *Role, Stance, and Footing: a Frame Analysis of Leaders' Talk in a Small Group Discussion*. Washington, D. C.: Georgetown University.

Koester, A. 2006. *Investigating Workplace Discourse*. London: Routledge.

Kretsedemas, P. 2000. Examining Frame Formation in Peer Group Conversations. *The Sociological Quarterly*, 41(4): 639-656.

Kweon, S. 2000. A Framing Analysis: How Did Three U.S. News Magazines Frame about Mergers or Acquisitions?. *The International Journal on Media Management*, 2(3/4): 165-177.

Labov, W. 1977. Therapeutic Discourse. New York: Academic Press Inc.

Lessa, I. 2006. Discursive struggles within social welfare: Restaging teen motherhood. *British Journal of Social Work*, 36: 283-298.

Levi, J. N. & Walker, A. G. 1990. *Language in the Judicial Process*. New York: Plenum Press.

Lovell, T. (Ed.). 2007. *(Mis)recognition, Social Inequality and Social Justice*. London: Routledge.

Macgilchrist, F. 2007. Positive Discourse Analysis: Contesting Dominant Discourses by Reframing the Issues. *Critical Approaches to Discourse Analysis Across Disciplines*, 1 (1): 74-94.

Marshall, G. 1998. *A Dictionary of Sociology* (2nd edn.). Oxford: Oxford University Press.

Martin, J. R. & Rose, D. 2003. *Working with Discourse: Meaning beyond the clause*. London, Continuum.

Matoesian, G. 1993. *Reproducing Rape: Domination through Talk in the Courtroom*. Cambridge: Polity Press.

Matoesian, G. 1997. "I'm sorry we had to meet under these circumstances": verbal artistry (and wizardry) in the Kennedy Smith rape trial. In Travers, M. & Manzo, J. F. (Eds.), *Law in Action: Ethnomethododlogical and Conversation Analytic Approaches to Law* (pp. 137-182). Aldershot: Darmouth Publishing.

Matoesian, G. 2001. *Law and the Language of Identity: Discourse in the Kennedy Smith Rape Trial.* Oxford: Oxford University Press.

Matoesian , G. 2005. Nailing down an answer: participations of power in trial talk. *Discourse Studies,* 7(6): 733-759.

Minsky, M. A. 1975. A Framework for Representing Knowledge. In Winston, P. (Eds.). *The Psychology of Computer Vision.* New York: McGraw Hill.

Neubaucer, D. W. 1988. *America's Courts & the Criminal Justice System* (3rd edn). California: Brooks/Core Publishing Company.

Nielsen, M. F. & Wagner, J. 2007. Diversity and continuity in conversation analysis. *Journal of Pragmatics,* 39(3): 441-444.

O'Barr, W. M. 1982. *Linguistic Evidence: Language, Power, and Strategy in the Courtroom.* San Diego: Academic Press Inc.

Olsen, M. E. 1991. *Social Dynamics: Exploring Macrosociology.* New Jersey: Prentice Hall, Englewood Cliffs.

Pan, Z. & Kosicki, G. 1993. Framing Analysis: An Approach to News Discourse. *Political Communication,* 10: 55-75.

Philips, S. U. 1983. Book Review: Form of Talk. *Language,* 59 (2): 429-431.

Philips, S. U. 1998. *Ideology in the language of judges.* New York: Oxford University Press.

Pick, D. 2006. The Re-Framing of Australian Higher Education. *Higher Education Quarterly,* 60(3): 229-241.

Pomerantz, A. & Fehr, B. J. 1997. Conversation Analysis: An Approach to the Study of Social Action as Sense Making Practices. In van Dijk, T. A. (Ed.), *Discourse Studies: A Multidisciplinary Introduction*

(Vol. 2): *Discourse as Social Interaction* (pp. 64-91). London: Sage Publications Ltd.

Prego-Vázquez, G. 2007. Frame conflict and social inequality in the workplace: professional and local discourse struggles in employee/ customer interactions. *Discourse & Society*, 18(3): 295-335.

Radbruch, G. 1963. Fünf Minuten Rechtsphilosophie. In: *ders.*, *Rechtsphilosophie*, 4. Aufl. Stuttgart 1963, S. 335ff.

Rawls, J. 1999. *A Theory of Justice* (Revised Edition). Cambridge, MA: the Belknap Press of Harvard University Press.

Ribeiro, B. T. 2006. Footing, positioning, voice. Are we talking about the same thing?. In Fina, A. D., Schiffrin, D. & Bamberg, M. (Eds.), *Discourse and Identity* (pp. 48-82). Cambridge: Cambridge University Press.

Rachels, J. 2007. *The Elements of Moral Philosophy* (5th edn.). New York: McGraw-Hill, Inc.

Rumelhart, D, E. & Ortony, A. 1977. Representation of Knowledge. In Anderson, R. C., Spiro, R. J. & Montague, W. E. (Eds.). *Schooling and the Acquisition of Knowledge*. Hillsdale, N. J.: Erlbaum.

Sacks, H., Schegloff, E. A., & Jefferson, G. 1974. A simplest systematics for the organization of turn-taking for conversation. *Language*, 50: 696-735.

Samaha, J. 1997. Criminal Justice (4th edn.). Opperman Drive: West Publishing Company.

Sanders, J. & Hamilton, V. L. 2000. Justice and Legal Institution. In Sanders, J. & Hamilton, V. L. (Eds.), *Handbook of Justice Research in Law* (pp. 3-27). New York: Kluwer Academic / Plenum Publishers.

Sarangi, S. & Roberts, C. 1999. The Dynamics of Interactional and Institutional Orders in Work-related Settings. In Sarangi, S. & Roberts, C. (Eds.), *Talk, Work and Institutional Order: Discourse in Medical, Mediation and Managements Settings* (pp. 1-57). Berlin: Gruyter.

Schank, R. C. & Abelson, R. P. 1977. *Scripts, Plans, Goals and understanding*. Hillsdale, N. J.: Erlbaum.

Scheff, T.J. 2005. The structure of context: deciphering Frame Analysis. *Sociological Theory,* 23(4): 368-385.

Schegloff, E. A. 1989. Harvey Sacks—lectures 1964-1965: An introduction/memoir. *Human Studies,* 12(3-4): 185-209.

Schegloff, E. A. 1991. Reflections on Talk and Social Structure. In Boden D. and Zimmerman D. H. (Eds.), *Talk and Social Structure* (pp. 44-70). Berkeley: University of California Press.

Schegloff, E. A. 1992. Introduction to Harvey Sacks. *Lectures on Conversation* (Vol. 1). Oxford: Blackwell.

Schegloff, E. A. 2007. *Sequence Organization in Interaction: A Primer in Conversation Analysis I*. Cambridge: Cambridge University Press.

Searle, J. R. 1969. *Speech Acts: An Essay in the Philosophy of Language*. Cambridge: Cambridge University Press.

Searle, J. R. 1975. *A Taxonomy of Illocutionary Acts*. (Reprinted in Searle 1979. *Expression and Meaning*, 1-29. Cambridge: Cambridge University Press.)

Shuy, R. W. 2007. Language in the American Courtroom . *Language and Linguistics Compass,* 1/1-2: 100-114.

Smith, F. 2006. *Erving Goffman*. London: Routledge.

Smith, F. L. 1993. The Pulpit and Women's Place: Gender and the Framing of the "Exegetical Self" in Sermon Performance. In Tannen, D. (Ed.), *Framing in Discourse* (pp. 146-175). New York: Oxford University Press.

Snow, D., Rochford, E. B., Worden, S. & Benford, R. 1986. Frame alignment processes, micromobilization, and movement participation. *American Sociological Review,* 51: 456-481.

Snow, D. & Benford, R. 1988. Ideology, frame resonance, and participant mobilization. *International social movement research,* 1: 197-217.

Solan, L. M. 1993. *The language of judges*. Chicago: University of Chicago Press.

Solan, L. M. & Tiersma, P. M. 2005. *Speaking of Crime: the Language of Criminal Justice*. Chicago: The University of Chicago Press.

Strega, S. 2005. The view from the poststructural margins: Epistemology and methodology reconsidered. In Brown, L. & Strega, S. (Eds.), *Research as resistance* (pp. 199-235). Toronto: Canadian Scholars' Press.

Stygall, G. 1994. *Trial Language: Different Discourse Processing and Discourse Formations*. Amsterdam: John Benjamins.

Tajfel, H. & Turner, J. 1986. The social identity theory of intergroup behavior. In Wotchel, S. & Austin, W. G. (Eds.), *Psychology of intergroup relations* (pp. 7-24). Chicago: Nelson.

Tannen, D. 1989. *Talking Voices: Repetition, dialogue, and imagery in conversational discourse*. Cambridge: Cambridge University Press.

Tannen, D. 1993. What's in a Frames: Surface Evidence for Underlying Expectations. In Tannen, D. (Ed.), *Framing in Discourse* (pp. 14-56). New York: Oxford University Press.

Tannen, D. & Wallat, C. 1993. Interactive Frames and Knowledge Schemas in Interaction: Examples from a Medical Examination/Interview. In Tannen, D. (Ed.), *Framing in Discourse* (pp. 57-76). New York: Oxford University Press.

Tannen, D. 2007. *Talking Voices: Repetition, dialogue, and Imagery in Conversational Discourse* (2nd edn). New York: Cambridge University Press.

Thornborrow, J & Wareing, S. 1998. *Patterns in Language: Stylistics for Students of Language and Literature*. London: Routledge.

Tiersma, P. M. 1999. *Legal Language*. Chicago: The University of Chicago Press.

Triandafyllidou, A. 1995. *Second Project Report: A Frame Analysis of Institutional Discourse*. Report produced for the Sustainable

Development Research Project.

Tyler, T. R. & Lind, E. A. 1992. Procedural Justice. In Sanders, J. & Hamilton, V. L. (Eds.), *Handbook of Justice Research in Law* (pp. 65-92). New York: Kluwer Academic / Plenum Publishers.

Umphrey, M. 1999. The Dialogics of Legal Meaning: Spectacular Trials, the Unwritten Law, and Narratives of Criminal Responsibility. *Law and Society Review*, (33): 393-424.

van Dijk, T. A. 1977a. Context and Cognition: Knowledge Frames and Speech act Comprehension. *Journal of Pragmatics*, (1): 211-232.

van Dijk, T. A. 1977b. *Text and Context: Exploration in the Semantics and Pragmatics of Discourse*. London: Longman.

van Dijk, T. A. & Kintsch, W. 1983. *Strategies of Discourse Comprehension*. New York: Academic Press, Inc.

van Dijk, T. A. 1980. *Macrostructures: An Interdisciplinary Study of Global Structures in Discourse, Interaction and Cognition*. Hillsdale: Lawrence Erlbaum.

van Dijk, T. A. 1985. Semantic Discourse Analysis. In *Handbook of Discourse Analysis (Vol. 2): Dimensions of Discourse*. London: Academic Press, Inc. (London) Ltd.

van Dijk, T. A. 1989. Structures of Discourse and Structures of Power. In Anderson, J. A. (Eds.), *Communication Yearbook 12* (pp. 18-59). Newbury Park, CA: Sage.

van Dijk, T. A. 1997a. The Study of Discourse. In van Dijk, T. A. (Ed.), *Discourse Studies: A Multidisciplinary Introduction* (Vol. 1): *Discourse as Structure and Process* (pp. 1-34). London, Sage Publications Ltd.

van Dijk, T. A. 1997b. Discourse as Interaction in Society. In van Dijk, T. A. (Ed.), *Discourse Studies: A Multidisciplinary Introduction* (Vol. 2): *Discourse as Social Interaction* (pp. 1-37). London, Sage Publications Ltd.

van Dijk, T. A. 2001. Discourse, ideology and context. *Folia Linguistica*, XXX/1-2: 11-40.

van Dijk, T. A. 2006. Discourse, Context and Cognition. *Discourse Studies*, 8(1): 159-177.

Verschueren, J. 1999. *Understanding Pragmatics*. London: Edward Arnold Publisher Ltd.

Watanabe, S. 1993. Cultural Differences in Framing: American and Japanese Group Discussions. In Tannen, D. (Ed.), *Framing in Discourse* (pp. 176-209). New York: Oxford University Press.

Yuan, Chuanyou. 2007. *Avoiding Revictimization: Speech Shifting from Police Interrogations to Police Interviewing*. Guangzhou: Guangdong University of Foreign Studies.

Zhong, Caishun. 2009. *A Discursive-psychological Study of Judges' Judicial Behavior*. Guangzhou: Guangdong University of Foreign Studies.

General Information on the Cases

Case No.	Nature of Cases	Case No.	Nature of Cases
01	Extortion	19	Theft and fraud
02	Bombing	20	Fraud
03	Causing death negligently (death compensation)	21	Assaulting deliberately
04	Fraud	22	Robbery
05	Assaulting deliberately and robbery	23	Assaulting deliberately and criminal reconciliation
06	Illegal medicine practice	24	Refusing execution of judgment and adjudication
07	Theft	25	Fraud
08	Robbery	26	Assaulting deliberately
09	Theft	27	Pyramid sales and false imprisonment
10	Spreading obscene objects for profit	28	Abandoning a baby girl and causing her death
11	Sales of fake and shoddy products	29	Smuggling ordinary goods
12	Murder	30	Theft
13	Unlawful intrusion into a resident's house	31	Illicit manufacture of explosives and bombing
14	Fraud	32	Fraud
15	Endangering public security	33	Theft
16	Causing traffic casualties	34	Illegal capital raising
17	Theft	35	Illegal capital raising
18	Fraud and theft		

Appendix II

Figures

Tables

Index

Y